Tale of Tala

Tale
of Tala

Chaker Khazaal

⊞ hachette
A.Antoine

Published in 2017 by Hachette Antoine

© Hachette Antoine & Chaker Khazaal, 2017
Sin El Fil, Horsh Tabet, Forest Bldg 965
P.O. Box 11-0656, Riad al-Solh, 1107 2050 Beirut, Lebanon

info@hachette-antoine.com
www.hachette-antoine.com
facebook.com/HachetteAntoine
twitter.com/NaufalBooks

The situations in this book are inspired by real events.

Cover artwork: Jeffrey Robinson
Edited by: Allen Douglas Carter
Layout: Marie-Thérèse Merheb

ISBN 978-0692942833

Available on Kindle and online stores.

To those born to be winners...

Chapter One
Part One

I lived my life believing that there are three kinds of people: winners, losers, and those who lived in between victory and defeat. In that third category is the sort of person who keeps trying. They accept defeat, but understand it as a temporary state of being. But I lived to be a winner, and that's how I wanted to die.

"Meet my son. Henry," Dad would say in his deliberate, confident voice to the room full of New York's social elite. "He's the heir to all I've built." He would gesture to the room and furnishings—Baker sofas and Brunschwig & Fils's Westbury Bouquet glazed chintz—and its reveling occupants with a vague sweep of his hand. It's clear he means to imply much more than just the party or the home in which he and my mother were hosting it.

I was born in New York City in 1977, an only child to a powerful family. My father was a successful banker, and my mother had her own fashion design company. They were both well-known, and in our Upper East Side townhouse, they often hosted many of the most influential members of the city's social scene: artists, musicians, bankers, politicians and socialites. The finest wine was poured and the most exquisite food was served, fuel for all sorts of interesting conversations. From the mundane to the scandalous, my young ears ate it up.

As early as the age of eight, I would be allowed to stay up and join these parties. My mother would dress me in the latest styles, and, downstairs on the first level of our home, she would delight in showing me off to her friends. Andy Warhol, Jean-Michel Basquiat, Leonard Cohen, Annie Leibovitz, and other such giants on the New York social and cultural scene were the sorts of guests my parents hosted. I was too young to know the true significance of these distinguished guests, but I marveled at their styles, poise and, sometimes, their odd and eccentric mannerisms. Even at that young age, I could tell which of the visitors were guests of my mother. They were an eclectic group, creative and colorful. Kind and insightful. They would ruffle my hair and spend time to talk to me as an equal. My father's guests all had the same suits, the same haircuts and even smelled the same. For an eight-year-old, it wasn't hard to decide which side of the room was the most fun.

My father, one of Wall Street's royalty, intended for me to continue his legacy as a banker myself. He had high expectations and, as with everything else in his life, he planned my future to the last detail. He'd put me in the best schools, hired me the finest teachers, and would not abide but for me to be at the top of my class. My mother, on the other hand, hired a piano teacher from Julliard and routinely had me accompany her to galleries, concerts and even the occasional smoky coffee house around New York. I have my parents and their high expectations to thank for the identity with which I grew up.

I lived up to those expectations. I was an exemplary student, a natural artist, and I never compromised on anything. I was focused, worked hard, never got into trouble, and, most importantly, never embarrassed my family. I was a winner.

When I was young, my only real opportunity to explore my own interests was at night after I'd gone to bed. My mother would tuck me in, and then stay until I would finally pretend to fall asleep. Once she had kissed my brow and quietly closed the door behind her, I would dig my diary out from beneath my mattress and write. In my secret diary, I would, from the perspective of a precocious, privileged boy, poke fun at the people I was meeting at my parents' get-togethers. For instance, I took youthful glee in my mother's friend Rita's habit of getting drunk and starting alcohol-fueled fights with her husband. According to the media though, Rita and her husband were the sweethearts of America and the ideal to which modern couples aspired. I would write about my mother gossiping about Barbara: She owed money to her fashion company while maintaining that all was well financially with them. I was fascinated by the contradictions and pretensions of the society into which I was born. That's what I wrote about.

I first wrote in my secret diary when I was ten, and it remained my secret until I turned thirteen. Our housekeeper found it and promptly showed it to my mother. Enraged by its salacious contents, my mother destroyed it. She didn't look me in the eye the whole time she ripped to pieces the tattered notebook that contained a full three years of scathing, juvenile observations. I was sure I would never hear about it again. However, that same night, I overheard my mother telling my father "You know, Richard, our Henry is a great writer. What an imagination. I think he's a natural talent, a real storyteller."

"Good for him," my father replied. I could hear the derisive curl to his lips. "Don't encourage this talent. Math, economics, trade, the market. That's his future." My father's tone would brook no argument. My mother must have known I was listening because after I had quietly returned to my room, she came, sat on the edge of my bed and silently held me for a long while.

Writing was my way to express suppressed thoughts and feelings. My writing was the way in which those unspoken words finally found their voice. It was empowering to hear my mother recognize my talent, and devastating to hear my father express such disdain for it. My father was the head of our household. While my mother helped me see that my dream was to be a writer, my duty was to my father and his legacy.

I went to college to study business, and life took me away from writing. I spent my first years at Columbia University studying something I didn't particularly enjoy, but I still excelled at it. It is what my father expected from me, and I could not oppose him. I am not sure why, but fear got the best of me. Some days, all I wanted was to quit school and escape to a remote island where I could write, where I could be the man I wanted to be. Although I had stopped writing, I fantasized about it constantly, but never had the guts to pursue it. My mother could see the pain in my eyes from abandoning my dreams.

"How was class today, Henry?" she asked after watching me hang my scarf and coat, "Did that economics prof post those grades?" My mother could always tell when something was wrong.

"Just fine," I lied. "He did, and I did better than I thought on the mid-term," I added and forced a smile. I could tell she wasn't convinced, but I repeated myself,

"I'm fine." She knew I had no interest in what I was studying and it was wearing on me. Mothers speak the silent language of their children, even when their children are in their sophomore year.

For me, life was made of rules, mostly set by my father. He was a very firm man, and his reputation was the most valuable asset he had. He cared about it a little too much. It was what he lived for, what he cared about the most. My mother and I had to adhere to his parameters and meet his expectations. Even the girls I dated had to be approved by him.

I had become enamored with a girl in school, but when my father found out she was on a scholarship and came from a middle-class family, he forbade me to see her. He asked me to see a different girl, Ramona, who was the daughter of another well-known banker. Ramona and I dated. Our fathers were happy, but we were not. Actually, we didn't connect at all as she was into big, muscled men, and I was athletic and more on the lean side. She enjoyed older guys, but I was her age. She was really into fashion and tabloids about which I was entirely uninterested. But we dated and made it work as best we could. We were more like friends, but still attended family events as a couple. We held hands, but never kissed. Well, we kissed once and the lack of chemistry was painfully obvious. We shared a tacit understanding that we would pretend though, and we were good at pretending. I was trained to live my life to please my old man. I was programmed to do that.

My life completely changed when I was twenty-one years old, and I was only a few months from graduating from college. It was a January evening and it was snowing outside. My mother and I were watching TV, and my father was on a business trip in Arizona when the phone rang. My mother answered it. After a short silence, her face became ashen. She fell to her knees, all the air rushed from her, and she wept. I hurried to help her, then, holding her tightly around her shuddering shoulders, took the phone. I don't recall those next moments when the voice on the other end of the line must have explained what had happened. There had been a plane crash. Life took another turn for both of us.

The days, weeks, months, and years following that phone call would be a chain of life-changing events. First, it was a daunting task to organize my father's funeral. Everyone wanted to attend and to be involved. They did not allow my mother and I to mourn properly. They did not give us the space we so desperately needed; in the days preceding the funeral, visitors stayed with us day and night. They wanted to comfort us, and many wanted to suck up to my mother, knowing that she would be inheriting my father's wealth. At last, the funeral went on as planned. Hundreds of people attended, and we all participated in burying a man who left a legacy behind: his work, and his family.

That same evening, I drove my mother home and we both sat in silence in the living room. We just looked at each other, unable to express how we felt. We shared, quietly, our vulnerability, our mutual sorrow, our tacit, profound, and complicated emotions. We took comfort in each other's presence as we both explored our feelings for the man, my father, her husband.

Despite how harsh my father was to me, I have to admit that he taught me the art of winning. He raised the bar high. To him, it was all a battle to be won. To my mother, he was a strong man in which she took much pride. We both mourned in silence. Until I broke it.

"Let's go to the cottage," I suggested.

Our cottage was in upstate New York. We could spend a few months there. I wanted to spare my mother from everything that reminded her of my father: New York City, the house we lived in, and all the people around. Getting away for a little while would be just the thing.

"What about school?" my mother objected, concerned.

"I can study by correspondence and come back to do my finals before graduation."

My mother conceded. We packed, and the next morning, we were on I-87 headed north to the cottage. We listened to Frank Sinatra, my father's favorite. We did not talk to each other much, our mutual silence was comfort enough. My mother would sleep for a bit, and then wake. Sometimes she would start crying. I let her be and I tried to concentrate on the road, telling myself that if she needed me, she'd let me know. But, in fact, I was focused on one thing that made me feel selfish. All I wanted was to get to the cottage and start writing. I thought of it as my emotional escape, and now that the man who'd forbidden me from pursuing my passion was gone, I was free to explore it.

We reached the cottage, and I rushed to my room that overlooked the backyard. I sat at the desk that I once used for studying. This time, there were no textbooks, no study notes, no equations. There was a stack of blank paper, crisp and white, and I was determined to fill each and every page, writing until I was satisfied. I was motivated by the pain of losing my father, and the freedom of finally doing what I loved the most. The first two words I put to paper were "Imprisoned Dreamer".

I can't remember how the next weeks went by. All I recall is that desk, and those pristine sheets of paper that were being filled by stories from my childhood, my upbringing, and how a dreamer was imprisoned in my body. The dream to become a writer had been trapped in the body of a business administration student trying to excel, to please his father and thereby the social circles around him. I wrote about love, dreams, expectations, lust and taboo. My mother knew that I was writing. I think it made her nearly as happy as it made me.

I wrote all night long, and, during the day, I studied for my finals. I was trained not to lose, and did not wish to have my ultimate dream deter me from the education I had started. I still didn't want to disappoint my father, whose scrutiny I could still feel over my shoulder, but I was also determined to have my dream see the light.

That year, I graduated at the top of my class, and at the same time, I had completed the manuscript for my first novel based on true stories of my youth: *Imprisoned Dreamer*.

Thanks to a connection of my father's, a literary agent pitched the book to publishers, and within a year, my book was published. It was a huge success with record sales. People my father had known were very influential and helped promote it. I was interviewed on TV, radio and at conferences. People loved the way I wrote about my experiences, and it was satisfying to see they enjoyed the side of my dad that only my mother and I knew. I talked about him with the utmost respect, but he was the man who imprisoned my dreams and I didn't hide that. The book motivated new writers and dreamers. It helped to raise questions about the notion of parents deciding what their kids should do in life.

It was a success! People would recognize me and stop me on the street to ask me what I was planning next. Admittedly, my charisma and good looks helped. I was doing what my father had trained me to do: to excel, to be highly respected, to be a winner.

My mother could not have been prouder. She saw me happy with my success, and now all that was missing was for her to see me get married and have a family, and to see her grandchildren. But those things weren't on my list. I was high on success. I enjoyed all the excitement, the events and parties. It was such an exciting time that I did not wish to commit to any woman. I couldn't let anyone imprison my dreams in life.

Imprisoned Dreamer was my first book, followed by many others. I wrote stories that people related to. In 2001, I published my second book, *Impossible Love*. It was inspired by my first failed relationship; the vibrant, exciting relationship that my father had put an end to, due to my girlfriend's inadequate social standing. Not surprisingly, writing that novel reopened old wounds. Before I sat down to begin work on that story, I didn't suspect how much I would endure: mourning for and raging at my father's memory and recognizing what he had taken from me despite all he gave.

As of 2016, at thirty-nine, I had reached the height of my success. I'd made a fortune well beyond what my father had left us and I was the most eligible bachelor in New York. It was exactly the way I'd imagined fame: parties, fans, flashing cameras, red carpets, book signings. Through it all, I stayed grounded though. I had the odd drink when I partied and occasionally dated, but without any commitment.

I did not want to get married, though my mother had been growing increasingly insistent in the last few months. It was in this way that I just couldn't give my mother what she really wanted. Living a charmed life like I was, I was enjoying the attention of countless fans and some select attention from few women. My mother knew about them, of course. I wonder if she knew that I spoke about her with my dates. I was entirely sincere when, even in the din of a busy club, I would talk to a girl empathetically about my frequent visits to my incredible mom. It was genuine, but it did work those few times, and the girl and I would be enjoying breakfast together the next morning.

The year 2016 wasn't entirely about success. Up until then, I had released a total of six novels and each made it on the bestseller lists. My last novel was released in 2011, and I had been working on my seventh novel for five years. My publisher and agent had been calling me almost daily, asking for my latest manuscript. I just kept telling them I was working on a new masterpiece, but that didn't satisfy them long. The expectations were high; so was the pressure. Creativity does not thrive under such pressure. I knew that when writers experience that state, writer's block, they should stop writing. That's the suggestion I gave people, but I did not follow my own advice. I wanted to release the novel. I missed that rush, that high I only got from success.

My novel, *Fair Fear*, was released in January 2016. Within a few days, the press had already labelled it with cheap superlatives like, "the most derivative drivel on the shelf" and "one of the worst novels in the history of literature." People shared on social media how terrible it was, how boring, how repetitive. People delivered scathing criticisms as only the anonymous can:

@bookworm12 It wouldn't have been so bad if it had say, plot, character and some redeeming qualities. *#FairFearsucks*

@literarycrit If this were a movie, it would go straight to DVD. *#Hasbeenauthor*

@literallyliterary I've lost all faith in my favorite author. Read to the last page hoping for more. #Disappointing *#FearFairFear*

The weeks following the book release were hard on me. No one wanted to interview me. No one even cared about the book, sales were so low. As I would walk down the street to visit my mother, like I did at least twice a week, I would see people looking at me with that enraging sympathetic look. I hated it. I was not bred to be a loser. I was born to be a winner, and this was the first time I'd ever truly felt defeat.

"What's the matter," my mother asked, touching my cheek and looking at me the same way she would when I was a child. My shoulders slackened and, with a sigh, the tension left me for the first time in days. She was always able to make things feel like they were going to be okay. If not for her, I didn't think I could find this sort of relief anywhere, from anything. I needed her.

"It's alright," I said, trying to sound convincing. My mother could read my mind though, and her brow knitted in loving concern. That expression, however well-meant, hurt more than any derisive tweet or bad review. It was not the sort of look one gives a winner.

"It is," she insisted, taking my hand and squeezing it. Her hands were still strong, though her knuckles were noticeably swollen from arthritis and there were spots on their parchment-like skin. I almost believed her. "I enjoyed the book," she went on. "Really. I'll bet a lot of people did. Don't listen to those embittered critics." I, of course, did not take her testimonial at any value; mothers are unconditional supporters to their kids after all.

That's when I stopped going to see my mother. I started to spend time alone at home. Drinking. I tried to figure out what to do next. I could not think. I just kept seeing that expression on my mother's face. I know the look was mere concern, but it seemed to me like pity. Whenever I looked at my phone, I would either see rude, merciless posts about my book or, perhaps worse, meaningless messages of support from fans and friends. My book was a failure; my natural writing ability had failed me. I was not meant to be one of those people who lives between victory and defeat. I could not understand what went wrong.

Weeks passed. Day after day, I watched the window's dusty, square beam of sunlight creep across the floor and the empty bottles grow in number around my unkempt condo. I didn't recognize the unshaven man with the hollow mien looking at me from the other side of the bathroom mirror. The respites from reality my drinking afforded me grew shorter and shorter. The relief that was, at best, fleeting, became eventually nonexistent.

The spring of 2016 took an eternity to arrive. The gloom and the cold weather did not help my state. I was very much looking forward to winter's end. I lived in a fog. You see, when you are trained to be a winner, losing is like a virus. It infects and spreads until it kills you.

With the first blossoms of spring, I was finally able to gather the strength to visit my mother. I shaved and put on my most fashionable clothes, thinking of my days as a boy when my mother would dress me in the chicest outfits she could find—in boy sizes— and proudly parade me before the artistic and social elite who attended her parties. She was the one who encouraged my writing from the beginning. She was the one who believed in me, pushed me, and never left my side. Her maid opened the door to tell me that my mother was still sleeping. I went to wake her up, she always loved that.

By the time I got to her bedroom door, a buoyancy had returned to my spirit that I hadn't experienced in a long while. I missed my mother so much. Why had I been away so long? The first smile to find my lips in weeks dissolved the instant I took my mother's hand. Cold and limp, her hand didn't squeeze mine. It never would again. She had had a heart attack and died in her sleep.

How could 2016 get any worse? I had lost it all. I lost my career with the failure of my book, I lost the admiration of the public, and now, at the worst possible time, I lost my mother. How could I go on? Anger set in. When I looked in the mirror the next morning, I was wearing a fearsome, determined expression. A winner. A winner or nothing, I vowed furiously.

In the days that followed, I occupied myself with my mother's funeral. Then, I called my publicist to arrange a TV interview. The press was interested, not because of my most recent failing book, but because of my mother's death.

There I was, in front of a camera, studio lighting bearing down on me. I knew the viewers were only interested in sadistically observing my suffering after the loss of my mother. They did not care about me as a writer. They cared about the story of now, the plight of a has-been celebrity struck low.

Despite my book being a piece of trash, my miserable and publicized situation got people to buy my work, maybe out of sympathy. The media had shed a lot of light in the past years on how close I was to my mother, so the whole story of a successful writer turned into a failure and then tragically losing his mother was an utter sensation.

I was tired, hopeless and profoundly sad. Despite my publicist being entirely against it, I was sitting in the garishly lit television studio, trying to appear composed with one leg casually slung over the other. The TV hostess looked up from her teleprompter from which she'd read the last volley of insensitive and vapid questions and drew a breath to ask yet another. I interrupted.

"I've quit writing."

My tone was cool and I stared indifferently at the hostess as she blinked, speechless for a moment. My publicist, on-set as usual, buried his face in his hands.

Before the hailstorm of questions could resume, I casually removed my lapel mic and left the set.

I walked past the crew and my publicist and headed straight home where I poured myself three fingers of whiskey. I was used to drinking in the middle of the day. I turned off my phone which had been whirring furiously since my announcement. My publicist rang the doorbell a few times, then knocked anxiously. I ignored it.

Hours went by, and the next thing I knew was waking up on my couch right before dawn. In the bathroom mirror, that stranger was waiting. I saw a defeated person. A loser. I wasn't equipped to live like that.

"Who are you?" I demanded of him savagely. "What? Nothing to say?" My knuckles were white as I was gripping the sink with such rage. My breath came in furious hisses through my clenched teeth as I stared at the man in the mirror. He only stared back with an accusatory scowl. I pressed my forehead against the cool glass to calm my breathing, trying to will myself out of this downward spiral.

I implored the man on the other side of the mirror. "You still have so much to live for. You've still got money. You've accomplished so much. More than most could ever wish for."

My angry reflection snarled and replied with venom in his voice. "You succeeded only to fail. And such a failure! And who do you have to share any success with anyhow? Your mom is dead. Any recent success was because she died! You have nobody. Nobody. You're the worst kind of loser there is. A winner or nothing? You're nothing."

I threw cold water on my face with shaking hands. An idea came to mind. I rushed to my bedroom and started packing a suitcase. I was numb. I was packing without any destination in mind. It was a new feeling for me. I always planned my next steps in life. I always had a target, and knew how to reach it. This time was different.

I ordered a taxi to the airport. When the driver asked which terminal, I said, "I'll let you know shortly." On my phone, I quickly looked up flights and found one bound for Amsterdam. I booked it, and, without thinking about it any further, emailed my agent and team to let them know I would be away for the next few weeks.

On the plane, I finally took some time for introspection, scrutinizing the man I had become in the last weeks. I wanted a break from him. I wanted an escape from myself. I decided to live the next few weeks doing things I was always forbidden or too scared to do.

Up until that dark time, I was always the well-behaved man. I'd limited myself to living tamely, despite my success. Sure, like everyone else, I'd met a few girls and enjoyed parties and a few clubs, but why did I hold back? I was set to change that. I thought of the outrageous things I could be doing. I wanted to experience the taboos and things I grew up disdaining because of family and societal expectations. I had nothing left to hold me back: no career, no family. With the death of my mother, I realized, I free off the weight of a conscience.

That long plane ride took my daydreaming mind to the wildest places and fantasies. I would live like a bad boy. The gloves were off. Sex, drugs, wild parties. And nothing tame or vanilla. I was free to explore. I was not the writer, Henry, anymore. I was not the well-behaved Henry. For the next weeks, or months maybe, I would break every rule I'd known. I would act on every fantasy I had.

Chapter One
Part Two

I had heard once that you'll find what you're looking for when you stop looking for it. It is the sort of thing you hear when the discussion is about love: when someone has failed and failed to find a lover, if they just stop looking, the partner of their dreams will miraculously show up. I didn't buy it. Not for a minute. What I sought is what I got. What I didn't go looking for, I just didn't care about. What I was looking for was trouble. That's exactly what I found.

If my mind hadn't been fixed on my most self-indulgent and libidinous fantasies that I had planned to soon make reality, I may have noted more details of my trip from Amsterdam Schiphol Airport into the city proper. I'd have noticed calm waterways lined with cottage-style homes; soccer fields speckled with children in brightly-colored uniforms; an ancient, sprawling cemetery; and then incongruously modern office buildings. With all of Amsterdam's gothic architecture juxtaposed with modern, the city was unlike my comparatively drab Manhattan. Looking back, I might have paid more attention to the vibrant colors, old-world architecture as well as the pleasant, thoughtful, bicycle-riding, social-minded Dutch. However, I was preoccupied by my yen for what I imagined to be the darker Amsterdam and all the pleasures and taboo adventures I hoped to find there.

I planned my itinerary for my first day of excess. I would go looking for drugs—something I'd never done before. I would then come back to the hotel for a little rest and get myself groomed and shaved—making sure that every part of my body that I wanted stimulated was clean and smelling fresh. I would then go out, visit a club, get good and high, and bring a girl back, or two, or a few. It all depended on how I was feeling at the time. I would deny myself no sensation nor pleasure that presented itself.

Drugs. Like I said, I'd never bought drugs before, let alone in a new city on an unfamiliar continent, but it was number one on my itinerary. Alcohol had been my drug of choice, but I intended to expand on that. The only information I'd garnered on drugs was from television and movies, and also a little from the times I'd been part of the odd Monday-morning bragging sessions with college classmates. I admired those classmates, even then, who bragged about the "pot" they'd smoked or the "blow" they'd snorted before they picked up girls at the club. I would never have had the nerve to consider drugs, much less embark on an excessive, hedonistic bender like the one upon which I'd just embarked.

Even at my thirty-nine years, I felt like a twenty-year-old, full of youthful excitement. Unconcerned about my naiveté and utter ignorance regarding the city, I struck out on foot. The Red Light District was not far and I was sure I'd have luck there. I had barely the vaguest idea of what I was looking for. I didn't see anyone in a trench coat peddling illicit wares. There weren't any caricatures of shady individuals leaning on street lamps or gangsters flanked with looming thugs. I was at a loss. Tourists strolled along cobblestone walkways on either side of the quiet waterway and mopeds buzzed gently around foot traffic.

"IGNORE STREET DEALERS," blinked a sign. It was the sort of sign that might be more at home warning highway drivers of a lane reduction or construction ahead. I blinked back at the sign and there was a friendly, smiling man suddenly at my elbow, indicating the sign with a tilt of his head.

"Some asshole has been passing off white heroine for coke," the man informed me amicably. "My stuff is totally safe," the man dressed in casual, athletic-emblemed attire assured me, "How much do you need?"

I looked at the imploring sign, then back at my new acquaintance. I was so inexperienced, I had a handful of bills clumsily out of my pocket before I even considered a reply. He regarded the wad of Euros and quickly waved it away. "Put that away," he urged gently and coughed a disarming chuckle even as his gaze followed the money back to my pocket. "How long are you staying in Amsterdam, sir? he asked.

"I haven't decided yet," I admitted. Then added, with a naive determination, "But not until I've sated all of my appetites."

"Poetic," he remarked, giving me an assessing once-over. "I have just what you need."

And he did.

Looking back, it was a gamble. I was lucky that he recognized me as a potential regular and didn't try to pass off flour or the deadly white heroine for cocaine. After seeing the determination in my eyes, and certainly the fat roll of euros, he must have foreseen the uncommonly large amount of money he was going to make off me. I would find him again and again in the days to come to top up my supply of coke and weed.

Carrying on with the first day's itinerary, I walked back to my hotel, an opulent place with astounding décor, doting porters and ingratiating counter staff. The only complaint I'd heard about this hotel was its close vicinity to the Red Light District, the very reason I found it the perfect center of operations for my escape into indulgence, my exploration of a new Henry. I stowed my illicit treats in the room's safe and spent a great deal of time preparing for my evening. Through the seemingly countless mirrors in the lavish bathroom, I watched myself shower, shave—both my face and other, more tender nether regions—, brush my teeth and groom my hair. It had been a while since I'd gone to a club, since college, in fact, but I knew how to capitalize on my striking features. The new Henry, when I looked at him in the mirror, looked well at home in his tight-fitting, loose-collared shirt. His keen, blue eyes observed me and he and I exchanged a wolfish smile. The young women at the club were going to eat up the salt and pepper at his temples and the lean, athletic build he'd maintained since college. He had the look of a predator in his eyes, a winner.

The relentless bass thudded in my chest even from the washroom stall in which I sat. I was facing the wall and leaning my elbow on the porcelain tank, trying to line up a tiny spoon burdened with a powdery heap of my first hit of cocaine ever. I spilled the first one, but the second spoonful was a success. It made my sinuses burn and my eyes water. Only moments after I blinked the tears away, I could feel a rush of energy. Other than that, I didn't feel all that different. I sniffed, wiped my face and proceeded out into the cacophony of the club. I'd found a tumbler of whiskey, still my favorite, and by the time I made it to the edge of the undulating crowd, I felt an overwhelming sense of confidence. I left my drink behind to follow my tingling loins into the throng of potential quarries, cocaine simmering in my brain. I decided, the moment a particularly lascivious blonde was grinding against my groin, that I loved the new Henry, and coke.

I felt, spoke and walked differently. I said precisely what was on my mind, and I felt the freedom to act on my every, and darkest, whim. Things, of course, went as planned and I ended up bringing a woman to the hotel. She wasn't precisely my type: a little too tall, bustier than I like too, with shoulder-length, dirty blond hair. But it didn't stop me from trading kisses and nips during our short stay in the elevator; in my current state of mind, she was perfect enough. I felt more virile, more... primal than ever. We clawed at each other's clothes and then skin. We never made it to the bed, the carpet, burning our knees and elbows, was more apt.

Both of us were floating on an alcohol, coke and hormone high. We were utterly free of inhibitions as only stoned strangers can be. As I rutted on top of her, sweat beading on my brow and upper lip, she took my hand and placed it on her hair. I first pulled gently, then I realized that the harder I pulled, the more she moaned and enjoyed it. Up until then, I had been the gentle man in bed. Not so, the new Henry. I found myself enjoying the notion of being rough and dominant. That's when I pulled at a fistful of her hair and sneered down at her, meeting her wild gaze. The feeling was, at once, alien and exhilarating.

The woman, whose name I never bothered to learn, then put my hands on her neck. I paused for a millisecond, during which time, I stepped outside of myself. I looked down at the tangle of sweaty limbs, flushed skin and bared teeth. I recognized that man, that alpha male in total control. There was not a hint of fear in his snarling, exultant expression. I choked her then. I slapped her. The woman yelped and she spread her legs all the wider for me. She even went so far as to beg, imploring me to go on.

"That's it," she gasped, her back arching and hips writhing as pain and pleasure twisted into an obscene euphoria. "That's what I need. Take it from me." Her cheek was ruddy from my last backhand and she touched the pain-hot flesh there with her fingertips. A devilish grin curled her lips and she rocked her pelvis, urging me to fuck her.

Intending to punish her with an especially powerful thrust, I reared back with a snarling grin on my face. My smirk fell and I glared down at my suddenly defiantly flaccid organ.

I was first embarrassed, and I felt like a failure. Failing was something I was escaping, and here I was failing at the most basic level: my manhood. It hit me to the core. I roared in frustration and pushed myself off her.

She tried comforting me, tried to make me feel better, as if sympathy were what I needed. It is a human pattern that when we face failures, we judge, and then we try to share sympathy, even if it's just to make ourselves feel better about the other's inadequacy. It is exactly what had happened when I failed with my book.

I rushed her out of my suite even as she, rattled, was trying to wrestle herself back into her clothes. The more she said that it was ok, the more aggressive and rude I became. I could not stand looking at her for the slightest second. She was my reminder that I had failed once again. I kicked her out.

I went to bed. Sleep was my only respite from that situation, that incurable feeling of failure. I woke up shortly after noon, hung over and tired. It took me few moments to remember where I was and what had happened the night before.

I got up and decided I needed to get out of that room. It was still raw in my hangover-sore mind. At a café close to the hotel, I sat where I could watch the tourists walk by on their way to museums, gothic churches and the Red Light District. I ordered myself a coffee, lit a cigarette—something I had never done before the previous night—and I explored the new-found pleasure of smoking with coffee as I ran through the prior evening's humiliating adventure.

Something about how she squirmed and talked dirty turned me off. Something about her expression of pleasure ruined it for me completely. I kept seeing that sympathetic look on her mascara-streaked face. Even when I remembered my hands squeezing her throat, the sympathy was still there in her eyes. She was feeling sorry for me, pitying me. It was the sort of look reserved for the runners-up, for the unfortunate. For the losers.

In my mind's eye, I slapped her. I slapped the sympathizing look right off her face. I watched her face change from wide-eyed shock to primal fear when I raised my hand again. She saw me then, recognized me. Sympathy turned to terror and then I was fucking her. Fucking her savagely, holding her down where I could watch every look of fright and panic as I implacably, relentlessly took what I wanted.

The sensation of the erection straining in my pants under the table snapped me out of my daydream. I went to take another pull on my cigarette but it had burned down to the filter. My coffee was cold, my cigarette was all ash, and my dick throbbed angrily. My hangover was forgotten.

I'd cracked the code. What turned me on was control, and, often, the complimentary feeling to control is fear. That's what intensifies the pleasure of control, seeing the fear in my sexual partner's eyes.

Once back in my suite, with the imagination of a writer, I pondered the concepts of control and fear. I replayed the night before but changed that one thing about it: the fear. I was getting another hard-on, and was enjoying myself until I was interrupted by a knock at the door.

"Housekeeping," chirped an implausibly cheerful voice.

"Damn it! Goddam idiots," I said aloud. I looked about my suite to see that, after last night's activities, it *did* require some tidying. I opened the door to find a girl whose crisp little maid's uniform hugged her svelte figure in a most appealing way.

"Would you like your suite cleaned?" she asked with a smile.

She was petite, had her hair in a bun and was the picture of innocence. I, on the other hand, was in my robe, with an erection threatening to reveal itself, and my mind in the filthiest of places.

When she walked in, I shut the door behind her. It wasn't a conscious decision to make this young maid the first victim in my study of the control-fear equation. I came from behind her, looming; she tensed, dropping the towel that was slung over her arm. She looked beyond me at the closed door, reached for the knob and stammered, "Sir, I need my—" I grabbed her hand, and squeezed. She was afraid. And my dick had never been harder.

I did not want to rape her. I feared the consequences of rape. Tricky situation. Difficult fantasy. So, I gave her a hundred euros and let the housekeeper go. I figured a good tip will keep her mouth shut about the encounter. It actually did.

Still shaken and excited, I started formulating a solution to my situation. I would start hiring girls, I decided. At least, if they're paid, I can do what I want. I'd be the client and they'd follow my rules.

I showered, and made my way downstairs to the lobby. I wanted to talk to the concierge and ask for a service where I can hire girls. At first, I was shy. Maybe it was the old Henry holding me back. Then the new Henry, the bad boy, broke through.

"What's a good agency to hire girls?" I asked, shirking my characteristic tentativeness.

The expression on the man's face barely registered a response, no shock whatsoever. After all, it is Amsterdam. He smiled and gave me a business card. The agency probably provided him with a stack of them.

"May I use your phone?" That question got a pause out of him. Here is a hotel guest making a call to hire a girl right in front of him. I bet that was a new one. I couldn't have cared less.

"Petite girl. Preferably 5'5 or shorter. Hm? Hold on," I said, then covered the receiver and turned to the concierge. "What's 5'5 in centimeters?"

That elicited a blank stare before he replied with a tang of sarcasm in his voice, "Sir, let me check that for you. Right away." A few ticky-tacks of the keyboard and a click of the mouse and he pointed at the screen.

"Shorter than 165 centimeters," I informed the representative from the agency. I favored the concierge with a wink and went on, "A brunette, please." The concierge diligently pretended not to hear my every word.

"Yes. Can she be here in two hours? I'm at Sofitel Legend the Grand Amsterdam." I covered the receiver once more and hissed at the concierge, "They couldn't think of a longer name for this place?" Then, a thought struck me and, back into the phone, I added, "And please. I want a girl who isn't really into, you know, BDSM?" I spelled out the acronym as casually as I could and the concierge tried to hide an eye-roll. "No, someone young and new... inexperienced. Ok? Excellent. Oh, whatever the price is fine." I gave the voice on the other end of the phone my room number and handed the phone back to the concierge. He then made a point of gracefully returning the phone to its cradle and smiling broadly at me.

I tipped the concierge exceedingly well. He pocketed the money and then favored me with a wink of my own. I left and ate my late breakfast quickly so I could return and prepare for my much-anticipated encounter.

From my room, I called the concierge and asked for what might be considered strange items: duct tape, scissors and a steak. Rare. And a bottle of their finest red wine. He did not question and had the items sent to my room within the hour.

I put the duct tape by the door and the steak knife by the chair where she would be sitting. I'd cut into the steak and smeared the blade with blood for effect. I took the rope belt from the bathrobe and coiled it on the table. I closed the curtains, dimmed the lights and lit some candles. I decided on casual clothing: jeans and a t-shirt. I looked in the mirror and rubbed the dusting of coke from my nose after snorting a nice, long rail. I was ready.

There was a knock at the door. Here she was.

A petite girl, just like I had asked for, walked in. I could almost smell the fear emanating from her, which, in turn, started getting me excited. I locked the door behind her.

She tried to hide her fear behind a desperate smile. "Don't smile," I demanded coldly. The smile dissolved. I relished the way that intensified her fear. Her eyes grew wide and she avoided my gaze.

She walked in and saw how I'd set up the chair and the tape, and then the knife. For an instant, her eyes went wide and she looked toward the door as though to bolt. I stood before the door. No escape. I instructed her to take a seat on the chair by the table where the knife sat, the rope was placed, and the candle flickered.

She walked slowly, all tits and ass, trying to be sexy. She disobeyed me then. Instead of sitting like I had asked, she came over to me, turned and began to grind back against my pelvis.

I snapped.

"You will do *precisely* as I say," I roared. She nodded quickly in agreement, and did not even dare a reply.

She sat down, and furtively glanced at the door, the window, the phone, probably trying to figure out a way to survive this. I could read what was going on in her mind as her gaze flitted about the room. She was wondering what the bloodied knife was doing there. She was scared for her life. She was scared of *me*. I savored the feeling of being the object of primal fear.

At that moment, when her hesitation was most obvious, I pulled out a stack of cash. A pile of American hundred-dollar bills. Her eyes widened, but that exquisite fear was still there. The moment I stopped sensing fear, the deal was over. She did not know that.

"Will you hurt me?" she asked. It was probably her way to assure to herself that she would do whatever I wished for the cash, as long as I wouldn't kill her.

I watched her mind work at this problem: she knew I would not kill her. After all, I had called the agency, gave my hotel number and I would be easily caught.

She was unprepared when I placed the knife at her throat. She shivered. I unfastened my belt and lowered my fly.

"Put this in your mouth. If I feel teeth..." I implied the consequences of disobedience by letting the point of the knife press gently at her skin.

She did as she was told, and her trembling lips were a vivid sign of fear. The more fear she exhibited, the more I relished each sensation. She abandoned all other thoughts and feelings. She only felt my knife and my cock, not knowing with which I would penetrate her in the next heartbeat. Besides love and hate, fear is the strongest human emotion.

I took her by the wrist and dragged her to the bedroom where I wrenched the clothes from her, stripping her. Then I pulled her hair until I could see the pain twist her pretty features. She didn't struggle at all; she was either too frightened or needed the money very badly. I stopped. I tied her up. I got one of the lit candles and raised it over her nipple. The little nub of flesh crinkled and hardened when the wax seared it. A tear welled in her eye. I let out a long, contented sigh as I watched that single, lonely tear stain her cheek with a smear of eye makeup. First, calm overtook me, the first moment of ease I'd felt in months. Then, I felt an uncontrollable arousal. I looked down to find my dick jutting from my loins. It was the last thing she saw before I covered her eyes with a makeshift blindfold—her torn stocking.

I watched her tremble and impotently loll her head from side to side blindly as I straddled her and stroked myself. She didn't know from one second to the next if it would be her last. I came on her small, perfect breasts and shocked, blindfolded face.

Then I paid her and told her to leave. I left her there and sat in next room, idly staring out the window as she wiped her face clean with the back of her hand and left without a word.

As the days went by, a pattern developed. I would wake sometime between eleven and twelve o'clock, choose between a rail of coke or a bowl of weed (usually leftovers from the prior evening), shower and shave, then place my order for the adventure that night. The afternoons were spent visiting sex shops, attending BDSM-themed sex shows, and surfing the internet on my phone, all in the name of research. My cocaine-hastened brain took it all in and I would have my plans for the night.

It soon became old hat though. Money bought me some of the best coke, the best girls and bought the most wonderfully deplorable sex I'd ever imagined. With a mere stack of bills, I could inflict pain, utter control and humiliation on a beautiful, young whore. The excitement and the catharsis were growing increasingly short-lived. Like my other new vices, I needed another fix, more and more each time.

There was one encounter that stood out from the rest.

It was perhaps the most frightening thing to happen to me in Amsterdam. There was a young, dark-haired girl with soft, brown eyes. She had the type of features that made her look even younger than her reported nineteen. The fear on her flushed features as I thrusted into her was intoxicating. My comparatively large hands encircled her throat as I took her. The sound of her breath catching in her throat triggered a sudden and violent orgasm. I felt like it would never stop coming. The lewd sounds of my flesh slapping at hers filled the room as I fucked and choked her with equal savagery.

I looked at her again, my climax finally beginning to subside. She was still. Her jaw was slack and her eyes had rolled back under their lids. Her expression was profoundly vacant. Still inside her, I froze with panic. She wasn't breathing!

Suddenly, the girl croaked and dragged in a desperate, shuttering breath. Terror twisted her cherubic features and she wrenched at the two sets of handcuffs with which I'd secured her to the bedposts. It took me perhaps a dozen thrusts to burst a second orgasm into that same condom with her thrashing and begging me, screaming our pre-determined safe word at me and weeping.

That encounter cost me a pile of euros and still more for her to promise not to report me to the agency. I couldn't afford to be black-listed after all.

I did not wish to be a criminal, I just wanted to be bad. I found great pleasure in inflicting pain on others. I was deflecting my own pain, while being in a position of power and control. It was making me feel good, and that's all I cared about. I did a lot of drugs, drank a lot, and lost touch with reality—exactly what I came to Amsterdam to do.

Eventually, my office began trying to reach me. Through one of the credit cards I had used for business expenses, they found out where I was. The fact that my whereabouts were known made me feel uncomfortable. The new Henry was on an escape. This was a holistic experience, and everything had to be perfect. My office and some friends had grown very worried. I did not care. I was too busy escaping to care.

It was time to go, and this time I'd be more careful and not let anyone track me.

I packed my bags and stepped out of the hotel and directly to the taxi parked out front. "Where are you from?" I asked the taxi driver.

"Ljubljana, Slovenia, Sir," he answered cheerfully, with a thick accent.

"Ok, that is where I am going. Ljubljana it is," I said to myself. One may think that it is too random. It is, actually. But to someone who is eluding the world, and himself, it was the perfect way to disappear.

I got on the first flight to the taxi driver's home city. I knew what I would do. I would find the best hotel and pick up where I'd left off in Amsterdam. I thought about spicing things up, maybe hiring more than one girl, or a virgin. I had little to no limitations by then.

Snow-capped mountains greeted me on the descent into Ljubljana, Slovenia. Walking out of the airport, I felt like I was in a village. It felt remote and distant. I liked it that way. It *was* an escape, after all.

I took a taxi to the hotel I had found on my phone. The trip took me through stretches of farmland and evergreen forest, exactly the sort of place that is ideal for reflection and introspection. I did neither. During those thirty minutes, I was researching on my phone avenues for further escapism. The hotel, Grand Hotel Union, was exactly how I would imagine a Slovenian hotel, it was crowned with a copper dome roof and it overlooked a busy, cobblestone pedestrian square, a triple bridge spanning a river and, of course, a castle.

I checked in, and went for a walk. It really was a pretty city. It wasn't entirely dissimilar to Amsterdam, at least in how old-world it was; it had that ancient, European look and was more like Amsterdam than

Manhattan at least. There was something truly elegant about the cream-white buildings framing the cobble-stone streets. I passed graceful rococo arches and then commercial buildings that would have suited a science fiction movie set.

Upon my return to the hotel, I immediately befriended the concierge, knowing he was my most reliable resource for the sorts of things in which I was interested. He spoke the language (English wasn't as prominent here as it was in Amsterdam) and struck me as resourceful and discrete. At least I paid him enough for him to be and to consider himself an employee of mine.

I asked him, Dimitrij, to come up to my room. Of course he did; after all, he now worked for me. The money I gave him was probably more than he would make in a whole month at the hotel. I explained to him what I was into. "I like to torture girls, but no one is leaving this hotel as a corpse. Don't worry."

He was not surprised at all, and he very calmly said, "What does corpse mean?"

"A dead body," I replied, patiently.

He smirked, approached me and whispered, in a conspiratorial tone, "Sir Henry, if someone is dead, you just call me. We will always find a solution."

I knew I had my man there. Someone who will get me everything I desire, and who would take a bullet for me, for the right price. I tipped him a little more, and the greed in his eyes told me he was mine.

On his way out, he told me something quite interesting. "We don't have to go through an agency here. They ask many questions, and they care too much about their girls. I have a friend who has girls. They are all new to this. They are newcomers to Slovenia. No parents, no family."

"New to this is a good thing," I replied. "Let's see what your friend has. I need one for eight tonight. Money is not an issue. Understood?"

"Yes, Sir. Of course, of course."

I added, "I need chains, whips, nipple clips, candles, a saw, duct tape, marijuana, cocaine, and—"

He interrupted me. "I will get it all. Don't worry, Sir Henry," he assured me.

I knew he had done this before; after all, I am not the only guest who is into fetish and rough play.

A few hours later, there was a knock at my suite's door. I slipped under the door a note I'd prepared. It read, "Count to 30, then open the door yourself." I left the door unlatched.

It was as though my play in Amsterdam were simply preparation for my time in Ljubljana. I'd honed the order to these encounters to a script of sorts. It took planning to get to the point where I felt the type of control for which I so desperately hungered, no, ached. The type of control that made my heart race, and the sort of fear that made me hard.

I stood behind the chair I'd placed facing the door, waiting for my first Slovenian victim to arrive. I had to admit that after my talk with the concierge, I had wilder ideas and thoughts that started to scare me. This time, I found myself wondering, in those thirty seconds before the door would open, if I could possibly have the guts to kill a human being.

The thirty seconds passed and the door opened. To my surprise, in glided the most beautiful girl I had ever seen. I pushed myself forward on the chair, then remembered that there were rules I'd set, and remembered where my pleasure is gained. I leaned back once more and coolly watched her walk in. She exuded confidence, but also innocence, as this youthful, dark-haired vision gracefully entered the room.

Long, black hair, dark brown eyes, fair skin, and teeth like pearls framed by lush, red lips. Somehow, her casual attire didn't take away from her appeal. Most girls would have worn something sexy, like a cocktail dress or miniskirt. She wore a charcoal tank top, a plain, black leather jacket, and pair of artfully distressed jeans. Even dressed like that, I could make out her youthful form: lithe thighs under the denim, lean belly and pert, buoyant breasts under her jacket. Returning my scrutiny to her cool visage, I saw that she had a mysterious look to her. As a writer, I sensed big stories right off the bat. There was a story there; there was pain; there was a girl on a mission. It wasn't an encounter with a prostitute. It was an encounter with someone who had secrets. Secrets are simply untold stories, ones that are deep, dark, and intense. I had to know what stories she hid behind those wide, perceptive eyes.

This pause was not part of the script. The Henry I had unearthed knew that only through darkness can the choicest pleasure be gained. I was powerfully attracted to her. But that would change nothing. It meant that I had to be the most intense, darkest, and cruelest person with her. I would not hold back, not with her.

"Sit down." I said finally, indicating the chair behind which I stood with a calculated mixture of nonchalance and menace.

"Ok," she replied and kept her eyes calmly on me until she turned and sat. I was, for an instant, distracted by the sight of her legs crossing one over the other.

Behind her, I blinked away the distraction and issued a second command. "You don't speak unless I require a response, understood?" It was New Henry's voice. I took comfort in its iron confidence and it was easy to delve deeper into my newly found persona then. I hid behind the New Henry and basked in the freedom my new self afforded me.

"Sure," she said with a smile.

I rounded the chair and slapped her hard on her face.

With absolutely no sign of fear or pain, she straightened and looked emotionlessly at the wall.

"Do you know that you are at my mercy? That I can do whatever I want to you?"

She did not reply. She did not show any distress. She looked down indifferently.

Her indifference irritated me. The lack of fear bothered me. I grabbed a fistful of her silken hair and dragged her to the bedroom. There was no resistance, only indifferent compliance. That was different, all the women I had been with had resisted, naturally. She did not. It was as if I were dragging a dead body.

In the bedroom, I forced her jacket off and then ripped her clothes. She was unmoved and looked away, heedless of my abuse. She showed neither resistance nor fear. Someone in her position ought to be at least concerned by the prospect of having to leave the hotel with a ripped tank top. Not so, my new plaything.

I tied her up to the bed with the chrome chains supplied by Dimitrij. I gave her a few, experimental lashes with my freshly-procured whip. No response. None whatsoever. She was taking each lash and not reacting at all. The more she resisted, the more it provoked me. I sat at the edge of the bed, lit a cigarette, and paused for but a moment before nearing the glowing ember to her face. She did not even move. I brought the burning cigarette close enough to her cheek that she could certainly feel the heat from it, but I could sense no fear. I put out the cigarette in the ashtray, enraged. How could someone be this fearless? Was she even human?

I was annoyed and disappointed then. She must be well-versed in S&M play, contrary to my requests. "You've done this before," I growled impatiently.

"No, Mister." she replied evenly. Her accent was Arabic.

I slapped her again, "Liar!" She did not reply.

"Why don't you answer?" I raged.

"You said I am a liar. You did not ask if I were a liar. You asked me to talk only when you ask questions, Mister," she said with a soft, unshaken voice.

I lost my mind. The whip left angry welts across her stomach, marred the perfection of her youthful breasts, and was utterly ineffective. I dropped the whip on the floor and, with the fire of rage burning in my eyes, assailed her with open-handed slaps to her face and closed-fisted blows to her stomach. Again, no reaction. She took my beatings as if it were something to which she was accustomed. The girl stared up at me, with an unimpressed lift of a brow. I sneered down at her, froth at the edge of my mouth and sweat gleaming on my brow. It was unacceptable and inexcusable, and maddening. I was incensed. She was bruised, yet kept the same expression she had first worn when she walked through the door into my room, into my life.

I had enough. "Get out," I snarled, seething, before unlocking her restraints and derisively dropping her fee in a pile of bills on the bed and storming out of the bedroom.

Without a word, she passed me and zipped her jacket up over her shredded top. The door clicked closed as she made her unhurried exit.

I sat on the couch overlooking the living room. Why was I so absurdly infuriated? This girl had left a deep impression. I could not come to terms with her lack of fear. A storm roiled in my chest. Frustration wasn't the major one. I was intrigued, something I had not felt in a long time. Intrigue can be a feeling with no explanation. It is the journey toward explaining the unknown that matters the most. "I don't even know her name and I want to take that journey," I chided myself.

I poured myself a glass of whiskey, and looking at the window outside, I watched the ancient, Slovenian streetscape but didn't truly see anything past my churning tumult of emotions. "Where is she from? What's her story?" I asked myself. As a writer, one gets to understand a person by simply looking at their eyes. Writers tell stories; and where better than eyes are stories kept?

In that stranger's eyes, I could sense a story of great love and sorrow, and defeat. "Why are you obsessing over a hooker? Forget about her. Go get another girl," I implored myself.

I found myself calling the concierge, my new employee. "Dimitrij, come up here."

"Yes, Sir Henry, I will be right up." And true to his word, he was in my suite only minutes later.

"You know the girl you had just gotten me?" I asked, my voice brittle with agitation.

He blurted a hurried answer. "Yes, Sir Henry. Was she no good? I saw she left early. I will make sure your money is refunded. Don't worry about it. I am very sorry. Very sorry."

I interrupted impatiently, "Shut up. Listen. I want her back."

He was confused but, of course, he did not object. "Ok, Sir Henry. She will be back."

I stated, with a voice of cold iron, "Tonight."

The fifty minutes of waiting and agonizing in between his leaving and her returning felt like a year. I doubted she would come back. She did, however.

This time, she knocked the door and I opened. Again, unflinching and confident, she walked in and did not utter a word. "What's your name?" I asked.

"Tala. My name is Tala," she said.

"Where are you from?" I asked.

"I am from many places," she answered with a look that finally showed fear. Had I touched a nerve? Was her origin a source of fear? I knew that all my next questions would be about that.

"Where are you from, exactly?" I insisted.

She furrowed her perfect brow in confusion. My interrogation, unlike our primary encounter, was quiet, almost gentle. I wanted to understand the reason behind her lack of fear. How could she be so passive and unafraid when faced with cruelty and violence? What made her so strong? What made her fearless?

She did not answer my question and I didn't press the matter. I wanted to take a break from this questioning. I had set a rule: I would never allow my playthings to drink alcohol or do drugs. I wanted the fear to be natural, untainted and sincere. There was another rule against socializing or telling them anything about myself, or knowing their story. The principal rule, never learn names, had already been broken. All rules with Tala were to be abandoned.

It was obvious that I could not get her to talk, so I figured alcohol might help. "Do you drink?" I asked her.

"Sometimes," she answered.

"Would you like to have a drink with me?"

"As long as you're paying, it's up to you how we spend the time. I don't mind."

"Money is not an issue. What would you like to drink?" I asked. She pointed at the bottle of red wine sitting on the table by a bowl of fruit.

While I uncorked the bottle, my attention was still riveted to her. She sat down, quiet and aloof. I was at a loss as to how to start a conversation, so I popped the cork and poured her a glass and I poured myself another whiskey. Her presence had an odd effect on me. The way she sat and watched me, was she as intrigued with me as I was with her? If she was sore from our earlier encounter, she showed no sign of it, physically or otherwise. I hadn't wanted to get to know—to understand—a woman this urgently for a long, long time. How would I bring the conversation back around to her past?

"In which part of Ljubljana do you live?" I asked, before considering that I would have no idea where any particular neighborhood might be located in the city.

Was that a smirk at the corner of her lips? "I don't know. I'm not exactly new to Ljubljana, but I have a driver and I never had the chance to learn the names of the different neighborhoods," she replied, indulging my queries for the moment.

"Where are you from?" I asked.

"Lebanon," she answered before she could stop herself. "I'm not supposed to say," she added, apprehension evident in her wide-eyed expression.

I walked to her and placed my hands gently on her shoulders, looking at her sympathetically. "It's okay," I breathed. I could feel her shoulders relax under my touch. She felt comfort in my gentle touch, I sensed. She needed compassion. We had that thing in common. Even after just having met her, I could tell that we might have a great deal in common.

A winner always recognizes another winner. We were both masters of victory, or so I thought and believed. Even more easily, a defeated winner can recognize another defeated winner, and I knew it as a matter of fact that we shared that as well.

Before long, the shoulder patting graduated to a hug, and then, to my surprise, I felt Tala placing her head on my chest as I made room to sit by her. I wondered if she was feeling what I felt. My heart was racing, so was hers.

I never expected this chemistry. It shocked me. We lingered in that warm, almost desperate, embrace. Those moments, with her head on my chest and our arms wrapped around one another, brought me more pleasure than all of the preceding weeks' escapades put together. She finally disengaged and stood. She was lost; that, I could read in her eyes. She carried her glass of wine and stood by the large windows. Tala, framed in the huge windows' waning light, the glittering backdrop of the old-world city behind her, looked at me from over her shoulder. I stared back, and to my surprise, a smile blossomed on my lips. It was the first smile I would share with her, and the first genuine smile I had had for a long time.

We fell into a comfortable silence, she drinking her wine, I sipping my whiskey. We did not feel the urge to talk, though the silent communication between us was a constant, deep and profound.

Tala was the first to break the silence. "Where are *you* from?" she asked me. And then, for the next hour, I would tell her my story. She opened the second bottle of wine herself, and I lost track of how many whiskies I'd sipped through. She listened, but from distance. I found respite in just telling my story and having someone, especially her, listen. We were both in a wayward state in our lives, each in our own way. Our circumstances were different, our motivations and origins were just as dissimilar, but we were adrift in the same way: I by choice and she by circumstance. There is no prostitute who was born to be one.

I ended my story with my arrival in Amsterdam and did not wish to continue. By that time, Tala had become a bit drunk from all the wine, and in the next few hours until dawn, both our lives would change forever.

Perhaps because she was so tipsy, without my even asking her, she said, "I failed my husband, my family, my entire life. And what am I now? I am a prostitute."

I did not like the mention of her husband. I wasn't sure why I felt that pang of jealousy, that insecurity, but I did not care. The instinct and desire to win took over again—something I haven't felt for a long while. But winning what? I did not know. I wasn't sure if it was the whiskey, or if I had gone mad.

"Why are you a prostitute?" I asked. I thought it might lead to her telling her own story.

She simply said, "I am forced to be a prostitute. That's who I am now. I am making some money. I need to find my husband. I am saving money for that. My body is all I have got left."

I had enough questions that I would still be asking until dawn and longer. I still don't know why I made that commitment that night.

"I'm going to help you, Tala," I promised her. "You don't have to be a prostitute any longer." She cried and buried her face in my chest once again. I could feel the warmth of her tears as I held her gently shuddering shoulders. "To every problem," I whispered soothingly, "there is a solution. We need to seek it. We will find it."

In my arms, she looked up at me, her eyes wide and glistening with happy tears, and said, "To answer your question, I am a Palestinian refugee from Lebanon, but I came to Europe from Turkey. My husband is still there, in Turkey."

I was right. There was, indeed, a story—one hell of a story. Tala laid down on the couch, more relaxed than I'd seen her all night. She started narrating her story. I listened to a tale that, even as I listened, I understood would change my life. It is the Tale of Tala, the story that would inspire me to write again, the story that would bring Henry back, the compassionate, gentle Henry. The story Tala shared in that hotel room in Ljubljana would lead us on a mission. And for people born to be winners, missions are meant to be won. It would be the subject of international news headlines and it would be an inspiration to the vulnerable, persecuted and helpless all over the globe.

Chapter Two

As a writer, I have learned that in order to get the story out of someone, you need to make them feel you are part of it while assuring the storyteller that you will never judge. The relationship between the writer and the would-be subject of the story is a complex and sacred one. A writer must be on the storyteller's side, and a sense of trust and comfort needs to be established from the point at which the first words are spoken.

It is sometimes difficult for someone even to start telling their story. They often struggle with how to begin. A story is a chain of events, and often, its protagonist can struggle to determine which event defines the beginning, the catalyst that would bring about the resulting adventures and challenges, the victories and defeats.

It was nearly midnight when Tala felt comfortable enough to start telling me her tale. Before that though, I had to alleviate any fear there was, which wasn't much. Her fears were three, only three. The first, we had already overcome, and that was her reticence to share with me where she was from. In a moment of ease, and with the help of wine, she had told me. Her second fear was her employer, the man who had brought her to me. Being a man of means, that was an easy obstacle for me to overcome.

I, of course, had the concierge's private number by then. "Sir Henry? Is everything okay?" he asked, concern causing his usual affable manner replaced with tension.

"Yes, Dimitrij. Don't worry. I really like this girl you brought me," I said, my hand idly reaching out to touch Tala's thigh. "I want to keep her for my entire stay, which could be days, or perhaps weeks."

"I will make the—"

"Yes. Arrange it. Whatever it costs is fine," I said, staring at Tala where she was reclining and nursing another glass of wine. Of course, Dimitrij didn't mind, as long as I was paying. After all, the effusive concierge's only concern was the money. Tala heard every word, and I could see the signs of relief on her face. She was a bird set free from her cage. The sight of those wide, surprised and grateful eyes gave me satisfaction beyond words.

Tala's third source of fear was, naturally, where to begin and what she could safely confide in me. To each story, there is a beginning, and what better place to start than one's childhood? It always comes back to one's upbringing. It defines the raw, unhewn state of a person before being shaped by the chisel that is life's experiences.

I put down my phone and paused to regard her. She seemed impervious to all that had happened that night, unaffected by the brutality. So strong, so beautiful. What had she endured to have the capacity to forgive the treatment I gave her earlier that night? When she looked at me from where she lounged, with her wide, expressive eyes, she must have seen beyond the man who'd treated her the way I had. I watched her run the tip of a finger around the rim of her wine glass as she looked, her captivating face framed by full, lustrous, black tresses. She directed a demure look at me from under long, kohl lashes and I was transfixed for a long moment. Finally, I gently urged her, "Tell me more, Tala. Tell me about your childhood." I took up the bottle of wine—neither the first nor the last of the night—and refilled her glass.

"My name is not Tala. It is Fatima. I changed it," she started as the wine was poured, then went on.

"I was born on January 21, 1990. My parents were Palestinian refugees and conservative Muslims who lived in a refugee camp in Lebanon. They named me

Fatima. Neither my father nor my mother gave me attention while I was growing up. My mother considered me an 'omen of evil' because I was not born a boy, and was the sixth girl my parents had. My father wanted a boy so he married a second wife; together they reared my brother, Ibrahim. My mother blamed me for my father's second marriage."

Fatima, now Tala, paused and her disposition shifted from melancholy to blithe. She giggled before stating, "My birth was unwelcomed, but I was a pretty girl." She tilted her head and looked at me with an enticing narrowing of her fascinating, brown eyes, "And don't you think I grew into a beautiful woman?" I contemplated her, and she seemed to thrive under my scrutiny. There was a playful challenge in her gaze. I took my time, admiring her raven hair, her lush lips, her bare shoulders. Her selection of tank top and jeans only served to make her body all the more enticing. She had the type of body that men and women both turned to look at wherever she went and, clad in tight denim and form-fitting cotton, every curve was put on fascinating display.

"Yes," I finally replied, "You did, Fatima."

"Call me Tala, don't address me with the name Fatima," she said firmly but not unkindly.

I very nearly didn't hear the rest of the story. Fatima, no, Tala was almost more than I could resist. She met my hungry stare with a cleverly feigned, wide-eyed innocence. She knew precisely what she was doing to me. My loins tingled in anticipation, and I leaned close, drawing her near with one arm. In that moment, Tala seemed to be experiencing similar yearnings; her eyes drifted closed, and she tilted her head to kiss me. At the last instant, before her lips would finally complete our embrace with a kiss, she turned aside and laid her head on my chest.

"I grew up in poverty," Tala explained, deftly evading my kiss. The only indication that she was aware of her effect on me was the way the edge of her lips quirked in a private smile. It took every ounce of my willpower to not pursue another kiss, and more. She knew it. But she had her story to tell, and I was eager to hear it, to know more, to know *her*. Undeterred, she nestled against me and continued. "My father worked as a carpenter in the camp. He could barely earn enough to feed his many children," she went on, pressing close, a natural affection that made my heart swell in my chest. "Because he was a refugee, he could not get a job outside the camp as Palestinians were unable to obtain work permits in Lebanon."

"I grew up feeling contempt for my circumstances. As the unwelcome child and omen of evil," she said with a sneer that did nothing to mar the beauty of her face. "I had to work hard for even the tiniest fraction of the love and attention my parents gave my sisters. I would even fake illness. When I was five, so my mother would take care of me and show me just a little affection, I pretended to be sick. It's not what I got at all. My mother said, 'Enchallah Tmooti W Trayhane Mennek Ya Wejj El Nahes.'" Fatima looked up at me to see my confusion, and she translated the Arabic, "I wish you to die, you face of misfortune." The venom in her voice when she repeated her mother's words disturbed me, and my heart went out to her.

Before I could offer my words of consolation, she went on, "My stepmother and Ibrahim lived on the floor above our two-bedroom, broken-down flat. In the Palestinian refugee camp, flats were cobbled one on top of the other, newer flats built on top of older flats. There was no space within the one-by-one-kilometer camp to do anything else. The two families sharing my father did not associate much at all. My father's second wife was younger and prettier than my mother. He spent more money on his son and his new wife than he did on us, his family downstairs. I would see him going up the stairs with cake in his hands while my sisters and I ate bread and thyme."

"When I was six, I snuck out of our flat to go up to Ibrahim. He was almost four. My stepmother was watching television as my half-brother slept in his comfortable bed. My sisters and I shared a lumpy mattress on the floor downstairs. I entered the room without my stepmother noticing and I was alone with Ibrahim." Tala's eyes drifted closed, and a warm smile found her lips as she fondly remembered her brother. "I started talking to him, 'You know that I love you. You know that whatever they say, you are my little angel.' He woke up then, and I started to get up, worried that he would cry like he always did when waking. Instead, he gave me the brightest, most innocent smile, just for me." Tala snuggled close, sharing with me the warmth of the memory.

There was a longing, a fondness for everyone she described—even her father—that belied her sometimes bitter words and tone. When life is most difficult, we can find solace even in an imperfect past. The future is unknown and frighteningly imminent: the past is familiar and holds no menace any longer no matter how foul.

"I started playing with Ibrahim, and we had such fun. I sat on the floor by the bed, and he was at the edge, laughing at the funny faces I was making. When he reached for me, he fell; he fell hard on his head." Tala's chest rose and fell with a heavy sigh. "He cried, of course. Loudly. I didn't know what to do, run away or help. It was too late. His mother walked in and even as she took up Ibrahim to comfort him, she cursed me. Her shouting brought my mother and two of my sisters up from the downstairs flat. Their shouts joined the storm aimed at me. My stepmother was crying, and so was my half-brother. He wasn't bleeding, but it was unforgivable that I even approach my family's trophy, Ibrahim."

"That night, my father hit me on the face and yelled at me, 'How dare you even come close to Ibrahim! How dare you touch him! It was because of you he fell!'" Tala's voice was brittle and close to breaking when she got to this part of the story. "Before I slept that night, I closed my eyes and tried to find an explanation, an excuse for the way I lived. Even as a child, I always thought that my family's cruelty was because life had been cruel to them. We were refugees, now into our fourth generation in the camp and we were poor. I tried to excuse my parents' behavior with those reasons in mind. I was the sixth girl and the sixth failed attempt to sire a boy. In our Middle Eastern society, only a son can hold the family's name, not a daughter."

Tala shifted to the edge of the couch, leaning forward to refill her glass. For a moment, she distracted herself from the solemn memories she'd just exhumed by rolling the rich, burgundy liquid, swirling it contemplatively. As she raised the glass to her generous lips, she considered me from over its rim. After that short interlude, she sat back and nestled under my arm once more.

"I remember when I was thirteen," she began, unconsciously combing the fingers of her free hand through her luxuriant, ebony hair. "My body had grown womanly, and it didn't take me long to realize that I could take advantage of my figure and my beauty." It was with neither pride nor shame that she told me this. It was true, of course. How could anyone dispute her attractiveness? "I was getting attention. It was such a new experience."

"All through my early, teenage years, it seemed like every man in the camp stared at me. Boys were very nice to me. They often smiled, offered assistance and even helped me with homework or chores like carrying grocery bags. They would follow me, groceries in hand, through the narrow alleyways between the buildings. It was like a maze we lived in," she commented, recalling the labyrinthine series of dusty, arms'-span-wide alleys that were the principal means of passage around the camp. "I would catch the eye of a boy—there were groups of boys, young men, who would hang out together on corners, and they'd always offer to help—I'd make sure to get my bags from him before we arrived at my home. It wouldn't do to have my family see. Often, though, gossip still managed to reach my mother. She would yell at me and forbid me to leave the house for days."

"I was enjoying my beauty and the attention," she admitted matter-of-factly, "That is, until my father interrupted that enjoyment. He forced me to wear a hijab, a head scarf. I had to wear conservative clothes that hid my figure." Tala sighed heavily and stroked her hair fondly, frowning at the memory. "I had a lot of pride in my hair. It was my best feature. My father wanted it covered, for modesty. Although I thought about taking off the hijab at school, I couldn't. I knew my friends would gossip and, as it always did, it would reach my mother's ears. Or worse, it would reach my father's."

"Like all of us in the camp, I attended UNRWA schools," she said, then elaborated, "United Nations Relief and Works Agency. It's an agency that provides infrastructure in camps like the one I grew up in." Coiling a glossy tendril of hair through her fingers, she reclined against me. The warmth of her body was, all at once, exciting and comforting. I never wanted the night to end; just sharing this simple intimacy with Tala made my skin prickle with goosebumps. The bond I was feeling with her was astonishing. I devoured every morsel of information she offered me. I wanted to know everything about Tala, each fact and anecdote. My instincts told me that her story would change my life. She had my rapt attention.

"Some boys still gave me attention, despite my frumpy and concealing clothes. It wasn't on the scale I was used to though. Boys prefer to look at a girl who is wearing tight jeans rather than a girl wearing a baggy skirt." With the precision of a dancer, Tala languidly lifted her leg, pointing her toe ceilingward to prove a point by showing me her long, graceful limb clad in

saw us huddled under the stairs, trapped by the fire raging behind him. In a heartbeat, he was there, his strong arms around both my sister and me. The comfort and safety of his embrace, in that instant, drove away my crippling fear. Bilal looked back to where the flames were licking at the walls, and then around for an exit. He took our hands, pulled us to our feet, and guided us to the back of the building. There was a single door at the end of the short hallway, and it was locked. With the smoke choking us and the heat lashing our backs, Bilal kicked the door completely off its hinges. Sunlight! His grip was iron as he pulled us by the hands to the safety of the street."

We were both out of breath. I wiped perspiration from my brow with the back of my hand and desperately drank the last of my whiskey in one, audible gulp. Tala reclined and laced her fingers on her chest, exhaling a long sigh. A faint blush colored her flawless cheeks, and she said, "I didn't know how to thank him. In the light of day, with the burning building behind us and panic and chaos all around, it was like I saw Bilal for the first time. I was looking at the man who saved my life. It was then that I fell in love with him, the first time I ever experienced real love. With my hand tight in his and his protective gaze on me, I finally found peace and security." Tala's voice trailed off with that, and her eyes glistened as she barely kept her tears at bay.

I didn't share Tala's sentiment at that moment. I got up and, using my bladder as an excuse, walked to the bathroom. I was bothered by the fact that Bilal managed finally to prove himself to her. Sure, he saved her life, and for that I was grateful, but it still rankled me to see the obvious devotion he inspired in Tala. I was being silly, I knew. I blamed it on the alcohol. As I pissed, I thought to myself that I would be her Bilal now. I would save her this time, and she would look at me with that beautiful expression of gratitude. Me. Not him.

As I washed my hands, I stared at myself in the mirror, "I'll bet I'm better looking than him." I was sure of it. I dragged my fingers through my hair, fixing my stylish cut to be just so. Ready to face her once more, and prepared to be her new savior and lover, I gave myself one last glance in the mirror and turned to join my Tala.

She was elegantly strewn across the couch, her face cradled in her arm, and she smiled dreamily at me as I crossed the room to her. I touched her cheek fondly and then sat at the edge of the couch, putting her head gently on my lap. Nuzzling my leg, she continued to tell her story.

"The war ended in August 2006, and the end of the war signaled the beginning of the love between Bilal and me. In refugee camps, love was as complicated as the rest of life. Conservative families still banned their girls from talking or going out with boys," she said. The mention of their love made my heart grow leaden in my chest, but I stroked her shoulder and played the role of the rapt audience. She continued, "Before engagement, two are not allowed to go out together, and premarital sex is a grave sin. It would wound a family's reputation." Tala waved a dismissive hand at the thought, "I did not care much about all that. I happily met Bilal at the school regularly. We spent time on breaks and sometimes we'd write love poems to each other. We were discrete, of course, and only a few people knew about our new relationship. Our close friends helped. When I was out with Bilal, my best friend would lie and tell my mother that I was with her."

"He respected me," Tala went on, "And he told me that when he turned eighteen, the following year, he would come and propose in front of my family. I would dream of that day, the day I became the center of attention day and night for my beloved husband-to-be. That would be the day I left the home and family that treated me like the omen of evil, a jinx. That hope made me patient."

"Bilal came from a poor family too, but he did everything he could to keep me happy. Besides going to school, he worked at a garage to get enough money to buy me a mobile phone. It was how he and

I communicated. I, of course, had to keep it secret from my parents," Tala told me, her cheek warm on my thigh.

"His father had told Bilal that he could start considering engagement when he was eighteen. The following year, in September 2007, our wait was over. It was time. He went to his parents and told them that he wanted them to visit my parents and ask for my hand. Bilal was the oldest of his brothers, and he had started studying at the local university. He was on a scholarship thanks to his excellent grades. He was good and kind; he always helped the elderly, never got in trouble, and was polite to everyone. His parents agreed, and his mother paid us a visit. She told my mother that she and her husband would like to come and talk to Abu Ibrahim, my father, about me. My mother, feeling the pressure from her friend, agreed and told her to come that evening. I was above the clouds with happiness, and my mother knew it. She did not tell me how worried she was to open the discussion with my father.

"That evening, Bilal's parents came. They were summarily rejected by my father. I could see by the glare he gave me that, in his eyes, I was once again a curse. His first excuse was that I was the youngest and my older sisters must be married before me. At that time, three of my sisters were already married, which meant I had to wait for the other two. My father then told Bilal's parents that he would rather wed me to someone who can properly take care of me. His last objection was that he didn't like the fact that I would be living with my in-laws and would have to wait for Bilal to finish university. He added, insultingly, 'For the little hope that he would even get a decent job.'

"My father was well aware of how men looked at me. It was the reason he insisted on my hijab, after all. He was hoping that I would be the one who would marry a rich man rather than a refugee," Tala said. "The next day, Bilal and I met in our usual spot, a café just outside of the camp. I was still so upset I cried when I saw him, I wanted so badly to be held in his strong arms. He alone comforted me. Nobody else would. 'I'm as disappointed as you are by your family's decision,' he said to me, 'But we'll be married, Fatima. I know it. Be patient. Promise me you'll be patient.' I let hope begin to fill my heart. 'Yes, Bilal,' I agreed, 'Maybe it won't be so long a wait. My sisters are pretty, and my family is respected. I'm sure it won't be long before they're married.' Bilal's smile was infectious, and I leaned forward in my chair, eager now for every optimistic and confident word my love was offering.

"'It will only be four years until I'm finished with university,' he said, excited, 'I'm sure I will get an excellent job. You know the marks I get at school. Then I will take you out of this place. We'll have a home of our own, a new life, a family...' I was never so optimistic about the future as I was at that moment when Bilal described the future he was going to earn us. All I had to do was wait four short years. My sisters would certainly be married by then, and he would have a well-paying job straight out of university. Of course it would happen! There was no question in my mind when he looked at me the way he did. I was so in love."

Tala regarded me from where she lay in my lap, and I silently stroked her thick, lustrous hair, "I remember it was 2011, the year Bilal graduated from university. My sisters had gotten married. All that was left was for my love to get a decent job and he would come back and propose to me. I had waited all that time patiently. I did not attend university," she explained, "By the time I finished high school, my father was diagnosed with diabetes and, being the only girl left in our house, I was obligated to stay home to take care of him. His vision was failing, and his health was slowly deteriorating."

"Our family could not afford proper medical care for him, and the local organizations didn't manage to help. This was 2011, around the beginning of the Syrian conflict and many people were fleeing Syria to Lebanon. There were budget cuts for UNRWA, the organization that ran our schools, medical services, and social services. There's a saying: 'What bleeds leads.' It seemed that we, the Palestinian refugees, were yesterday's cause. Media was reporting on the war, and we were deemed old news." Her tone wasn't resentful; she was simply disappointed. "When social media is saturated with news about the Syrian War and the new refugees, money is donated to their cause rather than ours. We've been without a home since 1948, and because of the way the Lebanese government—and society in general—limits our ability to get lucrative jobs, we need agencies like UNRWA. We are excluded from social security; we are refugees." She shook her head, her brow furrowing with the sort of frustration that is born from years of enduring unfairness. "Most who work for them do very good things, and I'm grateful, but, at the same time, there are flaws with the system. The latest, freshest crisis either finds the most donors for its cause, or the existing funding, like in this case, gets reallocated." She glares at the ceiling and adds, "And I won't even tell you about the possible fund misappropriation and how there are no anti-fraud systems in place."

Tala drew in a long, chest-heaving breath and expelled a cathartic sigh. "My father," she said after gathering herself, "was unwell, and we couldn't get him the proper care he needed." And with the story back on track, she carried on. Of course, the subject returned to Bilal, the man who still had an iron grip on Tala's heart, the heart I quickly realized I wanted for my own. "Bilal, on the other hand, finished his degree in computer science. He was one of the best students in his class." I was keenly aware of the fervid expression on her angelic features when she summoned up memories of Bilal. I could feel my teeth clench and my stomach tighten reflexively at each mention of his name. "He used to say that his motivation was his growing love for me," she said, her words a twisting knife to me.

"He spent the majority of his time studying, but he worked on the side so that he could afford to take me out." Her smile was coquettish as she remembered those times, but the subsequent memory darkened that smile. "Bilal was slammed with a harsh reality. He could not get a job. As a Palestinian refugee in Lebanon, he was not permitted to work in many fields. Also, it was a time when Lebanon was facing millions of Syrian refugees flooding into the country. The workforce collapsed. There was no work for him."

"He took me out for lunch at our regular spot, the café outside of the camp. There was none of his characteristic flirting. He was being serious and wouldn't meet my eyes. He was ashamed to tell me that he could not find work. I had known already, but was hesitant to ask about it because I thought, correctly, that it might be a sensitive topic." When I took secret pleasure in Bilal's failure, I felt the sour tang of guilt as much as jealousy. Tala continued. "He explained to me how hard it had been to find a job, how impossible it was. He reminded me that he still had every intention to marry me, but he simply couldn't face my parents, nor would he have a house for me. I would have to live with his family, and that was something my parents would not abide. And really, I had no desire to live with his family either."

"The lunch had the essence of a funeral. We were burying hope," Tala's eyes drifted closed, and she paused long enough for me to wonder if she'd drifted off to sleep. With eyes still despondently shut, she broke the silence. "I remember how I behaved after he told me that he could not propose to me. First, I talked with my family. 'I knew you were wasting your time all these years,' my father said, 'You'd have been better off with any one of the men that came to propose.' And my mother said, 'You're looking for the love that is just for novels and film. It is time for you to accept one of the proposing men instead of clinging to this childish hope. Bilal is not for you.'"

Tala was reliving this defeat bravely. Her jaw was defiantly outthrusted, and her lidded eyes still maintained a vivacious dignity, closed against the negativity of her parents' remembered words. "My father said, 'And that Bilal's job dream was a joke, being a Palestinian refugee. I was too generous with my patience. It is time for you to marry. You'll marry the first man who comes to propose and is able to support you and the family too.'"

"I told Bilal what my father said, hoping it would motivate him to do something, to find a solution. He thought about emigrating, but even that required money to pay one of the smugglers, and it also meant that he would be separated from me. He rejected the thought.

"I grew desperate, but I stayed firm. On the one hand, I would sabotage any proposal that came my way. For example," Tala said, her eyes fluttering open and sparkling with mischief, "When Mohammad came to propose, I showed up with chewing gum in my mouth, and I acted crazy, smacking my gum and giggling. Mohammad was from a good Palestinian family, and he had Canadian citizenship too. He would have provided a good life. Mohammad's mother told my parents that they'd just come for coffee and thanked us for hosting them. When he and his family left so awkwardly, my father yelled at me. My mother beat me. 'He was here to propose! I set up the meeting with his mother!' she screamed at me," Tala said with an odd, thinly veiled sense of pride.

"I would go back to Bilal and tell him about these proposals," Tala continued, "It got him so angry and scared." Sagely, she said, "Out of fear comes many ideas. The pressure, together with the fear, made Bilal lose his mind and begin something that would change his life, and mine."

"It was 2015, and many changes were happening in the Middle East: Syria was at war, and terrorist groups were flourishing. Terrorist organizations needed people, and they were quite aware that youth in the refugee camps were perfect targets for recruitment. Young men in those communities were discontented, frustrated, and, most importantly, desperate. Drugs were starting to become increasingly common in the region, especially in the refugee camps. That desperation, together with the instability of the region, made drugs more sought-after. It was an escape, and the youth were easily tempted in their situation.

"Bilal, who had never taken drugs, had heard of his friends getting addicted. When I gave Bilal an ultimatum: 'You have one month to find a solution to our problem, one month to make it possible for us to get married, or I'll have to accept the next proposal that comes to me.' He grew understandably desperate. He started visiting a café that was known for being frequented by drug dealers. It wasn't far from the camp. Bilal didn't want to buy drugs; he wanted to find the supplier. Eventually, he met Abu Ali.

"Abu Ali had heard about Bilal. Bilal was known to be a genius with computers. He was an excellent student, and people in the camp knew this. He'd received one of the rare scholarships. Abu Ali saw an opportunity in Bilal."

I watched Tala's face screw up in rage as she spat the name, Abu Ali, that first time. I had an idea of what the wretch had in store for Bilal, for which I ruefully praised him, but, judging from my new lover's reaction to his memory, there was more. Enthralled, I listened on.

"The demand for drugs had been growing, and Abu Ali needed help selling the in-demand drugs to customers in the camp. Bilal was resourceful, capable, and, of course, desperate. It was a match made in hell. Bilal started meeting Abu Ali to pick up the drugs and then he would return to the refugee camp and sell them to his friends. He began with just a few bags of marijuana and hash, but soon he was carrying backpacks full of all sorts of drugs into the camp. Word of mouth made for growing business, and Bilal's determination led to his risking his life.

"This all happened in the span of a month," Tala said, her voice cold as iron, the recollection opening old wounds. "During that month, he became strange with me, distant. 'I'm busy making us money so you and I can get married,' he said cryptically when I questioned him about it. I didn't pursue the subject again. I wanted so badly for us to be together and, despite my anxiety, I still hoped for the best."

"Bilal was making serious money. After four weeks, he had made a few thousand dollars already. He surprised me with jewelry: a ring, a necklace, and three beautiful, golden bracelets. He was excited that day," Tala said, her voice almost failing her as her throat tightened with sorrow, "He told me, 'I'm ready to propose! Your father can't possibly deny us now. I have enough money saved to show him I can provide for you and your family both. We can be married! And get a place of our own, so we don't have to live with my family.' I believed him. I didn't doubt for a moment that we would be together at last, at long, long last."

"That same day, a young man in the camp overdosed and died," she said in a muted whisper. "Being such a small community in the refugee camp, it was impossible for something like that to be kept between four walls. It didn't take long for the young man's father to learn from a friend that it was Bilal who sold him the drugs. The addict's father didn't want to admit to the community that his son overdosed. He maintained that his son had had a sudden heart attack. Within hours of the poor, young man's death, we'd heard about the overdose. The addict's mother told her neighbor, who promised to keep it a secret. The compulsion to gossip was far stronger than the commitment to the promise. And, the next neighbor heard the news in the same way, and then the next."

"Drugs are not discussed openly in the refugee camp. They are taboo." The way Tala uttered the word gave it more gravity than it would get in other cultures. At least I assumed it was the cultural context.

Taboo maintained its true meaning when Tala used it: off limits, outlawed, unthinkable. I could imagine hushed tones, upturned noses, gravely shaken heads. "If they are spoken about at all, it is discreetly. My father didn't even discuss the notion of drugs; he simply stated, with a quiet intensity that implied that he would brook no argument, 'You are not marrying Bilal.' He meant to kill any hope I had."

"I met Bilal that afternoon at our regular spot. When he arrived at the café, he had my gifts and was excited to show me the gold he bought. I wiped tears from my eyes and tried so hard to match his excitement, but he saw through my paper-thin smile. 'What's the matter?' he asked. But he knew. 'You heard about that man who overdosed.' It was a statement, not a question."

"'I don't blame you,' I hurried to assure him, 'You made money and risked your life and morals for us, for our love.' I was lost. It was all because of the ultimatum I'd given him. He only did this because he wanted me for his wife and was afraid of losing me. My parents had dashed all hope, and I suspected I'd wasted my life on a pointless dream.

"Bilal's words calmed the storm raging in my troubled heart. 'I will not give up. I will marry you. I will.' He was so confident, so determined. I believed him. I had to. 'It is time for us to run away. We will leave the camp and Lebanon. Just give me a few days, Fatima. I have saved enough money for us to run away and live. I promise.' I would give him his few days, or more if he needed. His promises gave me back the hope my parents had so swiftly taken from me. He promised me, and I believed in him.

"That evening, when Bilal returned home, his family was waiting for him. Of course, his parents had learned that he had been selling drugs. It was a horrible fight. Bilal was always a good boy. His family was angry, but it was their shame and disappointment that hurt him the most. His father told him that, as soon as the camp officials gathered their evidence, they would be coming to arrest him. The burden of his family's humiliation and dishonor weighed heavily on his shoulders, a feeling he'd never experienced until then.

"Bilal left his home, left the camp, and messaged his drug supplier. Promptly, Abu Ali called him back, 'Sorry to hear about your trouble,' the drug dealer said, though he did not sound surprised. In fact, I believe he was expecting the call. Perhaps he'd heard about the overdose and suspected Bilal would call soon, or maybe he always knew it would come to this, and he had planned for it. Naively, Bilal felt relief when Abu Ali offered rescue. 'Go ahead with your plan to run away with Fatima. I will help.' the dealer informed him.

"Abu Ali wore tailored French suits, designer sunglasses, and Italian leather shoes. He only drove German luxury cars, was always accompanied by shifty-eyed cronies, and he constantly favored those around him with toothy, cocksure smiles. He tipped exorbitantly and laughed raucously. He held court wherever he went, be it leaning against his chrome-be-decked Mercedes-Benz surrounded by his collection of associates, or sitting at the back of the café hedged by that same, vigilant retinue. He was a businessman. At least that was the image he tried to portray, and it only took the right amount of money in the right hands to be sure nobody asked too many questions. Again, desperation being the origin of corruption, he needed only pay off the Lebanese local authorities, and that bought him the sorts of friends who would protect him. The powers that wouldn't dare to approach Abu Ali.

"Bilal, in serious need of help now, was grateful for Abu Ali's offer. I received a text from Bilal about Abu Ali's plan. It was the middle of the night when I read, 'Tonight. We run away tonight! Pack your things and be ready.' I was, at first, ecstatic as I read those long-awaited words over and over. I did not think about the consequences or the true price of Bilal's so-called friend's proposal to help. I did consider the impact it might have on my family though: their reputation in the camp, and what people would say." Tala fondly stroked my forearm as she spoke. Her voice grew brittle when the topic turned to Abu Ali.

Knowing what I already did about Tala, I knew the story was going to go to some very unpleasant places thanks to this deal they were making with that obliging, exploiting criminal. However, love is a drug too, and Tala and Bilal were as high on it as Abu Ali's customers were on cocaine and heroin. Tala and her fiancé let love hamper their judgment, and based their decision to run away solely on the promise of Bilal's drug-dealing benefactor. Any second thoughts the two might have had were overshadowed by their desperation—desperation being a tool of evil. The young couple fell victim to it.

"Right before the morning's prayers were called, I slipped out of my family's home. I left a note for my parents, apologizing. I explained that I was running away with Bilal, but they shouldn't be ashamed as we would be getting married, so what we were doing was Halal." Fatima looked up at me and clarified, "Meaning approved by God, not taboo," then went on. "In only a few hours, I would be married to Bilal. He arranged it himself. It was official. We had witnesses, and it was officiated by a Sheikh." She cast another look up at me, gnawing her lower lip and wrinkling her nose. "You have to understand; the rules are specific when it comes to Muslims and their marriages. A girl of legal age is permitted to get married without her father's approval. In Islam, it is allowed, but certainly not encouraged. The issue was that *culturally* it is entirely unacceptable."

"I later learned that my family was tormented. They were angry, ashamed and did everything they could to find me. They suffered from my decision. My father, already not well, fell very ill. He could not take the news. It was his reputation. Refugee camps, even today, remain very conservative when it comes to many issues, especially when it relates to women." Tala sighed wearily but persisted. She was determined to finish this part of her tale for me.

"Bilal and I stayed at an apartment that Abu Ali secured for us. We were so anxious about what would happen next, but we found sanctuary in each other. The flat was where we spent our first days as husband and wife. We tried to forget the rest of the world and lose ourselves in our affection. We both had one friend each with whom we confided and received news from home. We were told that our families were searching for us and that, if we got caught, I would be killed for the shame I'd brought to my family.

"That was where our story would take a fatal turn. Bilal and I would be tricked, and our love would be put to the test for survival.

"A few days after we had gotten married, Abu Ali came to the apartment. We had not left it for fear of discovery, and he was the one bringing us food and anything else we needed. He played the part of concerned friend perfectly. That's when we told Abu Ali that we had to get far from Lebanon. It was a small country where it was simply a matter of time before we would be caught. My life was in danger.

"Finally, the moment Abu Ali had been waiting for arrived. He had a plan, and it was going precisely as he thought it would. 'Well first, you two need a honeymoon. So, I'm treating you to a trip to Turkey,' he began, his teeth flashing white as he smiled too broadly, 'After your honeymoon, I will come meet you both in Turkey. I have some business to do there. Then we can find a way to get you two love birds to Europe where you can start a new life.'

"It was a relief to hear such news, and exciting to have a honeymoon!" Tala said, her eyes bright with rage rather than the elation she must have felt during the moment she described. "We were naïve. We thought that Abu Ali was truly a friend. We trusted him," she said, as much misery as ire in her voice. "It was a time we had heard of a great many migrants and refugees crossing from Turkey to Europe. The civil war in Syria, which everyone expected would be over very quickly, had been going on for four years. Turkey was the means of escape for millions of refugees—at least three and a half million by that time. Half would stay in Turkey, and the rest would carry on to Europe or elsewhere. For a refugee, the idea of safety and peace keeps them alive and hopeful. That is what Abu Ali promised us."

"We left Lebanon in February 2015 and headed to Istanbul. Abu Ali arranged our visas, travel, and accommodation. It was the first time Bilal or I had ever been on a plane. A trip on an airplane is commonplace for someone like you, Henry, but for us, it was a miracle. It was like a dream. I thought I might be frightened, but I was far too excited by the promise of our future. Lebanon always felt like home, though it wasn't. It was a temporary home. Present, all the time, was a sense of conflict, of unrest. That's how it was with Palestinian refugees. We were born there, but we belonged to Palestine, a place to which we could never return, or even visit. We could not work or even go to proper schools. Our ID marked us refugees. Now, we were embarking on a trip that would change all of that. It was a journey away from our refugee status. Bilal held my hand, and I rested my head on his shoulder. We both felt, for the first time in our memories, that our futures were truly bright."

As I listened to Tala, I realized I had no idea where the story would lead. There was a stark bitterness to the curl of her lip, a narrowing of her expressive, brown eyes when she spoke of her hopes. I think I hated Abu Ali as much as she did and I had yet to hear what he did to Tala and her husband. I knew that pain and misery were to come, and it ached to know it. After all, Tala was a prostitute now, and where was Bilal? I knew things went very wrong for my Tala.

The first light of day made the pale limestone walls of the Slovenian architecture outside our window glow a bright amber. Morning was here. I was not tired though. I was enjoying this story I was being told and the company of the storyteller even more. "Are you tired?" I asked Tala, directing her attention with a tilt of my head toward the sunrise illuminating the old city. She shook her head, turning lazily to regard the still-sleeping city beyond our window. I felt she wanted to continue, and I was her devoted listener. Her words had been trapped for so long. It was a genuine catharsis to share those words that, until then, had never been spoken.

An unspoken word is like the thorn of a rose: it hurts. Only with its removal can the flower be held without pain.

Chapter Three

New beginnings. They bring with them all sorts of expectations, emotions, and challenges. Myself, I have always cherished those times; if we allow them to, they can be opportunities for the future. A new beginning is a blank canvas ready and thirsty for paint. For many though, fear and worry come along with it. Remember those three sorts of people I spoke about? Winners embrace the change and even those latter, negative feelings, choosing to observe the adversity and use it for motivation and even inspiration. Losers, on the other hand, get sucked into the mire of distress and fail to enjoy that stage of being for what it is. Those who live amid victory and defeat experience the grey, uneasy space in the middle of anticipation and doubt—two feelings between which it becomes difficult to distinguish.

"We began our descent into Istanbul," Tala
recalled, the eagerness she felt at the time complicat-
ing the expression on her cherubic features with the
grim awareness of what was yet to come. "I squeezed
Bilal's hand tightly. When I saw the sprawl of the
ancient and modern city, I couldn't take my eyes from
the window where the city was rushing at us. From the
sky, the city was, at once, beautiful and overwhelming.
The broad mouth of the Bosphorus was spanned by
vast bridges, edged with docked pleasure craft, and
surrounded by a city that was a dense saturation of
shoulder-to-shoulder terracotta-roofed homes, busy
shoreline roadways, and ancient and modern architecture. Istanbul was dominated by towering, hulking,
and magnificent mosques, their elegant spires stabbing at the sky. My heart was overcome with emotion
with the startling jolt of the airplane's wheels touching
down on the runway. I clutched Bilal's hand as I found
myself fighting both exaltation and panic."

"I had no idea what to expect in Turkey except
for what I'd gleaned from the Turkish soap operas my
mother watched constantly. They were translated into
Arabic from Turkish and were always playing on the
small television in our flat. I looked forward to seeing the Turkey I'd seen on television. I took comfort
in Bilal's confidence as he pulled me along the gang-
plank into the terminal. If he felt any doubt, I couldn't
see it behind the brilliant smile he gave me. That's

when I focused on my excitement. We were on our honeymoon! And we were going to start a new life in Europe! Most importantly for me, I was with the love of my life, embarking on a journey that would lead us to a better life.

"We breezed through customs. Abu Ali had prepared all our documents. I had my jewelry, and we had money. Bilal's savings and the funds Abu Ali had provided us for hotels, cars, and restaurants. We were greeted by a driver who took us to our hotel. On the way, Bilal and I watched through the windows as we were swallowed up by the old-world architecture looming over us in the narrow, cobblestone streets. Then, surrounded by vibrant, wide thoroughfares lined with busy market stalls and thronging foot traffic, I let myself fall into the mindset of a tourist, marveling at the colorful, crowding architecture and lively streetscapes.

"Bilal and I took turns pointing out the sights, laughing and embracing in the back of the luxury sedan. Our driver couldn't help but smile, witnessing the two newlyweds in his rear-view mirror as we cuddled ecstatically and forgot our apprehensions and fears for perhaps the first time in our lives. Everything was perfect; we existed only for each other, and this was just the first stop on our way to the life we'd always imagined.

"The hotel was gorgeous. It was like a palace. I'd never seen anything like it: polished marble on every surface, pillars of that same marble supporting the chandelier-laden ceilings, and gilded furniture in every foyer, lushly upholstered in reds and burgundies. The staff was used to seeing the wide-eyed amazement on the faces of their guests, but I'm sure we were the first whose amazement was as acute as ours. It was the first time we were openly affectionate; we did not have to hide any longer. We were married and on our honeymoon. We belonged right there, in that elegant hotel, together and plainly in love. We were giddy, and our steps were light as we followed the bellhop to our room. We embraced our hope and realized everything was going to turn out better than we'd dreamed. We marveled at our good fortune and what seemed like a profoundly promising future. Our affectionate laughter echoed through the marble hallways, and, with the bellhop studiously regarding the ceiling, we embraced in the elevator's mirrors, surrounded by scores of our amorous reflections. We paused when the elevator chimed, signaling our arrival on our floor. I was flushed as I adjusted my hijab, which Bilal had accidentally tugged askew, and I smiled mischievously as the door opened. By the time we were shown to our suite, we had elicited many knowing and amicable glances from other guests; they recognized newlyweds on their honeymoon.

her head tilted as she considered me and my mere of a hint of an apology. There was no response, no indication as to how she felt about my mistreatment of her earlier. Instead, she entered the room with a confident, imperious grace. I made to rise to meet her, but she laid her palms on my shoulders and pressed me back down onto the porcelain edge of the massive tub. I opened my mouth to end the silence but was halted with a gentle touch of Tala's slender finger to my lips.

Tala turned away from me and looked over her shoulder, gifting me with a sensual arch of her back that left me mesmerized by the curve of her hips and the excruciatingly way her jeans hugged her backside. A heavy-lidded, devilish smile curled her lip and dimpled her cheek. She was the center of my world at that moment, and she knew it. With aching deliberateness, she began to draw her t-shirt upward, revealing the perfect slope and valley of her lower back inch by exquisite inch.

My hands rose and gravitated, of their own volition, to touch the flawless skin between her shoulder blades above the strap of her simple, sheer bra but, with a mere flick of a sultry, rebuking glance, I was helpless but to pull my hand away. She turned on tip-toes of perfect, dainty feet, deftly unclasping her bra. With a coquettish smirk, she held the cups of her simple, white bra with one arm and stepped closer. Tala nudged my knees apart and edged closer until her one thigh pressed insistently against the growing lump in my jeans. "Patience," she chided, then demanded sweetly, "Take off your shirt." Under her spell, I complied without a thought and had my shirt over my head and tossed onto the floor in a heartbeat. Still clutching her bra to her chest, she took a languid step back and lifted her chin to indicate my pants, "Now the rest," she instructed, "All of it." I shimmied out of my jeans and boxers before I heeled off my socks. The porcelain was shockingly cool under my rear, but the sensation was miles away, lost as I was in the presence of Tala and her formidable beauty.

She paused and thoughtfully captured her bottom lip in her teeth, looking my body up and down brazenly. Her attention paused for a long moment on my lap. "Oh my," she gasped, mocking chagrin and considered my state of arousal. Despite myself, I felt a blush heat my cheeks. My timid reaction made her laugh. Her teeth flashed whitely and she shook her head, chuckling. "Naughty boy," she scolded lightheartedly.

"Now," she all but purred, turning her back letting her bra flit to the polished marble floor, "Help me with my jeans." All I wanted to do was to rip those jeans from her body and make mad love to her, but, at that point, I was entirely dedicated to her every wish. She unfastened her jeans, and I reached out to peel them down her hips. The merest touch of her skin triggered a jolt that coursed along my fingers, arms and through my body directly to my loins. When she stepped from the puddle of her jeans that lay about her ankles, she was Venus herself, departing the scallop shell.

Her body itself commanded my attention, and she knew it. From over one shoulder, she observed me, luxuriating in my scrutiny. It was more than admiration when I let my gaze travel up her shapely legs to her slightly parted thighs and to her perfectly sculpted buttocks. I wanted to lean close and kiss one dimple above her bottom and then the other, but before I could act on my reverential impulse, she turned. Her fingers entwined in my hair and caressed my scalp as she drew me close, my forehead cradled against her stomach. I caught a fleeting glimpse of lean stomach and dark, tidy thatch of pubic hair before she hugged me close to her midriff. "You've drawn me a bath?" Tala sighed, pleased, "So thoughtful."

As she stepped by me, over the lip of the tub, she caressed my stubbled cheek with the tips of her fingers. "Join me," she half whispered and half gasped as she lowered herself into the steaming water. My imagination had not prepared me for the reality of the vision before me when I turned to join Tala. I swallowed audibly, taken afresh by the sight of her. She was resplendent with graceful arms adorning either side of the large tub, her hair damp and clinging to her shoulders, and her breasts, buoyant just under the surface of the warm water.

The heat was a shock to my excited genitals as I lowered myself into the huge bathtub across from the object of my thoroughly incited desire, but I didn't hesitate to do as I was bidden. Our legs entwined and caressed one another as we both settled comfortably. Tala wound her hair into a loose bun behind, knowing precisely what the action did for my view of her. Warm water beaded on the smooth skin of her chest and ran in rivulets from the olive skin below her shoulders to the slightly paler flesh of her breasts.

The sun was cresting over the slate and copper rooftops of the old-world buildings outside the window. It illuminated the lighter brown highlights in Tala's hair and made her glistening skin glow like burnished gold. "Would you like me to continue my story?" she asked, her regard following mine to the sunrise and the view through the window. We had not slept, and, despite having been drinking all night, were both beyond that point of drunkenness and into a heady, euphoric—yet profoundly lucid—state of mind.

"Yes," I said, in defiance of my body's yearning for her and the urgency of my engorged organ nearly breaking the surface of our bath water. "Yes, please." The knowing smile on Tala's lush lips let me know that she was well aware of the delicious turmoil I was experiencing after her enticing performance. "You were on your honeymoon in Istanbul..." I offered.

The mirth dissolved from her face, her eyelashes drifted to her heat-flushed cheeks, and she nodded. At that moment, in my mind's eye, I could almost see her hijab materialize and block all but her striking, but dour face. "Abu Ali arrived in Istanbul, and life became hell." A shared bathtub, soaking in the morning sunlight, was an incongruently sublime setting for the devastating story Tala was about to tell me. I was shocked at what I would soon hear. Anyone would be.

"Abu Ali told us that we would be leaving for Europe in just a couple weeks, but before that, Bilal would need to go somewhere for a little job. When Bilal inquired about this 'job,' Abu Ali assured him that it was something relating to his skills in computer science. 'It's a European firm,' Abu Ali said, 'You do some work for them, and they will help get you and Fatima to Europe. They might even give you a job if they like your work.'

"I implored Abu Ali, 'Why can't I go with you?'

"He invented an excuse: 'The job is in a remote area in East Turkey. It is best that you stay here at the hotel. Take some money,' he said soothingly, giving me a thick envelope of cash, 'Go shopping. I'll make sure a driver is with you at all times.' I didn't like the idea at all, but I eventually gave in and accepted the money. Bilal was as hesitant as I was, but he had to look out for our future. We had nothing but that future to look forward to after all. Abu Ali added, 'Oh, and there will be little access to phones. Very poor reception.'"

"And they left," Tala said softly, the words nearly catching in her throat. "That was the last time I saw him," she said shakily, "That was the last time I ever saw Bilal." Her eyes welled with tears, and then, despite her efforts, one escaped and ran defiantly down her cheek. She closed her hands over her lovely face and cried then. I did not know what to say, so I leaned close and drew her around so her back was to me. I wrapped myself around her in a comforting embrace. She leaned her head back on my shoulder and held my arms tightly around herself, shuddering softly as she choked back tears. I respectfully chose to leave it to Tala to break the silence. Minutes passed while we embraced. I watched as a bead of water slid over her collar bone and disappeared into the valley between her breasts.

Finally, after collecting herself, she went on. "The next two days were fine. I went shopping with the money Abu Ali gave me, and I bought amazing clothes so that when Bilal came back, he would find me even more attractive than when he'd left. Many times, I considered removing my hijab; there were far fewer women wearing scarves than in Lebanon. I couldn't gather the nerve though. Every time I tried on a new outfit, there was a moment during which I stared at my long hair in the mirror. Before I stepped out of the change room though, I was always wearing my hijab.

The driver was with me as promised. I spent a lot of time watching television as well. I tried to fend off worried thoughts of Bilal and how he hadn't called yet. I had been warned it might be days, but that didn't put me at ease at all. I asked the driver about them, and he explained that it would be a couple of days before they even arrived at their destination. So, I patiently waited. And then came the morning that the hotel front desk called me."

"'Madam, what time are you going to be checking out today?' the receptionist politely asked me. I was confused, of course. I understood that Abu Ali had booked the suite for at least until he and Bilal would return, and I told her as much. 'I'm afraid the room is only booked until this morning, Madam,' the receptionist replied kindly, 'But if you'd like to stay longer, we can certainly extend your stay. We'll just bill the credit card we have on file for your suite.'

"'Perfect,' I said, relieved, 'Do that. I expect to be here at least another week. Thank you.' I hung up the phone, and it rang only moments later.

"'Good morning, Madam,' said the same voice as before, 'I'm sorry to disturb you again, but the credit card we were provided is no longer valid.' My blood froze in my veins. What could be the problem?

"'I'm sure my husband's employer will take care of this misunderstanding when they return,' I said, sounding far more optimistic than I was feeling.

"'I'm sure you're right, Madam,' the receptionist replied, sounding more patient than she likely felt, 'But we'll need payment for the room in the interim. We can refund it and charge your husband's employer when they return though, of course.' Panic wrapped a tight fist around my spine. I could barely breathe. What was happening?

"'I'll come down to the front desk and take care of this,' I promised, my brain reeling. There had to be an explanation. I hung up and immediately went through my things, collecting all the cash I had left after my shopping. If only I hadn't used the money for shopping! I brought the cash down to the front desk, but it was not enough for the five-day stay I'd hoped for, feeling that that might be long enough to get this sorted out. I paid for one more night and clung to the possibility that this was all a colossal misunderstanding. I could only hope.

"I went back to my room and tried calling Bilal's phone again. It went straight to voicemail; it was switched off. The worry mounted and, with trembling hands, I tried the driver's number. I was sure he would have some answers and would certainly know how to help. No answer. Staying in my room—I didn't dare spend more money leaving the hotel—the anxiety grew in my heart. I had perhaps one person in Lebanon I could call, but I maintained the hope that Bilal would call, or even Abu Ali, and I didn't want to worry a friend back home. I was sure the driver, at least, would show up.

"The driver never showed. Here I was, feeling torment over how events were unfolding; it was getting late, and I couldn't take it anymore. The uncertainty, the fear, the worries were eating me up. I barely recall even leaving the hotel that night. I walked the streets as though in a dream, or more accurately, a nightmare. I was lost and had only the vaguest of memories of that night. I remember walking aimlessly under the garish, neon lights of storefronts, looking blankly at my reflection in a display window and barely recognizing the pitiful creature there. My hijab was lopsided, and my eyes were frighteningly vacant. At one point, while I was standing at the edge of a curb, a taxi, gleaming gold in the dim light of the street, stopped in front of me. 'Are you alright?' the driver asked, concerned. I simply turned away and started walking in another random direction.

"By the time I finally returned to the hotel, I was more myself. I realized it was dangerous to be out in the middle of the night, especially in a city I didn't know. I cleaned myself up and tried to sleep. The next morning, I decided to call my friend in Lebanon—on the hotel phone, using a long-distance card, as my cell didn't work on the wireless network in Turkey. She was the only one I had told that I was coming to Turkey and I had spoken to her the day I arrived.

"'I'm so sorry, Fatima,' was the first thing she said to me. 'I was trying to get in touch with you for days! Your father. He has passed away. I'm so sorry.'

"Hearing the news brought me to my knees. I could hear the distress in her voice when she said, 'You mother, sisters, and your brother... Fatima, they're going to kill you if they find you. They blame you. His health got so much worse when you ran away.' I quickly said goodbye and hung up.

"I fell to the floor and cried—no, wailed— for hours. The few times my weeping let up, lessening to whimpering, sodden with tears and snot, I would try Bilal's number again and again, then Abu Ali's, again and again. I imagined I could hear a wicked, mocking sneer in the mechanical voice informing me that '...The number you are dialing cannot be reached right now. Please try again later.'

"The phone rang just as I was reaching for it to try Bilal again. Startled, I nearly dropped it in my hurry. 'Bilal? Bilal?' I pleaded into the receiver.

"'No Madam,' that familiar voice was a chilling slap to my face. Fresh tears coursed down my cheeks, and I choked on still more sobs of grief and worry. Pretending not to hear my anguish, the woman went on, 'Check out was thirty minutes ago. Would you like

Some tore their attention from their animated conversation long enough to leer at me as I walked up the short and grimy stairway. Their faces, illuminated by the neon sign that cheerlessly announced 'vacancy' above the door, took on a gaunt pallor and I hurried by them before they act on the unsavory impulses I imagined were on their mind.

"The lobby barely qualified as one. There was a bench on which an indifferent man casually smoked an appallingly acrid cigar, the smoke forming a wispy, bluish halo around his balding head. I crossed the cracked, checkered tiles to the counter. This woman could have been the sister of the woman from the kiosk. She was similarly rotund but had a more prominent mustache over her thin lips. She was precisely as pleasant as she looked. 'A cheap room?' she said, looking me up and down with an unimpressed sneer, 'Figures. You share your room with two other girls. They asked for a cheap room too.' The woman coughed moistly and produced a key which she slid across the worn counter toward me. 'The washroom is shared with the floor. No guests allowed and check out is at eleven. How many nights do you want?'

"I booked three nights and went up the dingy staircase. It was no surprise that no one offered to help with my suitcase. There aren't bellhops at miserable places like that. I could hear my roommates before I opened the door. The friendly, if distant, smiles they directed my way helped me to ignore the dank smell, peeling paint and uninviting beds. I let my suitcase thud to the dusty, linoleum floor before the only unoccupied bed, and, expelling a shoulder-slumping sigh, I sat on the edge of the lumpy mattress.

"I thought the two might have been sisters. There was something similar between them, though they were distinctly different in appearance. It was their eyes; no, it was *in* their eyes. They had seen heartbreak and had both suffered. Perhaps we, all three of us, might be mistaken for sisters.

"'This is Shireen,' the fuller-figured girl said, gesturing to her slim companion, 'and I am Dana.' I looked at Dana, surprised, and the first genuine smile I experienced in days blossomed on my lips. She introduced Shireen and herself in Arabic! From the slight difference in accent, I could hear that she was Syrian.

"'You speak Arabic!' I exclaimed, relieved to finally have someone to talk to in my own language.

"'So do you,' remarked Shireen and leaned forward from the edge of her narrow cot of a bed. I liked her immediately when she smirked at me after that amicable, sarcastic response. 'We're from Syria,' the slender, bubbly, young woman replied, but I had already guessed that from her dialect.

"'What brings you to Istanbul?' asked Dana, folding her arms self-consciously across her stomach. "A pretty girl like you shouldn't be stuck in a place like this," she said, glancing from a crack in the wall to a blotchy water stain on the ceiling and then back at me.

"'My husband and I came here because he has a job to do,' I lied. They blinked at me and then at each other.

"'Where is he?' Dana asked. It was only natural to ask about me and my story. The question shouldn't have surprised me, but I hesitated. It was clear that Dana could see the confusion, fear, and uncertainty on my face because she quickly volunteered her story before the pause became uncomfortable. 'I lost my family in the war in Aleppo,' she said, hugging her arms around herself at the memory. 'After they died, I managed to run away to safety. Like Shireen, my plan is to travel and make a better life.' That's when she surprised me with a mischievous smirk, 'I mean to find a tall, blond German to marry.' We all enjoyed a burst of cathartic laughter at that.

"Shireen took her cue and, leaning one elbow on her knee, told me, 'I'm from Homs. The Syrian War took my husband. I fled the conflict and came here to Istanbul to try and work to make enough money to get on one of the boats to Greece. Then, when I get as far as Germany, I plan to bring my parents and brother and sisters to join me.' She glanced at her companion, 'And I hope I can help Dana find a nice, strong German

man when I get there.' The laughter came even easier that time for the three of us.

"In the next days, I learned much more of Dana and Shireen's stories. Both came north to Istanbul with the expectation that they might have a better chance at finding work in a big city. They met during their journey and became fast friends. They needed a few thousand dollars, enough to get them onto a boat from Turkey and then make their way to Greece. It wasn't such a far-fetched scheme. The two stubbornly hopeful women had already been through far worse and survived.

"The amount of money they raised would determine how likely it was that they make it to Europe. With about one thousand dollars, they might hire themselves a rubber boat that may or may not make it across to the Greek island of Kos from Bodrum, Turkey. With five thousand dollars, they could get on a better boat with risks of its own, but fewer. When someone has nothing to lose, risks become irrelevant.

"When they arrived, Dana and Shireen had barely any money. Their plan to come to Istanbul, a big city, to make money didn't go quite as planned so far. They had been cleaning houses and getting paid—very little—under the table to save what little money they could. They ate at the houses they cleaned and did odd jobs where they could, but were barely making enough money to pay for the room they shared.

"I made up a story: 'My husband went to Bursa,' I explained, remembering the name of the nearby city from conversations I'd overheard at the hotel, 'and I am just waiting a few days for him to be done.' To their credit, Dana and Shireen tried to appear to believe me. They didn't pressure me for details.

"'Well, if you and your husband want to join us on our way to Europe, let us know,' Dana said.

"I smiled and waved the offer away with a brush of my hand. 'My husband is working for a European company. They will be taking us to Europe after he has finished in Bursa,' I said, wishing my story weren't made up and that I was as confident as I was trying to sound.

"I couldn't sleep that night, and I'm sure that the girls could hear me cry. They were considerate and did not bother me. I had left before my new room-mates awoke and returned to the hotel. 'No Madam,' the woman behind the desk said, 'No one has called.' I ignored the pitying look the clerk cast my way and left."

In the bathtub, I saw in Tala a sorrow I had never seen before. She made me think of a human being stripped of her soul. Suppositions formed in my mind as to how Tala eventually became a prostitute, but, I had no idea the turns and twists her tale would lead me on. She humanized the plight of refugees for me. My understanding of the subject until then consisted exclusively of information and visuals I'd found on television. I could see it so much more clearly—feel it, touch it. The suffering and fear were palpable now.

Tala was unaware of my epiphany and continued.

"While I wandered the streets, Dana and Shireen left to work, cleaning houses. I was lying on my rumpled blanket in my bed when I heard them return. They were still arguing when they entered the room. 'Why did you even listen to him?' said Shireen, her face flushed with anger. 'I've heard stories about *doctors* like that man. Sure,' she admitted, 'it's going to take a long time for us to make the money we need, but I'm not selling my body. Never. Not even if you give me a German passport for it.'

"Dana's mattress squeaked as she sat heavily down upon it. She wrung her plump fingers and said, 'At the pace we are going, it will take another year. He said he's a good Muslim, and I believe him. I've had worse bosses than him. He's kind and pays a little better than our other clients. He was right, after all. We are all born with two kidneys. We can live normally with just one. Five thousand dollars! For just one operation, we'd have enough to get us to Europe!'

"My skin prickled with goosebumps; I was terrified by what I was hearing. At first, it sounded like they were discussing prostitution with the mention of selling bodies, but they weren't speaking figuratively whatsoever. They were discussing *selling* their bodies!

Or at least parts of them. I might have spoken up and echoed Shireen's sentiments on the subject, but I did little more than greet them. I was troubled enough with my own problems. I was thinking of the misery I may have to face along, without Bilal. I missed him so much. I was worried... worried and heartbroken.

"I wish I had taken part in the discussion though. I regret not joining Shireen in warning Dana of the dangers of trusting people like that doctor.

"I thought through countless possibilities. Was Abu Ali like the doctor Dana was talking about? Could he be trusted? Where was Bilal? Was he as worried about me as I was about him? Was he all right? Was Bilal suffering? Was he alive?

"The argument between my roommates was still going strong as they both prepared for bed. Dana turned out the light, and as she padded across the tiled floor to her bed, she persisted, 'Why not just sell *one?*'

"Shireen expelled an irritated sigh, 'Are you crazy?' she yelled across the room, 'Don't even consider it. We will clean houses, and we will make the money to get out of here. It will take time, but it will happen. What you're talking about is dangerous. Now, go to sleep, and don't give the idea another thought. Okay? Promise?'

"Dana's response was nearly inaudible, but she answered, 'Okay.'

"The next morning, the girls were already gone when I awoke. I lay there, staring at the stain on the ceiling tile. Was it larger than it was last night? I focused my thoughts. I needed to think of a plan, but thinking that way meant that I was giving up on Bilal's return. I refused. I had to hold onto hope. It was easier to just not think of the future, at all. I still had the jewelry. It hurt to think about it. Those few pieces of gold were all I had from Bilal. Selling them wasn't something I wanted to consider.

"I left and went through the routine I'd established: I would walk directly to the hotel, and I would ask the clerk at the desk if Bilal had called or left any messages. Under the uncomfortable weight of their sympathetic stares, I would listen to the news that no, he hadn't called. Defeated, I would leave and spend another hour or so wandering the bustling streets. People brushed by me with a sense of determination guiding them, making their pace brisk with purpose. I, on the other hand, walked aimlessly, blind to the city's bustle, until my hopelessness lifted just enough for me to perceive the faint possibility that Bilal may have tried to contact me. That is when I would return to the hotel for the second, third and fourth time that day—sometimes more. The clerks, looking at me with growing annoyance, would allow my use of the phone to try Bilal again. I would then try Abu Ali and even the driver as well.

"Never. Never any answer.

"Lost in my thoughts and fears, I was a ghost on the streets of Istanbul. I had lost myself. The Fatima who always resisted and bent circumstances to my own ends and faced challenges head-on was dead. I was a grieving woman. All alone. Imagining, beyond hope, the return of my beloved husband.

"Finally, I found myself back in my bed in the hostel, contemplating the dirty ceiling tiles and my miserable situation. The door burst open. 'Dana?' Shireen called, her breath coming in gasps. 'Fatima! Have you seen Dana?' I sat up, startled, and shook my head quickly. 'I think,' she leaned one hand on the doorframe as she caught her breath, 'I think she may have gone to see that doctor. I thought she left for work without me, but she never showed up at the house. I don't know what to do!'

"I looked at her with despair that I truly didn't feel. Inside, I was empty. At that moment, I could not have cared less about Dana. When one's world is falling apart, it is hard to think of others. We often become selfish with our own misery. I was numb.

"Shireen, fearful of authorities like all undocumented people, could not call the police. That fear of authority is one reason criminals like the doctor choose people like Shireen and Dana for their victims. The small chance of legal consequences makes it safe for them, and the victims' desperation makes it easy for them to manipulate. A woman as displaced and despondent as Dana is the perfect target.

"When Shireen sat on Dana's bed, shaking, she laid a hand on a piece of paper she hadn't noticed before. Through tears she glared at the note and sneered fiercely at the words there, 'Liar!' she hissed, 'Filthy liar! She *promised* me she wouldn't go to that horrible doctor!' She balled the note in one fist and threw it at the wall, enraged and trembling, 'She went to him.' Slumping her quaking shoulders, she hid her tear-streaked face in her hands, 'Something is wrong. Something is wrong!' She let herself weep for only a few heartbeats longer before she allowed the rage to return. With a tight jaw and bared teeth, Shireen glared at the door, a plan forming. 'I have to help her. I have to save her,' she said, seething with determination.

"It shames me to admit that I didn't say a word to Shireen, neither to console her nor to join her in her rage and worry. She didn't wait for a response from me before she took up her purse and stormed out. What did she think she could do for Dana? I squeezed my eyes shut against the world and hugged my pillow to my chest like a petulant child clings to a favorite teddy bear. The world would have to do without me for the time being.

"My frantic sleep was interrupted by the door clapping open and Shireen hurtling through it. She collapsed on her bed and buried her face in the pillow.

The sleeve of her shirt was torn at her elbow, and blood stained her sheet from an abrasion on her arm there. I was shocked awake by the sight of Shireen's blood, and I shrugged off my own suffering at that moment to rush to her bed and lay beside her, one arm slung over her shoulder as I tried to soothe her insurmountable grief. 'What has happened? Shireen, please, what happened to your arm? Are you okay? And Dana? Did you find her?'

"Shireen turned from her tear-soaked pillow, her nose running and her mouth downturned in a dreadful grimace. 'She's gone. Vanished. The bastard took her. I know it!' She dragged the back of her wrist across her upper lip, sniffling and went on, 'I went to the doctor's house. He didn't even bother to deny it. He just,' she lifted her bloodied arm to show me her scraped elbow, 'threw me out of his house. This is from the sidewalk. He said he'd call the police if I ever came back and that I would be thrown in prison and deported back to Syria.' Shireen's chin dimpled, and her bottom lip quivered as she looked up at me with horror in her eyes. 'He didn't even deny taking her!' she repeated. Then, letting her face fall to the pillow again, her voice muffled, 'I don't know if I'll ever see her again. Do you think she'll come back?'

"I leaned onto her; my only response was to squeeze her comfortingly. It wasn't enough, but she sat up to embrace me, her fresh tears warm on my shoulder. I didn't realize until then how much I needed to be held. We both cried, clutching each other. Shireen may still harbor hope that Dana might be okay and would return. Dana was almost certainly dead though. Shireen would expect Dana's return less with every day that would pass.

"In that hostel room, two victims of life's harshness sat. Misery united the two of us. We had that in common. We found some little comfort in one another's arms and we were both so grateful for even that much. The two of us spoke into the night, comforting and sharing. I helped to remind Shireen that she still had family and promise of a future and she offered me support as well. Shireen was the first person I would trust with my story. I chose to believe her when she said, 'He will be back.' Just hearing it said aloud was comforting, though I knew she was just trying to make me feel better and that she knew it was surely untrue.

"All I could do was reply with equally reassuring and untrue words: 'Dana will come back. She is probably just recovering from the surgery and will return as soon as she's feeling up to it.' I knew that it was a lie. The doctor would not have reacted the way he had if Dana was okay and recuperating in a hospital somewhere. Instead, he just threw her out and threatened her. Yes, Dana was surely another victim of the organ traffickers. Desperation is a tool of evil.

"We slept together in that one, tiny bed. Our sleep was short and restless, and the next day, she and I went through the same routine as usual. Shireen went to work and I wandered the streets and checked the hotel for Bilal's call. After work, Shireen would return to the hostel, pointlessly hoping to find Dana waiting there, just as I would hope to have a message waiting for me at the hotel each day. It was, in fact, hopeless.

"My money was about to run out. My motivation shifted to pure survival at that point. That is what happens with human beings after a tragedy. First, we fall apart and then devolve to a plain, primitive survival. It is how we resist implacable situations like the ones Shireen and I were in."

I enveloped Tala in my arms, nuzzling her fragrant hair—sandalwood, I think—and rocked her gently. The water had grown tepid in the tub we shared. The sun was well above the horizon, and the city outside the window was busy in the heart of its morning rush-hour. Tala's tragic story kept bringing me back to my own: my mother, my book, my career. I fled, much like Tala had, from dreadful circumstances. To me, the parallel was uncanny.

"Are you tired, Tala?" I asked. She shook her head that she had leaned back on my shoulder, basking in the morning sun, pensive and quiet. Droplets of water glinted like a peppering of tiny diamonds on the flawless skin of her shoulders and arms. Taking advantage of the lull in Tala's story, I slipped out from behind this beautiful woman with whom I was beginning to recognize a powerful yearning, something fresh and authentic. It burned in my chest and only grew hotter with every moment I spent with Tala.

Donning a hotel bathrobe, I left the bathroom to ring the front desk and order us some coffee and breakfast. As I walked back to the washroom, my reflection in a hallway mirror made me halt. The Henry who narrowed his eyes at me from the other side of the mirror, scrutinizing me with the same recognition I weighed on him, was someone I hadn't seen in a long while. I felt like the Henry I was before my last failure: present and confident.

Tala was toweling off when I returned to the bathroom, her back toward me. She may have taken a moment longer than needed to dry her calves, bent at the hips, back arched and toes curled into a ballet pointe. I could tell it was for my benefit, and if she meant to rekindle my excitement from hours earlier, she succeeded. She straightened elegantly and wrapped the towel under her arms and around herself before turning to me as though she hadn't realized I had entered. "Let's lie in bed," she suggested, walking past me and my robe-concealed erection into the bedroom.

We faced each other, our heads nestled on plump pillows, I in my robe and she still in her towel, and she continued to tell me what would happen in the next months of her tale.

"Shireen got me jobs cleaning houses, and we worked together. We were both treated poorly by most of our employers. It wasn't surprising though; we were undocumented, desperate refugees after all. The situation was no better than the one I had left in Lebanon. I found myself in only another variety of displacement and misery.

"There was not one day that passed where I did not think of Bilal. I had gone to the hotel every day. I didn't even stop when the staff there were finally fed up with my incessant—and pointless—visits. They started losing patience and being rude, but I didn't care. It wouldn't stop me. My hope refused to let go.

"I did not sell my jewelry. They were a gift from Bilal! I made enough money to survive each day. While Shireen continued to work to save for her passage to Europe, I refused to do the same. I would only go to Europe when Bilal returned.

"He never did.

"Shireen and I, after that long, sorrowful night we spent comforting each other, became close friends. Like sisters—closer than I was with my true sisters. I could tell from Shireen's furtive glances whenever I brought up Bilal's name that she doubted he would ever return and was far too kind to share her suspicions. I couldn't blame her. Myself, I knew that her best friend, Dana, was certainly dead. Why would the organ traffickers, once they had her anesthetized and on the operating table, stop at just one kidney when she had so many more profitable organs? The thought made me cringe, but I knew the truth of it.

"Months passed. I had grown accustomed to horrendous treatment while at the homes Shireen and I cleaned every day. There was one house, in particular, that I dreaded going to. The man lived alone and hounded us as we tried to work. While we tidied and scrubbed his unkempt home, he would call us vile names and suggest we deserved whatever suffering we may have experienced as refugees. He favored me over Shireen. More than once, I had to brush away his hand when he grabbed at my thigh or breast. He would snarl and say things like, 'Oh, come on. Have you fucked a Turk before?' or, 'Don't pretend you don't like it. The way you bend over and show me that hot ass of yours, you're asking for it.'

"When Shireen was at another home, cleaning, I had to clean that bastard's house myself. I was terrified of what might happen if there weren't two of us. I should never have gone by myself, but I needed the money. Evil seeks out just this sort of desperation. When I was bent over his tub, my fingers gritty and sore from scouring the porcelain, I felt him enter the room. Then he seized my hair through my hijab and struck my face against the cold bathroom tiles.

I never looked back at him, not when he ripped my pants from me or even when he forced himself into me. Terror paralyzed me, and I gripped that grimy sponge so hard, I had to pry my fist open with my other hand after the ordeal."

How could Tala be retelling this part of her story with such a cool attitude? She seemed so dreadfully numb to the experience. Hearing all this stoked a hot rage in my chest. Here was a woman who had already lost everything and then this man, this bastard, came and selfishly made it so much worse. He was genuinely evil. How could someone do that? Even as I raged, I tried to maintain an attentive expression. I felt that she was aware of my anger though.

"I returned to the hostel, bruised and in tears. Shireen was incredibly upset. She helped me clean up and tried to convince me that everything was going to be okay. I wailed, hysterical, 'Another man has touched me! Bilal will never want me!' I'd seen it before. In the refugee camp, a girl at school was raped, and her family felt shame. She was to be married that summer, but her would-be husband's family forbade the marriage because she was a shameful rape victim. 'That's it,' I said, wiping away still more tears, 'I am selling the gold I have. You and I are going to Europe. I can't keep waiting for my husband, and you can't keep waiting for Dana. They are gone.' Even if Bilal ever returned to me, he would never want anything to do with me after he learned of my rape.

"Not an hour later, I was haggling with a shopkeeper nearby. 'Yes, Miss,' he said through a crooked smirk of yellowed teeth, 'They are worth more than two thousand five hundred American dollars.' He splayed his hands in mock sympathy, and I noticed him eyeing my hijab with a shadow of a sneer. 'But you're not going to get more than that. You are desperate. I can see that. I can guess from your accent and your pitiful, bruised face, that you are probably a refugee and undocumented.' He shrugged and began to count out the bills. I didn't say a word. After all, he was right. I realized, afterward, that the shopkeeper took as much advantage of me as the bastard who raped me.

"With what Shireen had saved and the money I'd gotten for the jewelry, we purchased tickets for a bus to the coastal city of Izmir. On the bus ride, I kept looking back down the road toward Istanbul. Reeling from my experiences there, I silently cursed the city. I turned in my seat and stared at the dotted lines down the center of the road to where they disappeared. That is where my future waited. With deliberate effort, I allowed hope to bloom. We were on a journey toward a new beginning, a better future in Europe. That was our mission."

There was a knock at the suite door then. It was our coffee. Fondly, I brushed a stray lock of hair from Tala's cheek and, with pursed lips, shook my head in amazement. "You are truly incredible. You've been through so much. I want to hear the rest. Every detail." With that, I left the bed and, cinching my robe, went to fetch our breakfast.

Upon returning, breakfast-laden tray held out before me, I was astonished once more by the mere sight of this angel adorning the expansive bed. Clad only in a bath towel, she made my knees weak with desire. Deeper than that, I felt excited. I pondered the thrilling agitation I was feeling and recalled what she had said only moments before about the future and new beginnings.

Tala sat up on the bed and leaned back against the quilted headboard, eyeing the breakfast tray with a hunger that she didn't know she felt until that instant. I positioned the tray between us and I took my place against the headboard as well. Tala bit into a croissant and I watched her as I sipped my coffee. I was no longer the man who fled New York. Tala returned me to myself. All I wanted was to take care of her and for us to spend the rest of our lives together. I could give her what she wanted. I knew I could. As much as she could give the same to me: a new beginning and a better future.

Chapter Four

There are points in life at which we no longer have anything to lose. When we live in those times, we have a dangerous freedom; we are free to do anything. We lose all concept of limitation; we are daring and ready for whatever life may bring. Don't be fooled though. It may sound romantic, but it is hopelessness and desperation that can lead to this liberation. Imagine what is possible when the choice is between survival and the dreaded alternative.

I have some experience along those lines. In fact, we all do—in varying capacities. My struggle wasn't as dire as some, but I had the opportunity to live without inhibition after hitting the proverbial rock bottom. I experienced failure that was crushing in that my fall was so far; I'd reached the pinnacle of my vocation just to plummet to a low I could have only imagined. That, along with the loss of my mother, was devastating.

Tala, too, had lost everything: her husband had gone missing, her family wanted her dead, and she had just enough money to buy herself passage from Turkey to Greece. How did she arrive here, in this suite, sitting, cross-legged in a sumptuous, hotel bathrobe on an expansive, opulent bed, drinking coffee and nibbling on a breakfast that probably cost more than she could make in a week? Why was I so taken by her? This refugee-turned-prostitute. The way she looked at me over the rim of her coffee cup had my pulse racing, my palms moist and the hair prickling on the back of my neck. Her mere vicinity made me desperate to both protect her and make love to her. Her story compelled me to fend off my urges, the same urges that had my loins aching for the entire sleepless night. But I listened.

"It was a nine-hour bus ride. I had a lot of time to think," Tala said, holding her warm cup in two hands. Her hair was still damp, and sable tendrils framed her aquiline features. I was amazed how bright her eyes remained after being up all night and weathering such intense feelings as she recounted her tragic tale.

"I spent most of the trip from Istanbul trying to put Bilal out of my mind. Of course, it only made me think of him even more. And that only made me picture how the love would drain from his eyes when he found out another man had touched me. How he would pull away, turn from me, detest me. I could

Better to say that the terror was so persistent that we had become numb.

"Shireen and I were sheltering from the sun under the shade of a faded blue awning at the market close to the port. I could see that the market owners were capitalizing on migrants like us and were peddling items like waterproof bags, life jackets, water bottles and assorted flotation devices, all at viciously inflated prices. We had been waiting a long time, and we were beginning to get worried that our connection, who was late, was not going to come at all. Just before panic could take hold, a gruff, Turkish man approached us. He was unshaven, and his clothes were unkempt. Threadbare jeans that had grown a dingy gray from blue hung loosely from his waist, and he wore a t-shirt faintly yellowed at the collar and armpits. 'Shireen?' he asked me. He never quite looked me in the eye. I shook my head and directed him to Shireen next to me who shifted from one foot to the other, scrutinizing the man. 'Fine,' he said to her, 'You have the money?'

"The money was all he cared about. He did not care about our well-being nor about any concerns we might have. After the business of the payment was dealt with, I asked him, 'What happens if the boat sinks?'

"'You swim or die. No guarantees. This is not a first-class cruise,' was his reply. It occurred to me that he was probably asked questions like that all the time. His boorish responses probably made it easier to keep the questions to a minimum. I'm sure that when one provides a service as dangerous as his, it's better not to get to know any of your customers, considering how treacherous the trip is and how risky the unlawful business can be.

"Shireen asked him, 'Lifejackets? Do you provide life jackets?'

"The man spat on the street and waved off the question, 'Listen, you're paying for a place on the boat. Nothing more. Understood? You can get a lifejacket or whatever you need from this market. Be there,' he pointed a finger in need of a nail trimming toward the seashore, 'by 5:00 a.m. Boat leaves at 6:00.'"

Tala was standing by the window, her white, hotel-emblemed robe tied snugly around her narrow waist. The garment was left carelessly open enough to allow me a teasing glimpse at the tender flesh of her cleavage. She was on her second cup of coffee, and she paused in her story to consider the morning traffic below. I watched her eyes drift close, and she leaned against the window. Her forehead pressed against her reflection in the glass. I almost spoke when the pause stretched for another moment, but she opened her eyes and met her own haunted stare in the glass. She went on.

and threw it as far into the sea as I could. The sea took it, swallowed it, just as it had a part of me that day.

"I blinked then. Shireen? I called after Thomas, 'My friend! My friend, Shireen! Have you seen her?' He was busy helping a shivering, blue-lipped boy from the water. Thomas wrapped the child in a reflective foil blanket and barely looked at me long enough to quickly shake his head. I looked at the few refugees still dragging themselves, exhausted and shaken, to the shore. None of them were Shireen. I searched the beach for at least an hour. She had not arrived before me. I knew then, with absolute certainty, I would never see her again.

"I buckled under the weight of yet another loss and sat heavily on the stony beach, buried my face in sand-gritty hands and wept for what I stubbornly promised would be the last time. I wasn't allowed the luxury of crying for long though. A tentative hand touched my shoulder. It was Thomas. 'You can't stay here,' he explained, pulling his hand away, perhaps remembering how some Muslims may react to even an innocent touch such as that one. 'The Greek coastal guards won't let you stay. Go to the UNHCR camp and register. Here,' he said, handing me a piece of paper, 'Directions to the registration center.' The Norwegian looked down at me, compassion in his pale, blue eyes. 'You were brave and strong to have made it to shore,' he said, 'Your friend would be glad to know you made it. She would have wanted you to be strong now and for you to make it to wherever you're going.'"

Tala had settled onto one of the chairs by the window, and I moved to the chair opposite her, leaning my elbows on the table between us. I moved the centerpiece, a small bouquet of flowers, so I could watch her face as she told her story. I stared into her eyes, but her attention was focused far away. Her brow furrowed with the ache of grief as she relived those dreadful events. Perhaps the sharing was a catharsis for her. It was painful, and she might be suffering, but the resolute set of her jaw kept me from interrupting.

"I should have thanked Thomas for his help and kindness, but I was too devastated to do anything but look away dismissively. 'Go,' he said, looking up the beach to where officially dressed men were walking our way, 'It's better to leave now than to have them tell you to go.' I did as he said without a second glance back. Determination burned in me. It seared the tears from my eyes. Despite my incredible fatigue, I stalked up the beach toward the street, damp, barefoot, and still reeling from the tragedy I'd just survived.

"I checked my wallet. It was still sealed in the waterproof bag I had purchased. Shireen had bought one just like it. There was a small group of people, cold and wet like me. I followed them up a short set of steps onto a low-walled, residential street. Whitewashed low-rises stood on either side of the street. A few people watched through their windows as we passed. A pinched-face woman glared at me, a shirtless man scowled from another window, and a young woman looked down from a balcony in her second-floor flat with what might have been sympathy.

"The group of us headed northward, the direction indicated on the paper the volunteers, like Thomas, had provided. Miserable, I fell back from the throng. Just off the main road, I found a small café from which I bought a cheese sandwich and a coffee. I sat with my little meal in the little ad hoc patio in front of the shop. I shivered, cold and tired, feeling the weight of the looks given to me by the café's patrons. Again, the reactions and expressions depended on the individual. Some diligently ignored me, some smiled empathetically, while a couple—both men—leered lasciviously.

"As I sat there, leaning heavily on the tiny bistro table, my clothes drying in the breeze and sun, a woman with a large sports bag slung over one shoulder halted in front of me. She had been heading in the direction of the rest of my group of refugees, and the bag was overflowing with donated clothes. I squinted up at her as the sun was behind the woman in the early evening sky. Her eyes were full of sincere concern when she looked at me. Without a word, she dropped her load and rummaged through the cast-off clothes before producing a pair of worn, canvas shoes. She placed them before me on the sidewalk, then stood and placed a hand over her heart before turning and following the stream of my fellow migrants.

"I watched her as she walked away, holding her wide-brimmed sun hat to her head against the wind with one hand while the other hauled her burden of hope and kindness. She may have been a local or a tourist-turned-volunteer. There were many of both on Lesbos, but the crisis was still overwhelming for the island's communities.

"The shoes were about half a size too large, but I could not have appreciated them more. With the stranger's gift tied snuggly to my feet, I went inside the café to clean up a bit. I did not have another change of clothes, but those I was wearing, damp with sea water, were gradually drying. I looked at myself in the mirror. It was startling to see myself without my hijab. It made me think for a moment of the last time I'd gone without it—a brief look back at my teenage years. I did not look much older than I had before my father made me start wearing the headscarf.

"I still had my beauty. My looks might have been the only thing I had left that I could call my own. It may have been immodest to be aware of my uncommonly good looks, but I feel it was a facet of my instinct for survival. I combed my fingers through my tangled hair and washed until I didn't appear *quite* so disheveled. My fingers caught in a particularly stubborn knot and a dark memory cast a shadow over my confidence.

"I remembered a cruel fist wrenching my hair, strong hands holding me down. I could smell the rancid garlic scent of his breath as he grunted and snarled next to my ear. I was crushed between his sweaty, rutting body and the cold, implacable porcelain tub.

"I rubbed fiercely at the tears threatening to escape my eyes and glowered at my reflection in the mirror. 'Who are you?' I demanded of myself. 'Are you Fatima in a refugee camp? Fatima in Turkey, happy and in love with her husband, looking forward to her future?' With narrow eyes accusing me through that mirror, my reflection challenged me, 'Are you the Fatima who lost her husband? Are you the Fatima who was—' I nearly choked on the word, '—raped?'

"With chest heaving from rage, I scolded that pitiful woman in the mirror, 'Or are you the Fatima who is now searching for a better life? The Fatima who will make it to Europe and succeed, finally? To win?' I nodded curtly at myself and turned to leave the bathroom, just a little less unkempt, a little drier, and a lot more determined.

"I tried to flag a taxi. A driver slowed, then he looked at me from air-dried and wrinkled clothes to my new, secondhand shoes, and he sped away. It happened exactly like that two more times, the drivers recognizing me as a refugee and then driving off. 'Didn't they tell you that taxis won't take refugees?' a woman's voice said. Her sunhat's brim fluttered in the breeze and her duffle bag, empty now, was slung over one arm. 'If they are caught giving refugees rides, they are charged and fined,' the woman explained, shaking her head.

"My shoulders slumped, and I watched another taxi drift by, the driver carefully avoiding eye contact with me. I frowned and produced the information sheet Thomas had given me. 'How do I get *here* then?' I asked, stabbing a finger at the registration center indicated with a dot on the map.

"The wind threatened to take her hat again, and the woman clasped it reflexively to her head. 'You walk,' she said, her attention drifting from the map to further up the street where there was a hunched-shouldered family trudging northward. Once more, she shook her head and then gave me one last glance before continuing on her way. 'Good luck,' she murmured, sincere and somber.

"I did that. I walked. The map was easy to follow, but, after hours on the road, I realized it would be no short trip to the UNHCR registration center. By the second hour of my trip, I had met other people walking the same road, refugees like me.

"A pair of young men, overstuffed backpacks strapped to their shoulders, marched at a faster pace than I was managing. They seemed hardly winded by the trek and uncommonly confident. By the time they reached me, I had heard some of their conversation, and I recognized the accent of one of them as Palestinian. I had questions, and that was my opportunity to get answers. I stopped when they got nearer. 'Hello,' I said, smiling and inclining my head, 'I am Palestinian too.'

"We introduced ourselves and were all pleased for the company as we fell in step together. 'I am Mohammed, and this is Fahed,' Mohammed said, gesturing to his friend. It turned out that they were from another refugee camp in Lebanon and made it across from Turkey just after me. However, they didn't suffer a capsizing as I had.

"It may have been a dangerous idea to trust these two men, but I was very short on companions since I'd lost Shireen, and Mohammed and Fahed seemed to know what they were doing. There is safety in numbers, and the sun was edging nearer the horizon. I did not want to be on this road by myself—after dark especially. 'So, what happens next?' I asked.

"'Now we get to UNHCR and get registered as refugees. It is best to tell them that you are from Syria,' Mohammed said, and Fahed nodded, 'Things will go better and faster. If you have any Palestinian documents, get rid of them before you get there.' He wiped

sweat from his brow. His t-shirt was stained with perspiration around the broad straps of his backpack.

"My feet were aching, but I didn't complain, not
after having suffered far worse than mere sore feet. I
had been walking at least three hours by then. 'How
much further?' I asked, casting a glance westward
where the sun was setting over low, misty mountains.
I could see lights of a small village nestled against one
of them.

"'We're about half of the way there,' Fahed said,
wincing apologetically.

"'Didn't anyone tell you anything when you
landed?' Mohammed asked.

"I shook my head, 'Not really. The volunteers
were far too busy helping rescue the rest. Our boat
capsized,' I reminded him. He nodded grimly.

"Thankfully, the walk in the night was uneventful,
and the three of us met other refugees, but kept our
pace quick with each other's help and overtook and
passed many other groups who were on the same long
march. We spent the next hours practicing our Syrian
accents and dialects. We even invented our Syrian
backstories so we'd have answers to their questions
at registration.

"By the time we arrived, my shoes were stained
from the weeping blisters they had worn into my
heels. We were at a port, surrounded by chain-link
fences and lines of refugees like us. The main source

of illumination was the towering ship that cast light from its decks and dominated the UNHCR registration center. The sight was a welcome one. It signified our next leg of this journey.

"The hundreds of people in the queue were from all sorts of countries, their appearances, and languages varying from one refugee to the next. Managing the lines were employees who were giving each a piece a paper officially giving them refugee status. That piece of paper served as their clearance to board the looming ship promising passage to Athens. The final destination, ideally, was Germany, the country that was most accepting of refugees. That was the dream for most of us.

"On the other side of the lineup, journalists gathered. They were looking for stories and images like those that had been circulating in the media. One would think the entire world would be sympathetic after seeing those pictures and reading the accounts of the migrants' struggles. But some became all the more intolerant and racist toward people like me. We were just looking for a better, safer life. Nothing more. Had they forgotten that many of their ancestors were refugees themselves? Even Moses, Jesus, and Mohammad were refugees at one point, fleeing a country for a better future.

"I made it to the front of the line. It was my turn. Tired and ready for the end of her night's shift, a woman waved me forward. That is the moment when Fatima became Tala, when her background changed from Palestinian to Syrian. I'd spent the last hours imitating the dialect from all the Syrian television I had watched, and I was ready. I was perfectly convincing as Tala, a Christian Syrian fleeing the war.

"Without hesitation or further questions, the UNHCR worker handed me my piece of paper. 'This is your refugee status documentation. Keep it. You will need it to get on your boat to Athens. Then you will need it when you board buses and then a train taking you to Germany,' she said. It was a string of words she must have uttered countless times, repeated so often they were a lifeless drone. But to me, they were the most welcome words I had heard in recent memory.

"The woman was already looking beyond me to wave the next person in line forward, but I interrupted with a question. 'The boat outside... Is that the boat?' I asked, my voice shaking at the idea of crossing still more water. 'I lost a friend crossing from Turkey,' I explained.

"Her eyes softened, and she nodded, 'Yes, Tala.' The sound of my new name felt strange but somehow reassuring. 'You will be on that big vessel. It's very safe. I'm sorry to hear about your friend. The boat costs 160 euros, and it will take you to Athens. From there you will board a bus to Macedonia. After that, your next stop is Germany.' The smile her news put on my face made her tired expression brighten. The UNHCR is full of well-intentioned and kind-hearted people like her. 'Good luck, Tala. Now, please, I need to take the next people in line.'

"I moved along, holding my documents and my questions.

"I was instructed to a holding camp and was told, 'You can sleep in the camp by the center because the next ship won't leave until five in the morning.' The last thing I wanted to do was to stay even one more night in a refugee camp. It was already late, and despite my aching feet, I decided I'd walk more.

"Lesbos was beautiful. I spent the next three or so hours listlessly walking the streets of the ancient port town. The streets were narrow and paved with cobblestones ground to roundness under centuries of traffic. I finally spent time saying goodbye to my friend Shireen. I stood at a low, stone wall and watched dozens of boats rock in the gentle sea—small fishing boats, slender sailboats, and flashy speedboats. Their riggings clanked softly, ringing like bells in the quiet, sea-scented night. 'Goodbye, my friend. I wish you were here with me. I promise to make it. I promise to live—to win this struggle. Whatever it takes.'

"I straightened, squared my shoulders and turned to start walking back to the port. It was only a couple more hours until the boat would start boarding. There was a car, idling in front of a line of row houses with brightly painted shutters. There was a man at the wheel, his coarsely haired arm resting upon the car's open window. I smiled. How fortunate that he was there; I needed to ask directions. 'Do you know how to get to the port? I need to catch a 5:00 am boat to Athens,' I asked, hoping the Greek man would know a little English. I didn't bother trying Arabic.

"The way he looked at me halted me for a heart-beat as I crossed the street toward him. 'You and thousands of other refugees, I'll bet,' he replied with a smile that made my skin prickle with goosebumps. I could feel his eyes roam over my body like cold fingers. This man was not going to frighten me though, and I walked straight to his car. 'I know where it is, yes,' he said, 'But why don't you let me drive you there instead of making that long walk?'

"Some may think my decision to take that offered drive was unwise and even dangerous. I had nothing to lose. Why would I hesitate after all that I had survived already? He had to rush to brush food wrappers and crumbs from the seat before I could sit.

"His little, Korean-made hatchback smelled strongly of cigarette smoke. I was glad the windows were open. The man leaned one wrist on the steering wheel and considered me thoughtfully. Perspiration beaded on his balding head and wispy-mustached upper lip. 'How much money do you have?' he asked.

"I replied with a feigned conversational air, 'One hundred and ninety dollars. I need to exchange it for euros.' For some reason, I had the feeling that the man would not hurt me, but I was still nervous despite my calm composure.

"'You won't make it out of Athens with only that much,' he said. The words rang true. He was sincere about that much, I was sure. 'The boat requires funds, the bus, the train, the food,' he went on. 'Listen,' he said, slinging one arm over the back of my seat. The odor of his underarms wafted up to assault my nostrils. 'There is a quick and easy way to make a few hundred euros. I will be as generous as you are.' He stepped on the accelerator and we were moving before I might decide to get out of the car. My first thoughts were not to get out though. 'No pressure. Just proposing. Just proposing,' the man assured me in Greek-accented English."

Tala turned to me, blinking away the remembered image of that foul car and its equally foul driver. "I'm thirsty," she said, "Will you please pour me some water?" She nodded to the decanter of water that was brought with breakfast by room service. I complied, of course. Tala watched my hand shake as I poured the water, the rage boiling up from my belly. As if she hadn't been through enough at that point in her journey! That man, like so many people, was the type to use others when they are at their most vulnerable—a trait in some that I detested. I hated it. I could never understand it.

Tala's fingertips brushed mine when I handed her the glass, and she favored me with a nervous smile. "Did you want to stop?" I asked, recognizing her reticence to continue, "If it's too hard, you don't need to go on. But I hope you will. I'm sure it isn't easy. It's difficult enough to hear; I can only imagine how hard it is to recount it."

The way she regarded me with her impossibly deep, brown eyes made me think of years, decades, of joy with this woman. I laid my broad hand on the bare knee she had allowed to slip from between her robe, and she pressed her own hand onto mine, "I'm nervous about telling you the next part," she admitted, but took in a breath and resumed.

"The man didn't say anything for a long while. I think he may have been reconsidering his choice to take advantage of me, in fact. But, then he looked at me again, and I could sense the lust and desperation. He was entirely unappealing: fat, unshaven, and balding. 'No,' I said, finally. 'I won't do it.'

"He did not respond, except to stare at the road ahead and accelerate around a turn. I thought I could sense aggression from him, anger and maybe desperation too. I thought I could smell bathroom cleanser then, however impossible that was. And fetid breath hot on my ear—the smell of garlic. I could barely

bellowed for quiet. 'Calm down! They have not blocked us. We simply have to wait!'

"I really wasn't clear on what was going on. I had waited this long; it was crowded, but comfortable—far better than most of my trip so far. I simply remained quiet, even when those around me were losing all patience and were growing loud and agitated. In fact, I slept. At long last, I slept.

"Waiting for me in my dreams was Bilal. I was looking up at him from the deck of a massive cruise ship like one of the many I had seen docked at the port in Athens. The railings were wrapped in gold streamers that crinkled under my palms as I hurried up to greet him. His smile was warm and uninhibitedly broad. I matched his elation and opened my arms, careening into his embrace. The sun was so bright that it made a halo around my love's face, and I kissed him. I kissed him with an intensity surpassing that on our vigorous, passionate wedding night. The weight of my suffering was lifted just as he lifted me from my feet. I could smell the familiar scent of him, feel the welcome roughness of his lightly stubbled chin. He was with me, finally. Sorrow and pain were crushed from me with the power of Bilal's loving arms.

"Gunshots.

"Screams shattered the perfection of my dream, and I opened my eyes just as the bus lurched suddenly into motion. Backwards. More shots were fired, and I gaped out the window at Macedonian guards pointing rifles at the bus. They didn't lower them until we were a good distance from the border crossing. They were firing at the bus to keep us from entering the country. They did not want refugees at all.

"It had become a trend in the world to treat the refugee crisis like some zombie apocalypse. Fear had won over humanity. But fear of what? We are just human beings fleeing danger and war. I never understood the passion with which people hated us. We were reviled and scorned. We were held accountable for the atrocities of a small few—people we neither know nor tolerate. It was easier to hate and fear us than to help us, or at least show compassion.

"We waited a few hours, and the bus driver turned to talk to us again. 'We are going back. If they show aggression again, I will stop right away and turn around. This isn't the first time this has happened. Don't worry. We'll try again.'

"This time they let us through.

"It wasn't long before we arrived at the bus station. The train on which I would travel to Germany was only a short walk from there. I did not want to think about where I got the money to pay for my train ticket, it was too painful. Instead, I found the correct platform and stood there, ready to be the first to board. Thousands of other refugees had the same idea though, and when the train was finally announced ready for boarding, each car was quickly filled to capacity. The remainder of the passengers had to be left on the platform for the next train which would arrive an hour later.

"The train would take me through Serbia and then Slovenia before arriving in Germany. Or, so I thought.

"At the Slovenian border, immigration officers boarded the train. They were dressed in black fatigues and were armed, though their guns were holstered. The men wore black baseball caps and pitiless scowls. All but one. That one wore a black beret with his pitiless scowl.

"The officers shouldered their way through one passenger car to the next, pushing aside anyone in their way. They were looking for something. 'That one,' the officer in the beret commanded, 'Her.' To my horror, he was pointing at me.

"I was taken from the train to the platform. Two officers held my shoulders and walked me to a car. The man in the beret was already in the car when I was shoved in to join him. 'I have an offer for you,' he said, giving me a wolf's grin.

"For someone who has lost everything in life, any offer might be a source of hope. His offer was straightforward: 'You are a beautiful girl. With a body like yours and face like that, you can make good money. And if you accept my offer, I will make sure you get your Slovenian residency. It is like the German residency.

We are all European Union. It's a sure thing,' he explained, 'unlike your application in Germany which may be refused there.'

"The immigration officer worked for a human trafficking and prostitution ring which reached all over Europe. They preyed on refugees.

"Refugees like me.

"I am very tired," Tala said to me, tucking a dark tendril of hair behind her ear.

"Of course you are," I said. She looked at me with an imploring look that I could not resist. I hugged her and kissed her brow, her cheeks, her lips. "Thank you for telling me your story, Tala. You've been through so very much." It had been over twelve hours since she walked through my door for the second time yesterday and began telling me her dreadful tale.

I made her a promise then, a promise I didn't know I would live to regret. "Tala, I will help you find Bilal. I will be by your side. You are never going back to those people."

I gave her hope, but she was skeptical when it came to trusting others. I could sense that, and didn't blame her, considering her past. I took her by the hand and brought her to bed. I watched her fall asleep, and I thought to myself: Here is a person who had lost everything, and now I am going to be her savior.

I believe I fell in love with Tala at first sight. I fell all at once and hard. So thoroughly did I love her that

I would promise her anything. I promised to help her find her husband. How could I accomplish that and remain her lover? I did not know. She gave me something these past several hours: Henry. She had awakened the old Henry, the Henry who wins and never loses.

It was up to me to give her something though—something to live for. I had no practical notions as to how to accomplish that goal, but I would start by loving her. She would never come to a place in her life again where she has nothing to lose. I would free her from desperation, from hopelessness. From that moment on, I would ensure that she never again experienced anything like the horrors she described.

Chapter Five

A man born to be a winner thrives on the mission upon which he embarks. There is no victory without it. To succeed at the mission, he starts with the will to take it on, then he considers the challenges in his way, and ultimately forms a plan to overcome those challenges and win. I am such a man. And I intended to be the winner.

My mission was in the forefront of my mind. It was taking up my every thought, and despite not having slept all night, I was not tired. I was staring at Tala, her slumbering form strewn across our bed like a young man's masturbatory fantasy come true. She was delightfully nude, and I watched as she shifted in her sleep. Her thighs brushed languidly against one another and one soft, creamy breast nestled against the sheets on which Tala slept. Though the sight of my lover made my loins clench with my craving for her, it was the mission that kept me too restless to sleep.

I left the bed quietly and headed into the living room. Evidence of our night's drinking, empty glasses and bottles, and remnants of our breakfast were still cluttering the table by the window. I was to help Tala find Bilal, the man who was married to the woman I love. A selfish, petulant part of me hoped that I would find Bilal dead, but I wasted no time feeling guilty over the thought. Instead, I spent my energy on devising a plan.

Would I go to Turkey? Lebanon? Would I contact my connections back home and put out a worldwide alert with the media? Such a thing might be an incredible boost for my public relations—I was suddenly interrupted by unexpected and surprising thoughts of a comeback. The seeds of a new book were already germinating, and I paced across the living room. Before I realized it, I had a pen and a pad of hotel-branded paper, and I was scribbling fervidly.

The first words I jotted down were, "Tale of Tala," the title of my new book. It was my first time writing since my last book—my failure. I had committed to giving up altogether, but writing was a drug. How could an addict like me resist the euphoria that Tala's story represented? I was passionate about the subject already, and after so many hours having been immersed in Tala's recounting of her story, I was enthralled even more.

I was putting words to paper as they rushed into my mind, by way of my pained heart. I started with how I met Tala and how my failing book led me to her. There was no failing for a winner like me. I was reminded that everything happens for a reason, and my prior book was just a way for the universe to bring me to Tala. Having rationalized all of that, and despite my lack of sleep, I felt invigorated and at home in myself. The old Henry was in full comeback mode.

I wrote and wrote. Hours passed as Tala slept, and I was filling page after page with her story—our story. My pen scratched across the elegantly bordered paper at a speed at which I had never before written. My handwriting became erratic and nearly indiscernible as my pen struggled to keep up with the racing prose rushing from my brain. It was as though love fueled my work, and passion drove my words. Tala was my muse.

I had utterly lost track of time, and I had already finished a good chunk of *Tale of Tala* when I heard the new book's namesake call my name.

"Henry?" she called from the bedroom. My heart stopped, and a flush burned my cheeks and neck. It was the first time Tala had ever called my name. Her voice was lethargic and tinted with a hint of concern. I padded quickly toward the bedroom.

After a pair of steps, I skidded to a halt and turned back to the coffee table to gather the pen and paper. Before I returned to the bedroom, I tucked the pad, face down, in the drawer where I'd found it.

Tala's hair was beautifully mussed, and she was lying back smiling lazily at me from her nest of creamy white pillows. She stretched with a feline grace, one arm extending languidly over her head, and her body arched, causing the sheets to drift from her bare form. The sight was like a delightful punch to my belly. The air rushed from my lungs all at once. Pretending neither to notice her state of nudity nor the way it affected me, Tala scolded sweetly, "It is already after five o'clock."

I watched as a graver expression chased the sultry smile from her face, and I braced myself for a question about what I had been doing those hours while Tala slept. I did not want her to know about my book and was desperately relieved to hear her ask, "Were you serious about helping me find Bilal?"

Inspiration had diverted me entirely from any planning. I crawled onto the bed and shrugged out of my hotel robe before embracing her and relishing her warm, smooth skin against mine. "Yes, I was—*am* serious about it," I assured her as I nuzzled her throat. "We are the same, you and I. Survivors. Winners. We will find him."

She sighed and smiled as she twined my hair between her fingers, silent for a long moment. I gave her hope. I gave her life back. No, I gave her a life. The suffering was over, the struggles finished, and the tragedies ended.

Tala slipped out from under me, and I reached after her in playful anguish, but the instant she closed the door to the bathroom, I was off the bed and in the living room. I had to find a more secure place to hide the burgeoning first draft of *Tale of Tala*. I hid the precious pad of paper deep in my suitcase where Tala would have no reason to look.

I did not wish Tala to know that I was writing her story so she does not question my integrity. It seemed that everyone wanted something from her, and I did not wish to be yet another man using her for a personal motive.

We finally left the hotel to seek out some food and to share a little time outside of our suite. The concierge, Dimitrij, was at his desk, casually chatting to a bellhop when he spied us exiting the elevator. "All is well, Sir Henry?" he called, his unsavory smile bordering on a leer. I wanted to kill him. I wanted to beat him until my knuckles were torn and his breathing stopped. He was certainly involved in Tala's misery and the sequence of events leading to my love's becoming a prostitute.

I pulled Tala against me fondly and kissed her brow, directing a deceptively dazzling smile his way. "Dimitrij," I said cheerily, "I need to talk to you later. Don't leave tonight without seeing me."

The man had no inkling as to the foul loathing I felt for him. If he had, his smile would not have widened as it did. It was a predator's smile, and I felt Tala tense against me when she saw it. I stroked her back and guided her toward the revolving door without another look back at the detestable concierge.

Ljubljana's charming streets took our minds off the sleazy Dimitrij and we quickly fell into the roles of tourists and lovers. We visited a café and snacked on burek, a savory pastry filled with cheese, and had cabbage rolls with some seasoned meat that, while unidentifiable, was delicious. Afterward, we held hands and meandered across cobblestones as the street lamps flickered on and the sun began to set.

We talked about places we had visited and discussed our favorites. I told Tala that my favorite was Jerusalem with its ornate churches, magnificent mosques, and its bustling, riotously colored markets. Tala was enchanted.

"Tell me more," she urged me. She had never been to her home country. Palestinian refugees were not allowed in the State of Israel or the West Bank. "I want to know everything," she implored. I told her about my favorite hotels, the roads, and the deplorable drivers.

She was initially riveted by even my most mundane accounts of Jerusalem's people and my tourist's experiences, but she grew quiet after a short while. I could tell Tala was distracted. Already knowing the answer, I didn't ask her what was on her mind.

Later, we were in a restaurant whose expansive windows afforded us an unobstructed view of the river when Tala finally asked, "So, how will you find Bilal?"

Behind my intent gaze, I winced at the question. I stalled to better contemplate my reply by straightening the elegantly hemstitched napkin in my lap while maintaining my attentive smile. I had to be compassionate. Bilal was the man who could take Tala away from me. I wished she could have just forgotten about it, about him, just for a little while. She deserved some happiness, some good times. "Lebanon," I told her, "That's where I will start. I will need to find Abu Ali."

Before that instant, I didn't have a plan at all. I leaned close and placed my hand on Tala's. "I need you to tell me something," I said, "Where was the café that Bilal used to meet Abu Ali? Had he mentioned it to you?"

Tala's brow furrowed in consternation. "Yes," she replied, "He did. I know it very well." A heartbeat later, she asked, "What if he went missing too?"

"When one embarks on a mission, one can't be deterred by 'ifs' and 'buts.' I'm going to have to start somewhere," I said.

Tala rolled her eyes and grimaced playfully, "So dramatic," she said, laughing. It was nice to see her smile. Her shoulders relaxed, and she squeezed my hand affectionately.

That's when I closed both my hands around hers. I tried to be as gentle as I could when I asked the dreadful question, "What if Bilal is dead, Tala?"

Glass shattered, and her wine cast a foreboding, blood-red stain among broken shards on the tiled floor. I cursed myself for asking the question and, before I could apologize, Tala clutched hard at my hand. "You are right. He may be dead." Her voice was tight in her throat, and her eyes narrowed with stubborn determination. "If he is dead, at least I'll know that he is in a better place than the world he knew." She defiantly refused to let the tears welling in her eyes spill to her cheek, "And I can think of him watching over me. I won't fool myself into false hope."

"There is no such thing as false hope," I insisted, reaching across the table to lift her chin with a finger. She met my eyes, and she smiled at me sadly. "Hope, itself, is beautiful, powerful, and sincere. It can be a window through which we can see what is to come. With hope, we can imagine what is next and achieve our goals. It is hope that makes our mission's success possible."

"What makes you so optimistic?" Tala asked.

I didn't fault her that incredulity. I trailed my fingertips across her cheek, tilting my head as I stared at her. "Because I was born to be a winner," I answered.

She smirked and rolled her eyes. "Again, so dramatic," she jeered good-naturedly, "I think I adore that about you."

One of the bus boys was tidying up the mess Tala had accidentally made on the floor, and I asked for the bill. On the way back to the hotel, we stopped at a boutique whose window display caught Tala's eye. "You like those?" I asked, gesturing to the clothes in which the mannequins were adorned. She gestured pointedly down at her jeans and leather jacket and chuckled.

"They're beautiful," she remarked, turning back to the fashions on display. "Skirts, dresses... And look at those shoes!" Indeed, I could imagine how her calves would look with those patent leather, high-heel shoes with their strap clasped around Tala's ankles. I swallowed audibly and cocked a brow as I looked through the display window. The clothes took on an entirely different quality when I pictured them on Tala. Everything was suddenly unbelievably sexy.

"Come on," I said, taking her hand, "Anything and everything you want." A laugh burst from Tala's sumptuous lips, and she shook her head, eyes sparkling.

"You're crazy," she noted, and she stepped ahead of me, pulling me into the store.

We were there until well after the store's closing time. Considering the money they stood to make from us, they didn't mind staying open for us whatsoever. I sat comfortably on a chaise lounge and enjoyed a private show of Tala modeling various outfits from fashionable-casual to chic-formal and from simple traditional to daring sexy. I cherished the time we spent shopping and playing dress-up, and especially the elated smile and uninhibited laughter. The act of furnishing my lover with her dream wardrobe was a true delight.

Our walk back to the hotel was even slower than our earlier meandering pace as both of us were laden with comically abundant parcels and garment bags. We laughed and stumbled in between halts to readjust our loads or pick up a bag that had tumbled from our heaps of merchandise.

We turned a corner and happened upon a small crowd. There was a band busking in the street which had garnered an audience. I heaved my load into a pile and motioned Tala to do the same. Skeptically, Tala looked at me, at the heap of shopping bags and then back at me.

"Dance with me," I commanded, laughing and reaching for her.

"Are you crazy? Right here?"

"Who cares?"

The band started into a fresh tune. A trumpet, accordion, and violin spiritedly entertained the group of tourists and locals, their syncopated rhythm keeping the traditional, Slavic modality bright and lively. The music undulated and whirled around us with a gradual and playfully relentless accelerando.

Tala and I laughed aloud, twirling and struggling to keep up with the musicians. The crowd parted around us and started to clap along with the music, encouraging us. I stared at Tala. She was flushed with exertion, gasping and laughing all at once. Neither of us had a clue as to how to dance to this music, but what we lacked in skill we made up for in enthusiasm.

I've never seen a more beautiful woman than Tala that night. Her dark eyes were wide with mirth, and her hair danced freely about her shoulders in luxurious tendrils. I took a mental picture of this scene and tucked it away in my memory as I knew I would want to include it in the book.

I was still thinking of how I might write about the events of the night when the music came to a rousing crescendo and was finished. The crowd and musicians all applauded Tala and me, and we happily took our bows, still laughing. The thrilling and romantic night was filling my mind with elegant prose, and it made me yearn to take down the words. It was intoxicating. As well, Tala was feeding my addiction to love with her breathtaking, delighted smile and melodic laughter. I was under the influence of my two addictions: writing and love.

Dimitrij was waiting for us in the lobby when we returned to the hotel. He took our bags and then passed them to a bellhop who piled our purchases onto a luggage cart. "Sir Henry," he said, "Welcome back."

I didn't respond except to surreptitiously hand him a generous tip and murmur, "Come join us upstairs."

When we all, Tala, Dimitrij, the bellhop and myself, arrived at the suite, I dismissed the bellhop and turned to Tala. "Please, Tala. Would you give Dimitrij and me a few minutes to talk?" She looked at me, then Dimitrij, and then turned back to me.

"Of course," she agreed, "I'll organize my new wardrobe."

I sat on the sofa and motioned to the chair across the coffee table from me. Dimitrij sat down, and I said, "Alright. I need you to ask your friend how much it would cost if I wanted to buy Tala from him." The words tasted sour in my mouth. This talk of purchasing a human being was disturbing.

"I will ask. I will ask. Of course, Sir Henry," he acquiesced.

"I'll need to know tonight. And her documents. The ones from the UNHCR. I'm assuming they have those too. That's important. It's part of the deal. I need her status papers."

"I'll be in touch very soon, Sir Henry," he assured me. The concierge, understanding that he might potentially make a very nice amount of money from this transaction, didn't waste any time. He left to see to my requests.

The door to the bedroom opened.

"Why are you doing this for me?" Tala asked, leaning in the doorway, arms crossed. "You know that when you find Bilal, I have to be with him."

I did not answer her for a moment. Then, I told her, "Because I want to help. I will treat you like a friend, even family. I respect you. I will not sleep with you. I will not disrespect what you have with your husband. I promise." I almost choked on that promise.

The sofa was a lonely place, made all the lonelier knowing Tala was just a few paces away in the next room. I had my writing though, and the ache of Tala's vicinity was only kept at bay by my writing. I could relive that time when we sat in the bathtub together for hours, when we shared the bed, and when I felt the electrically charged sensation of her flesh against mine.

"Are you writing again?" I heard Tala say from the bedroom door from which she regarded me, her head tilted curiously.

"Yes," I replied, "Just working through an idea I had a long time ago. You must be my muse." I flashed her a brilliant smile to distract her from the pad of paper in my lap. I casually turned it over and laid it down. I worried about her finding out that she was the subject of my next book. It was very important that she didn't feel that I was using her.

My next interruption was Dimitrij when he came up to the suite to report. "Sir Henry, my friend wants 50,000 euros for Tala. She is a very valuable girl for him."

"No problem," I said, trying to keep my revulsion from showing on my face. With every flippant remark about Tala, Dimitrij was growing increasingly vile to me. "And her papers?" I inquired.

There was the briefest of pauses before the concierge replied, his attention flitting toward the closed door of the bedroom. I hoped that Tala was sleeping. "My friend got rid of them," he said. Then, seeing the immediate and searing hot rage in my eyes, he added, "But I have another friend who sells Dominican passports. They are 125,000 euros. Tala can be a Dominican citizen with a passport. A real one."

I looked at Dimitrij and tried to imagine the low-lifes and thugs with whom he might be associated. I could only guess at the connections he must have had to be able to provide a passport as he described. He wet his lips as though anxiously salivating over the thought of his cut of that exorbitant amount of money. The refugee crisis seemed as lucrative to these bottom-feeding criminals as it was tragic to the displaced victims. Human lives and futures had become a commodity traded on the black market.

"Fine," I said through the grinding teeth of a tight, forced smile. I clapped him on the shoulder in a feigned gesture of camaraderie, "I'll have the 175,000 euros for you in a few days."

Dimitrij smiled so broadly I could see the glinting gold of his bargain-rate dental work. "You know," he said, amiably patting my hand on his shoulder, "Sir Henry, I don't get any cut of these transactions." I was both appalled and bemused by how easily and convincingly he could lie to my face.

I couldn't bear to touch him an instant longer, and I let my hand slip from his shoulder, disguising my rising rage with an affable chuckle, "Tell you what, Dimitrij, let's make a deal." A hungry gleam in his eyes betrayed his greed, but I pretended not to notice. "I will give you 10,000 euros if you get me that passport quickly. Also, I will be away for a few days later this week. Tala will be staying. You are going to be responsible for her. You will send someone with her anywhere she wants to go. Her safety and comfort will be entirely your number one concern. For this, I will give you 1,000 euros a day. How does that sound?"

I could see him tremble with all the excitement welling in him. He took my hand in both of his and shook it hard enough to make my teeth rattle. "Yes, Sir Henry, yes! I'm your man. Tala will be safe and happy.

She will want for nothing while under my care." He was elated. And why not? He was about to make more money than he could make in a year.

It was a relief to watch the intolerable sycophant leave. I knew I could only trust him as long as I paid him, but he would serve his purpose. It bothered me how much I needed his help, but he was a valuable tool for me to use in succeeding at my mission.

Slender arms wrapped around my chest from behind, and Tala was hugging me, resting her chin on my shoulder. "I knew you were my savior. My angel." She squeezed me tightly. I'd won Tala's trust. She affectionately hugged me, but chastely. It was such a change from the prior night when she was still playing the role of lover... prostitute. I was disappointed by how she so promptly agreed to my promise to not sleep with her. We'd shared a bed—shared a bathtub! We'd been so incredibly intimate. I could bring to mind every square inch of her perfect body: the turn of a calf, the dimple above a sculpted buttock, the wisp of downy hair between her thighs.

I had to step out of her embrace. Her touch was driving me mad with thwarted desire. When I turned and saw her beaming at me, her hands clasped gratefully together, the vision of sheer beauty and delight made me forget my frustrations. I laid my hand on her shoulder and smiled, "Let's celebrate, Tala."

And we did. The next two days were spent exploring Ljubljana like two honeymooners, holding hands and strolling through the old-world streets. The baroque architecture, elegant and timeless, seemed to lean benevolently over the narrow, brick streets as we wandered. We ate at fine restaurants, drank wine overlooking a tranquil, jade-green river, and watched the sun set from an ancient castle's watchtower.

"I don't think I've ever enjoyed myself more in my whole life than I have in these last two days, Tala," I told her. She stood beside me behind the stone wall at the crown of the watchtower as we looked over the city that was nestled under hazy, silhouetted mountains. Tala leaned her shoulder against my arm. I took the cue and draped my arm around her, and the dimming sunlight turned the red-tiled roofs below us to burnished copper.

From time to time, Tala would ask about my plan. "Have you given any more thought to how you're going to track down Bilal?" she asked. In the ruddy light of dusk, she was startlingly beautiful. Her loveliness made it difficult to lie to her, but I did anyway.

"Yes, Tala. I have a plan to find Abu Ali. I'm going to go to Lebanon—that is where I know I'll find Abu Ali." In fact, I hadn't given any plan much thought, and I didn't intend to leave until I had finished writing the story up to the point where I make the promise to Tala to find Bilal. I hadn't done much planning at all beyond finding Abu Ali at the café Tala had already identified. I was too involved in my writing. I needed my fix. It was, after all, my drug of choice.

I also wanted to be sure Tala was set up with her new passport and her Dominican citizenship. In this, Dimitrij came through. His profound love of money made him very dependable.

"Here is Tala's passport, Sir Henry," the concierge said, proffering a large, manila envelope. "It is growing more and more difficult to get these. They're selling fewer of them all the time. I fear that if you asked me for the same favor in a couple of months, it would have been impossible."

"Good work," I said and fished the passport out of the envelope. I scrutinized the quality of the document, searching for watermarks and any signs of inauthenticity. In truth, it was all pantomime; I had no idea how to tell if a document were forged or not.

Dimitrij crossed his arms and smiled his usual, broad and unsavory grin. "Miss Tala now has a nationality. For a refugee, a passport like this one is a precious thing," he said, indicating the document in my hand. "It's real," he assured me, "Expensive, but real." As always, money was at the forefront of his thoughts. I suspected the next words to come out of his mouth would also be about money. Once again, he didn't disappoint. "I brought the passport quickly, right?" he asked, conjuring in my mind images of a selfish child seeking praise and reward for having taken out the garbage or tidying his room. He was right though. I had promised him a bonus.

"Yes, Dimitrij," I conceded, "Let me go get your money." I was lucky to have contact with my father's family friends. Bankers and investors had ways of helping me to arrange large cash withdrawals, even overseas.

I left the living room and entered the bedroom. Tala was sitting on the edge of the bed. She had obviously been listening in on Dimitrij and me. I was firm in that I wanted Tala out of the room when I dealt with Dimitrij. She was waiting to hear the news.

I didn't address her at first. Instead, I lifted the bed skirt and pulled a shoulder bag from under the bed. I unzipped it to be sure the money I'd stowed there was undisturbed. It was. I rifled through the zippered pockets to find the fat envelope that held Dimitri's bonus, and then I smiled up at Tala. "The passport is ready and here." Tala gasped and stood up, her brow knitting in tentative excitement. Placing my hand on her shoulder, I gently guided her back down to sit on the bed again. "Let me just go get rid of him and I'll show you your new documentation."

The way she looked up at me with those wide, grateful eyes was thanks enough. "Tala," I explained, "I keep my word. It will all happen as I told you. You'll see." There was still doubt behind her eager stare. I bent and picked up the bag of cash before adding, "I'll prove it to you. I promise. People like us, we win."

As I turned and left the room, in a murmur intentionally loud enough for my ears, Tala said, "Always so dramatic."

I was still chuckling when I returned to Dimitrij, money in hand. "First, your bonus," I said as I handed the overstuffed envelope to the man. Then, handing him the cash-laden bag, I said, "And the payment for the passport."

To his credit, he wasn't gauche enough to count the money in front of me. The fevered look in his eyes betrayed his greed though, and I knew in that instant that he had inflated the price even before his bonus. He stood to make a great deal of money from me.

"Before you go," I said, smiling kindly, "I trust you have made arrangements for Tala? I will be leaving tomorrow for a few days. She will be taken care of, and she will be obeyed in all things. Correct?"

Dimitrij nodded vigorously. "Oh yes. Of course. She will have a driver and an assistant to help her and to look after her. They are waiting for my call. Rest assured, Sir Henry, your Miss Tala will be taken care of and will want for nothing." I had to trust him, and I felt that I had bought his loyalty. Even if I was wrong, he knew there was much more money to be made from me, and he would serve me if it meant more cash for him. My bank account was my insurance when it came to Dimitrij; without it, I couldn't be sure he would keep Tala safe.

Tala spent a long while admiring her new passport. "Why can't we smile in these pictures?" she asked me, thumbing through the first couple pages of fine print which she couldn't decipher as they were in Spanish.

"Something about needing to see the color of your eyes, I think," I replied. Though my mind was on my book and I was only partially taking part in the conversation. I wanted to get back to work on the manuscript. I had been writing every night while Tala was sleeping, and tonight would be the same. I needed to record the events of today, and I would be up to date before I flew to Beirut.

"Did I hear you say you were leaving tomorrow?" Tala asked. She closed her passport and held it possessively to her chest, looking at me with an unblinking, measured stare. It was impossible to know what she was thinking for certain, but I was convinced she was thinking of Bilal and probably her friend Shireen. She had lost everyone who was close to her. Bilal left her in a hotel just like I was about to leave her.

I was snapped out of my peripheral thoughts of the book when Tala looked at me with that grave regard. So, I crawled up onto the bed and lay beside her, and, placing my hand on her cheek, I whispered to her. "I know you're worried. You've been promised things in the past, and those promises were broken tragically. Bilal promised you he would come back, just like I promise I'll be back." With the edge of a finger, I lifted her chin. "Tala, I'll be back."

Tala's long lashes drifted low as she cast her gaze away. "I know you believe that..." she sighed. "But what you're doing is dangerous."

"Let me worry about that. I will not let you down. I'm going to return. And before I do, I will locate your husband," I said. "You know the combination to the hotel safe, right?" I asked, and Tala nodded glumly. "Good. I've put a very nice amount of money in there for you. I want you to take advantage of Dimitrij and his cronies. Go shopping. Go out to eat. Enjoy every luxury. I have also gotten you a mobile phone. I will be in touch constantly. The last thing I want to do is make you anxious because you haven't heard from me."

Bravely, Tala let a smile bloom on her lush lips. "Henry," she said. The sound of her saying my name still made me heady with desire. "We've grown so close..." She reached out and took my hand. In the second's pause that followed, visions filled my mind's eye: Tala in a white dress, holding a bouquet and smiling brilliantly up at me with tears of happiness glistening at the corners of her eyes; Tala reclining in our bed, her belly big with our child; Tala kissing me goodbye at the front door of our brown-bricked home.

But Tala left the thought unfinished. There was love in that sorrowful gaze. I was sure it was for me. I

opened my mouth to say something, perhaps to pro-
fess my own love, or maybe just to utter more reas-
surances. But Tala entwined her fingers in my hair
and forced her lips on mine, silencing me.

I was Tala's. If Dimitrij was mine, bought with
money, I was Tala's, bought with the tantalizing promise of love.

For another night, my desire, more urgent than
ever, was left raging. I wanted nothing more than
to make frantic and desperate love to Tala. I made a
promise though, and I had to prove to her that my
promises were meant to be kept. Instead, like the prior
nights, I would write. I was almost caught up to the
present in my telling of Tala's tale—our tale—and that
was the last thing I needed to do before leaving for
Lebanon.

If I couldn't have Tala, I at least had my other vice:
my book. *Tale of Tala* was as seductive as Tala herself.
With each day that turned subsequently into a new
chapter, I was becoming fanatical. Even while I experienced each event, I was beginning to imagine their
description that I would later type into the next chapter of the book. My life was more than inspiring the
story, it *was* the story, and I found that I was becoming more and more likely to base decisions upon how
they would read in my prose.

The taxi was uncomfortably warm on the trip to
the airport the next morning. "Very sorry, sir," the

driver said, shrugging, "Air condition... broke today."
At least that's what I thought he said. His English was
very weak. I thought to myself that I'd better get used
to the heat. After all, my next stop was the Middle
East. I leaned my face toward the breeze from the window that would only open half way, and I retreated
into my thoughts.

Did Tala truly have feelings for me? I was certain I
was in love with her. Absolutely certain. How could she
be in love with me? I could tell that she had feelings; it
was all over her face. But love? She had a husband. She
couldn't love both of us. Could she? What would she
have to gain from feigning love? One thing of which I
was certain was I did not want to share Tala.

The Ljubljana Airport was a blur. There were too
many thoughts rioting in my head for me to pay any
attention to the check-in, the shuffling queues, and the
uninspired airport staff. I had never been to Lebanon.
The book needed a journey, a quest. The element of
adventure and, perhaps, danger would add immeasur-
ably to *Tale of Tala*. But was I overconfident in thinking I could do this? I had to keep my promise. I had to
succeed. I had to win. I was a winner. A winner.

I was sitting on the plane, rattling the ice in my
now-empty, plastic tumbler, trying to pry a plan from
my brain. My second whiskey was long gone, and I
was trying to catch the pinch-faced steward's attention for a third. I did not know what to think. I couldn't

even define what my victory would look like. Would I be the winner if I found Bilal and reunited him with Tala? What if I found him dead? Would Tala be mine by default?

Neither seemed like a complete success.

Either way though, I would be a winner. The book I was writing was going to sell. I knew it. The story was strong, and it flowed from my pen quicker than anything else I'd ever written. At the end of the day, I was a writer. My books would define my victory. That's how I lived, and that's how I would always live.

After my third whiskey, my mind wouldn't focus long enough to form a plan for when I arrived in Beirut. In fact, I fell asleep. I hadn't been sleeping well for the entire week as I stayed up late writing every night. It was both a compulsion and a means to take my focus off my yearnings for Tala.

Dozing in my seat, I dreamt of her.

Tala was wearing that same white dress I had imagined earlier that day. It was, of course, a wedding dress. She was astoundingly beautiful, holding her bouquet and staring at me, soundlessly mouthing her vows to me. Her dress was intricately embroidered and bared her shoulders. Then we were at my house in upstate New York where I originally became a writer. Our kids were running across the toy-strewn yard, all breathless giggles and elated squeals.

"Welcome to Lebanon," the captain's voice calmly startled me awake, "The local time is..."

I pinched the bridge of my nose, wincing at a headache for which my third whiskey was responsible. A crick in my neck complained when I turned to look through the window at the growing picture of Beirut. It was a metropolitan expanse that looked to have been built directly atop the Mediterranean. From the sky, it was difficult to imagine the disorder and squalor Tala described. The city looked pristine from my perspective on the plane. The approaching landing strip jutted directly out into the vibrant, cerulean sea, and it was a welcome sensation to feel the aircraft touch down on it.

On the way from the airport, I observed that in my recent travels I could define a city by its contrasts. Beirut was a city of such contrasts. It was known as the "Pearl of the East" or the "Paris of the Middle East," but, at first, I could not see the comparison at all. The congested highway offered only a depressing view of dilapidated slums, concrete buildings with their dark, unadorned windows like the empty eye sockets of skulls, staring bleakly out at the endless lines of traffic. The image, despite the oppressive heat, made me shiver. The low-rise, slipshod structures were crushed together and separated only by claustrophobic alleys.

Tangled webs of power lines and cables canopied the walkways, unsightly and unsafe.

The sight brought me back to Tala's description of the refugee camp in which she grew up. In English, I asked the taxi driver if it was indeed the camp. He narrowed his eyes and peered at me through the rear-view mirror from under black, unruly eyebrows. With a derisive sneer, he said, "Yes. This is Burj el Barajneh, a Palestinian refugee camp." He looked like the name left a bad taste in his mouth, and he went on, "I won't drive you in there. I don't go there. Few taxis will."

As though he were doing an ignorant tourist a magnanimous favor, he explained, "You should avoid these camps; they're full of criminals. It's not safe. You probably wouldn't be seen again. Let me just bring you to your hotel. It's in a good neighborhood. You'll like it much better." When he looked at me again through the mirror and saw me contemplating the wretched camp with its sad, misshapen, concrete buildings, he sighed and shook his head.

We drove into a tunnel and then, when we emerged from the other side, I saw the other, starkly contrasting side of Lebanon. The modern, glass and steel architectures, pedestrian thoroughfares, green spaces, and trendy shops. It was an entirely other city than the one I had seen from the highway, the one where Tala was raised.

I arrived at my hotel and rushed to my room to write. I recorded the day's trip and my dream. My rough manuscript was growing, filling with our story so far—mine and Tala's. I flipped through what I'd written. It was shaping up nicely; I was especially proud of how I described her journey across the Mediterranean, and I read it over for perhaps the fifth time. Content, I squared the sheets and replaced the alligator paperclip. Only then did I turn my thoughts to my plan.

Tala had told me that, in Lebanon, people with money had the power to do anything, just like anywhere else in the world. I had the money, but I needed help. Luckily, cash can buy the kind of help I needed. I needed somebody local who could act on my behalf without raising the sort of suspicions that an American would. He would be crucial to the success of my mission. Finding and hiring him was first on my list. Next would be to find Abu Ali. If he didn't frequent the café where he met Bilal, someone there must know something. Any piece of information could help me track him down and bring me to the next stage of the plan.

I reminded myself that I had to be careful of whom I trusted. Any mistake could be fatal. I was not so foolish as to think my mission was anything but dangerous. My most important tool, my money, was also the thing that could make me a target.

I texted Tala to let her know I had arrived safely at the hotel. I didn't want her worried, but even more, I didn't want her asking too many questions. Communicating via text meant in-depth conversation. Such a conversation might have led to queries about my intentions for after I found Bilal. As of that moment, I wasn't sure myself.

The next morning, I visited a café near the hotel. With my growing manuscript and coffee, I spent hours reworking my text, writing and rewriting, while observing the café's patrons. I spent hours transferring my handwritten copy onto my computer. Once that was done, it was a far more manageable task to revise the chapters I'd written so far. I had little interaction with any of the other customers; none struck me as good candidates. I wasn't sure what I was looking for in an agent to help me in my mission, but I was convinced I would recognize him when I saw him.

Surprisingly, I discovered my agent the next night. There was a quiet lounge not far from the hotel, and I sat at the end of the bar. In the murky light, my face illuminated by my laptop screen, I was polishing some prose when the bartender came to clear my glass. "Another one, sir?" he asked, indicating the empty tumbler in his hand.

I looked at him from over my screen, and there was something about him. My instincts told me to strike up a conversation with him. After all, bartenders usually know many people, are usually excellent conversationalists, and are invariably discreet. It all came with the job.

"Yes," I said, "A double this time, please."

Efficiently, he set about pouring a fresh tumbler with a healthy double shot of whiskey.

"Where are you from?" I asked, watching him work.

"From here," he answered, placing my drink on the cocktail napkin next to my computer, "Beirut."

"How do you like your job?" I asked.

He blinked at me once, then again, tilting his head, curious. "It's okay," he replied after deciding how much he should share with this American stranger. "I want to get the hell out of Lebanon though. I don't make enough money," he explained, "The economy in this country is not doing well. The population was already crowded before the Syrian refugees all came in the last few years. It's been bad since the seventies, but it's been getting even worse more recently."

It was all I needed to hear. He was desperate to get out of the city and had little money. This was going to be easy.

"I have a business proposition for you," I told him. "I'm a well-known author from New York, and I'm looking for someone who is from here, to help me out. An assistant, I suppose."

"What's your name?" he asked without hesitation. When I told him, he picked up his phone to google it right in front of me. I watched his eyebrows creep further and further up his forehead as he researched me. I am sure he must have read about how wealthy I was, because he put his phone down and leaned one hand on the bar, leaning close, "Okay. I'm listening."

Before anything else, I would need to get to know this man better. I trusted my instincts quite a lot, but I needed to be sure. I had to be positive about his discretion. He would need to be quiet about the tasks I would be asking of him.

"Not here," I said, closing my laptop and packing it up, "Come have a drink at my hotel with me."

He paused, frowning at me.

I laughed. "No. An actual drink. It's not *that* sort of business proposition," I said, still chuckling.

"Oh," he said, shrugging, "Of course not. I didn't mean—"

"Never mind," I said waving his comment away. "You said you wanted to get out of Lebanon? This job will entail traveling. You want to come talk about it?" I stood, laid a few bills on the bar and tucked my laptop under my arm. "Coming?"

Minutes later, we were in the bar at my hotel, sitting at a booth where we could talk in private. It didn't take long for the man to start relaying stories about the challenges of living in Lebanon. I was quickly bored, but I persevered through his whining so that I could understand him—his motivation and therefore his trustworthiness. We were two beers deep into our conversation when I was confident that he was determined enough to make money and get out of Lebanon that I could trust him.

"What's your name?" I asked after I had heard enough.

"Tarek," he said.

"Tarek? I'm here in Lebanon to write. I need to hire an assistant for the duration of my stay. If I like the assistant that I hire, I will take him back to America with me and keep him on my payroll."

His eyes lit up, and he asked, "What does the job pay?"

"Ten thousand dollars. American dollars."

I thought Tarek was going to choke on his beer. He coughed behind a hand, recovering, then said, "I don't make this in a year. I will quit my job. Right now."

"Good," I said, "Let's exchange numbers. You'll meet me here at the hotel tomorrow at noon. Don't be late."

Tarek was twenty-seven. He grew up in Lebanon and had a university degree in business administration, but he was unable to land a job. Bartending was the only work he could find, and the pay was dismal. But he was good at it and had the sort of youthful good looks that helped a bartender earn tips. My job offer, however, was his best opportunity to make some real money.

In truth, I didn't actually have a plan for him beyond helping me in this stage of my mission. I only intended to use him to help find Abu Ali. I didn't mind helping him in the process though. I wasn't a bad person, but, I must admit, I was a selfish one. My mission was my first priority. I had to fulfill my promise to Tala, and, of course, finish my book.

The next day, Tarek arrived promptly at noon. I took him to lunch where I told him about my book, *Tale of Tala*. He listened to the story with building excitement. He even stopped me more than once for clarification, and then he even had suggestions: "You should have Tala forget about her husband and just marry the writer," and "The writer should kill the husband when he finds him."

"Wait," he said, frowning and tilting his head at me, "Is this based on a true story?"

I raised my hands, palms up. "You're too clever. I can't fool you. Yes, it is. And now *you* are part of the story."

"I am?" he said, blinking at me.

I went on to tell the story up until the part where I met Tarek the night before.

"I understand," he said, nodding thoughtfully, "Your mission is to find Bilal for Tala."

"Yes," I replied, folding my hands on the table between us.

"What happens next?" he asked.

"This is where I need your help. And, as promised, I will be generous with you if you work hard, and if you do well, I'll help you to immigrate to America."

He squared his shoulders, narrowing his eyes earnestly, "Mr. Henry, I am at your service. Anything you need, just tell me. It will be done."

I believed him.

"But, Mr. Henry," he continued, "How can we find Bilal? Isn't he in Turkey?"

"Listen very well. First, I need to find a man named Abu Ali. You are going to help me do that."

He nodded once and leaned back in his chair. He followed my instructions and listened intently as I explained. "I need you to start visiting that café I mentioned. You'll do that for a few days to see if he still frequents the place. Tala described him as perhaps forty-five or fifty. He has a mole next to his nose and a bit of a belly. He dresses very well, drives German luxury cars, and is never without his entourage of cronies and thugs.

Tarek shifted in his seat, nervous. "But, Mr. Henry," he said, "That area is Muslim where Hezbollah is in control. I'm a Christian. If anyone recognizes me or finds out I'm looking for Abu Ali for an American, I could be killed."

I patted his shoulder and said, sagely, "You can't start your mission with fear. You have a goal to achieve; think only of victory."

I felt a pang of guilt, manipulating the man like I was, but the mission was paramount. Besides, it did gave Tarek the confidence he needed.

"The problem is with a stranger suddenly being a regular at the café. It might look suspicious," Tarek said. Then he pursed his lips and peered at the ceiling, thinking. "If I'm asked who I am, I'll say I'm from out in the mountains of Lebanon, and I just moved here for a construction job."

"That's a good enough backstory," I admitted. "That ought to work."

The next day, Tarek, armed with his authentic-sounding backstory, went to the café for the first time. I was anxiously waiting for him at the hotel. To get my mind off the suspense, I called, rather than texted, Tala. It was so lovely to hear her voice. "It sounds like you're making progress," she said, "But be careful. Okay?" I agreed to be cautious and she added, "I have a friend nearby that could help."

"No, Tala," I said. "I won't chance involving anyone else. Not until we have to."

What I was really worried about was involving anyone who might know Bilal and Tala. I couldn't risk Tala's family getting word of where she was. Also, I wasn't ready for Bilal to find out that I was looking for him because I had yet to decide how I was going to proceed once I found him.

I planned to have Tarek watch the café for a few days. If he found Abu Ali there, then great. I would know that he is back in Lebanon and I would know where to find him. Then we would have to move onto the next stage in the plan: to kidnap Abu Ali and bring him to me.

If after a week, Abu Ali did not come to the café, Tarek was to start investigating. I didn't like this idea. Questions would lead to suspicion. That was the last thing I wanted.

On the first few days, Tarek came back with no news. I was spending my time in the hotel room, drinking and revising my book. To the next chapter, I added Tarek's returning without any luck. It was disappointing.

There are difficulties when one is completing a mission, ups and downs. Even winners aren't exempt. It is always important to focus on the victory and what it will take to accomplish it. When I felt hopeless, I thought of the end goal: finding Abu Ali, then Bilal, then finishing my book. Unbidden, the thought of losing Tala surfaced in my mind. It hurt, but I had started to condition myself to think more about my book than about my love for her. But at the same time, that love was fueling my writing.

I was fighting growing doubts when my phone rang. It was Tarek. "He is here," he said, excited, "He is inside."

Confidence returned in a rush, and I reclined on the sofa in my hotel room. "Good work, Tarek. There's going to be a bonus waiting for you when you get back," I said, mentioning the money first to lessen his worry about what I was going to ask of him next.

"What do I do now?" he asked.

"You follow him. Just follow him and see where he goes. I need to know his route when he leaves the café and where he ends up—where he lives."

Tarek was still distracted by my mention of a bonus when he replied, "Okay. I'll go find where he lives and report back."

"Wait," I said, "Tarek, don't be overconfident. Alright? You're going to be careful. You can't be found out. There can be no suspicion." I was worried about Tarek, yes. But I was just as worried about how his failure might kill my plan.

After I had hung up, I stared out the window. I had to plan the next stage. How was I going to kidnap him? Where would I keep him after I had him as my captive? He was my only hope to find Bilal, and now I was a step closer—an integral step closer.

I called Tala right away to tell her. I was excited to share the news. Tala couldn't help but start crying when she realized the first step had been taken, that Bilal was one step closer to her. "Thank you so much, Henry. You are my angel. I can't believe you are accomplishing all of this for me," Tala said, her voice hoarse from crying. "What is next?" she asked.

"Wait, Tala. I know very well where my plan is going to take us. You trust me, right?"

"Yes, Henry. I trust you. Now more than ever."

Abu Ali was in my sights. Finding him was an important victory.

One victory leads to the next, and a winner gains momentum with each win. The mission was one step closer to its ultimate success. Now it was up to me, a winner, to take each step toward my goal with caution and cunning, just like I did with that first victory.

Chapter Six

Danger is relative. It is what we make and think of it. For the winners, danger is just one more hurdle on the path to success, and only seldom do winners focus on it. Never would they let danger alter their plans. Danger begets fear, something I refuse to bring with me onto the battlefield of life.

Capturing Abu Ali was a dangerous enterprise. I realized that, but I refused to think about it. My thoughts were focused on the result: finding Bilal and, of course, finishing my book.

Tarek returned to the hotel, brimming with excitement. Excitement is another thing to avoid when on a mission. I would only get excited when I'd won, not before.

"What will we do next?" Tarek asked me. "It will be impossible to capture him at the café or his home. The café is far too crowded, and his home is guarded."

He had followed Abu Ali from the café straight to his home, perhaps thirty minutes away. "Alright," I said, "You'll take me back to the café right away. Take the same route Abu Ali took. I need to scout the road so I have every detail needed to hone my plan."

We got into his car, an unremarkable sedan, and I turned to regard him coolly, "Now, take the exact route. I need to think. Don't speak unless I ask." He nodded and looked away. Tarek understood who was in charge. I indeed needed to think. A plan was forming, but I needed to concentrate while we were performing reconnaissance on the route.

As we passed the refugee camp in which Tala was born, I made a mental note to go back and polish my descriptions of some key places and events when I got back to my hotel. How could such a beautiful woman have come from such ugliness? I couldn't picture Tala in that human wasteland. To call it a camp was also misleading. It was all concrete, dilapidated buildings built atop other dilapidated buildings which were constructed on still others. When I looked at the one-kilometer-square, appallingly overpopulated neighborhood, I could not imagine Tala ever setting foot there, let alone living there all her life.

From the bustling area around the café to Abu Ali's house, there was a stretch of highway that was dark due to a power outage. Our target's house was far too secure; Tarek was right about that. But I had the beginnings of an idea. I would need to hire more men.

When Tarek and I returned to my hotel, I broke out silence and said, "Very good work." The praise elicited a broad smile from my mercenary subordinate. I fought the urge to sneer at his self-serving attitude. "Go. Come back the same time tomorrow." I left the car and tossed a billfold on the seat behind me. If he wasn't entirely devoted to me by then, my approval and my money secured our bond.

That night, I wrote more in my book and edited parts I had already written. My view of the story was growing clearer, and I wanted to show that in my prose. Also, my plan was fleshing itself out in my mind. It helped to write; it made my head clear and my imagination to work. I felt like a character in an old movie, scheming and planning a heist or a train robbery. The stakes were high, but so were the rewards.

Prompt as usual, Tarek arrived at my hotel room the next day at noon.

"Listen very carefully," I instructed unnecessarily. The man was already sitting at the edge of his chair, leaning forward attentively. "You are going to find some people for me. They will be doing the kidnapping for us," I said. The words felt strange on my lips, but I did not hesitate or second guess myself at all. "They will be paid very well."

Too eagerly, Tarek replied, "That will be no problem. I know many people in Lebanon who need the money. For the price you are paying, you will get what you want." He raised both hands, palms up and shrugged, "And kidnapping is happening more often these days. In fact, I am sure I could find people to do it for just a few hundred American dollars." It was strange to hear such things spoken about so nonchalantly.

"We also need to find a house," I said, "A rental property where we can keep Abu Ali. The house should be in a remote area."

"No problem," he assured me, "We have money; we have the entire country. For the right amount, I can make you a prime minister." While I didn't laugh at his joke, his cocksure attitude was infectious.

I smiled though, and nodded, crossing my arms in a display of benevolent tolerance. "This will go smoothly as long as I plan it right, and if you and your men follow the plan—every detail," I said, one eyebrow raised. "I will suffer no variation from the plan without my authorization. Do you understand?"

My assertive posture and commanding tone sobered Tarek, and he folded his hands in his lap. "Yes," he intoned, "I understand."

"Good," I said and sat back on the sofa, slinging one arm over its backrest and crossing one leg over the other, "You will go to the café and wait for Abu Ali to arrive. You'll be waiting outside, parked across the street and observing from a distance. Got it?"

"From my car. Across the street. Got it," he agreed.

"When our target leaves, you are going to instruct one of the men you hired, to follow him. Your man will be on a motorcycle."

Tarek nodded and frowned, glancing around until he saw the pad of paper and pen by the phone next to him. He took them up and started scribbling notes. "First man... needs motorcycle... follows Abu Ali from café," he said, reading as he jotted down each point. "Got it."

I inclined my head, smiling my approval at the meticulous note-taking, then went on. "The motorcyclist will need to be young, someone who has an innocent look to him. Now, do you remember that stretch of highway where there is no light? Where the power is out?" I asked. He nodded, looking up from his scribbling only for an instant. "That is where your man will come up alongside Abu Ali's car and gesture to him to his rear tire. Understand? He needs to pretend concern and play the helpful young lad and point at the back tire as though there is a real problem. Do you have that?"

Tarek only paused long enough to respond with a "Got it," before he was back to taking detailed notes.

"The motorcyclist's job is done at that point. He needs to drive away once Abu Ali starts to pull over. This is to keep Abu Ali's from becoming suspicious. I will need two cars and four more men. Armed. They must be armed," I said, my voice cold with steel determination.

Tarek swallowed audibly at this but didn't waver. "Four armed men. Two cars."

"They will have been following from a distance. Once Abu Ali pulls over, the first car must cut in front of him, blocking him, and the second must come up behind him to prevent his escape. The men of the first car will take Abu Ali from his car, and the men of the second car will get out and keep their guns trained on our target," I said. My plan was becoming much clearer in my mind as I described it to my hired man. "The men of the first car will take Abu Ali at gunpoint. They will cuff him—don't forget to get handcuffs—and put him in their car. Abu Ali's car should be driven away from the road and left there. The two cars with your four men and Abu Ali will head directly to the house in a remote area that you will have rented. On the way, they will alert you via phone—with no explicit details—that they are en route. Then you'll come get me at the hotel and bring me to the house where they'll already have bound Abu Ali to a chair."

"Handcuffs... dispose of Abu Ali's car nearby..." said Tarek, feverishly scratching pen to paper.

"The two in the second car are to watch for anyone following. Should they be followed, they will need to take care of it."

Tarek looked up for a mere instant, understanding that I meant for the men to shoot anyone who tried to follow them, and then wrote down the last points of the plan.

"Any questions?" I asked, privately pleased with myself for having come up with the plan. This sort of thing was well beyond my usual realm of comfort. I, of course, have never been part of an abduction, let alone an abduction in a country where I'm unfamiliar with terrain, language, and culture. However, when I played through the scenario in my mind, I was, of course, confident that, if strictly followed, my plan will work.

"Yes," Tarek admitted, "What if somebody sees us?"

"If you do it fast, and as I described, it will be fine." The doubt in my hired man's eyes was troubling. I sat up and squared my shoulders. I projected confidence. I knew it. I was depending on it to quell the uncertainty I saw in Tarek. "After all," I said with a shrewd smile, "Didn't you say that kidnappings like this one were happening all the time in Lebanon? Don't you think other drivers or passersby would be more likely to keep it to themselves than get involved? It's a small gamble considering the payout. I think you'd be willing to do far worse to get yourself established in America. Am I right?"

I watched as he considered this, and the tension lifted from Tarek's features. It was the mention of America that really brought his fears to heel. "Yes," he said finally, his smile returning, "You are right. The plan is a good one."

I inclined my head, and said, "Thank you. So, in all, the job will require six of you: motorcycle boy, our two men in car one, the two in car two, and yourself."

When I looked at Tarek's notes, I was impressed by his neat penmanship, especially considering how quickly he had been jotting down my instructions. Each point was pleasingly bulleted and concise. He had filled the first page on the pad with point after point and flipped it over to the second page for still more. "Got it. What next?"

"Two things," I said. "First, you must be sure to keep my identity secret from the men. In fact, only the two men—the ones in the first car—who will be guarding Abu Ali will see me. The rest will not see me or even know I exist." I was silent for a moment, waiting for Tarek to look up. Holding his gaze, I repeated, slowly and with utmost gravity, "They won't know who you work for. They won't know of me at all. Understand?"

He nodded slowly, "Yes, Mr. Henry. Only the two who are guarding Abu Ali. Only those two will see you. The rest won't even know you exist."

"And even the ones who see me won't know who I am. Just that I pay them. Good? Good." I huffed a sigh, content that Tarek clearly understood. "One more thing. You and the men must understand this. If any of you are caught—not that I expect it—but if any of you are caught, you must *not* tell the authorities anything whatsoever. Trust that I will come and get you. You said it yourself; I can get anything I want in Lebanon with enough money. I will spend whatever it takes, bribe whoever I must. There is absolutely nothing for you or the men to worry about regarding getting caught. Got that? Just be silent and wait for me to pay the trouble away."

Tarek stared at me unblinkingly, and then a smile crossed his face. "I got it," he replied, shaking his head in disbelief. "You have thought this through. I'm so fortunate that you walked into my bar that day."

I waved away the flattery and scoffed, "Write. Write all of that down so you can tell the hired men everything. Be sure they are very clear on all of it."

Over the next few days, Tarek was busy gathering our team, which wasn't too difficult a task in Lebanon, especially as of recently. The country's instability helped our cause. The climate lent itself well to organizing crimes like this. People were desperate, many of them, and when crime is so commonplace, it's simply easier to get away with it. When the chances of being caught are low, it's that much simpler to find willing people.

Tarek was certainly earning his money. He found the perfect house; it was remote, not too terribly far from the city, and the landlord was placated with cash and a flimsy explanation that the place was going to be used by a writer visiting from America. Perhaps the story was too close to reality, but I was not worried. Tarek didn't name me, and the landlord never met me.

While Tarek was busy with preparations, I was busy writing. I also frequently spoke with Tala. She was spending most of her time in the hotel room, enjoying her solitude, sleeping in a lavishly comfortable bed, and being taken care of. Other than her one-week honeymoon, she had never experienced such peace and care. Now she had it.

Tala was anxious over what I was doing though. She kept asking for updates and grilling me on details. On the other hand, she was very grateful for my doing this for her. It was my ultimate hope that her gratitude would turn to love. Besides my book—writing this story in which I was living—my love for Tala was my utmost goal.

Days passed before Tarek called me with the news I had been anticipating. "He's here," he said, agitated, "This is the night."

I should admit, I got nervous. But it didn't make me hesitate. It was a matter of a remarkably short time before I would be face to face with Abu Ali, which meant a step closer to Bilal. "Good work," I said, keeping my own voice under control. It would not do to stir up Tarek's agitation any further. "Call me when he is en route, at which time you should be here at the hotel to pick me up. You are doing even better than I had expected. There will be a big bonus for you when this is all done, Tarek." I ended the call before he could reply.

Each minute dragged its feet to the next. I waited impatiently and paced across the living room. When the first hour had passed, I reached for my phone. I had not heard from Tarek yet. I stopped though, and I reminded myself that Tarek was doing as I instructed and he would only call when Abu Ali was secured. Tarek was to call when he was downstairs, and Abu Ali was confirmed captured.

My next impulse was to call Tala. Again, I had to stop myself from dialing. If I made that call, I would make her unnecessarily worried. I controlled myself and put the phone down. In its place, I picked up a bottle of whiskey and poured myself two fingers and clinked a single ice cube into the tumbler.

I sipped my whiskey and considered the view from my window. The Mediterranean was black as night beyond the golden lights of the harbor. It and I were both restless. I could see ominous whitecaps as the black water roiled. It was the same with me, restless and turbulent.

I was tense and chewing loudly on what was left of my ice cube when the phone rang, finally. I sprung at the phone but halted to take a long, tempering breath before I answered. "Tell me good news," I said, controlling my nerves and sounding as staunch as any career criminal I had ever seen on television or film.

Tarek was breathless. "It's done. He'll arrive at the house in just a few minutes," he said. Nearly keeping the disbelief from his voice, he added, "The plan, every step of it, worked perfectly."

I didn't know exactly how anxious I was until Tarek said those words, and relief struck me so profoundly that my knees gave out and I sat heavily on the sofa.

"Mr. Henry?" Tarek said.

"Yes, Tarek. Excellent work," I said, recovering in a heartbeat. Exhilaration made my heart race, and I sneered a smile into the phone. "You're downstairs? Waiting?" I asked.

"Yes. The engine is running."

"You are going to love America," I said, "You've made yourself so indispensable, I would be a fool not to bring you back with me."

"Thank you, Mr. Henry. Your plan was perfect."

"I'll be right down," I said. In the elevator, I went through the questions I would be asking when I interrogated Abu Ali. It occurred to me that I may have to torture him, or rather, have him tortured. I would pay one of the men to do it, of course.

"You should be proud of yourself, Tarek," I said as I got into his car. He had a handgun waiting for me on the armrest. I blinked at it, and he smiled.

"It wasn't in your plan, but you might want to be armed as well," said Tarek, beaming with pride.

I hadn't thought of that. "I assumed you would bring me one. It's only logical," I countered, taking up the weapon and making a show of checking that the safety was on. I had never handled a gun before, but I watched enough cop shows to know that much. "Good job," I repeated, "Perhaps *I'm* the one who is lucky to have found *you*." He smiled broadly at that. He was probably imagining what his life would be like in America. "How did it go?"

"Surprisingly, he was unarmed. If our men didn't already have their guns pointed at him, he might have gotten a gun from inside his car somewhere. We can't be sure. When the men took him, he struggled though. They hit him on the head and dragged him to the car. It took only seconds. Just like you said."

I shook my head, mentally commending myself for formulating the plan. "Great," I said, "Let's go."

It was about forty-five minutes before we arrived at the house. Throughout the entire, wordless drive— Tarek knew when I needed my silence by then—I thought about the possible outcomes of this night.

Part of me hoped that Abu Ali would say that Bilal was dead. I will have fulfilled my promise to Tala, and she wouldn't be anyone else's but mine. To be honest, that was my hope.

I spent the rest of the trip deciding how best to extract the needed information from Abu Ali. I knew what I would do. First, I would start with a more psychological attack—scare him, threaten him—then, if that didn't pry the right answers from him, we would begin with the physical aspect of the interrogation. There could be no reluctance on my part. I could not falter. He had to be terrified that he might not survive. Fear makes a man pliable. He would talk if he were panicked and scared for his life.

The house was unremarkable, mud bricks and red clay shingles. We were miles from the closest neighbor and nestled in the shadow of a low, scrub-strewn mountain. Tarek rounded the circular driveway, and we got out. My heart was pounding in my chest, but I didn't show the merest of signs of unease. I tucked my gun into the back of my pants and waved for Tarek to follow. I had to intimidate Abu Ali from the moment I walked in.

Just off the mosaic-tiled foyer was a den. The only light in the house was coming from there. The two men stood on either side of Abu Ali. With his hands cuffed to the legs of his chair, Abu Ali drooled blood onto his coarsely haired chest and substantial belly.

Blood and spit stained his tailored pants. The man looked up from the floor. One of his eyes was swollen almost completely shut.

We stared at one another for a long, electrified moment. I let the silence stretch taut like a piano wire. I did not utter a word, just lit a cigarette and slowly walked around him. Dispassionately, I exhaled gray-blue smoke through my teeth and considered him. His good eye, wide and distressed, followed me on my circuit around his chair. He was most probably wondering if he was going to live to see morning or not. I gave him exactly no reason to suppose one way or the other. The more uncertain and afraid he was, the more in control I was.

I broke the silence with a slow, deliberate question. "Do you speak English?" I asked, pointing casually at him with the two fingers between which I held my cigarette.

He stared up at me from under his sweat-slick brow.

I slapped him with my free hand, a cruel, derisive strike. I felt the satisfying clatter of his teeth when I connected with his stubbled cheek.

"Do you speak English?" I repeated, speaking precisely as calmly and pleasantly as I did the first time.

Tarek, from behind my left shoulder, interrupted and asked the question in Arabic.

Abu Ali still did not respond.

I placed the cigarette carelessly between my lips and reached unhurriedly back to retrieve my gun. Its heft felt exciting in my hand. I held the weapon before my face, contemplating it long enough for Abu Ali to regard it. I swung and struck him across the jaw with the butt of the gun.

My voice was saccharine sweet when I leaned closer and said, "One last time. Do you speak English?"

He nodded his head, spit a bloody tooth onto the floor, and with a heavy accent, answered, "Little."

I glanced over my shoulder at Tarek, indicating with a look that I would be relying on him as a translator. Then, I bent at the knees to look Abu Ali in the eye and, with a cold gentleness, asked, "Where is Bilal?"

Abu Ali's face changed. He understood me without Tarek's interpretation and looked at me, startled. "Bilal?" he asked instantly, feigning ignorance even after the revealing reaction to the name.

I sighed heavily with mock disappointment. "It's really too bad you aren't more forthcoming," I said, then waited for Tarek to translate. That's when I took a long pull on my cigarette, making the cherry burn bright and hot. I blew the ash from the heated brand and murmured, "Tell him we are about to begin."

Making a man talk when he might be killed for divulging the information he gives up is a long, arduous task. Over hours, we had to convince him that it would be far less painful to tell us how to find

Bilal than to face the repercussions of having leaked the information. We saw the light of dawn glowing through the slats in the window blinds before Abu Ali gave up what details he knew.

Abu Ali was a pitiful, blubbering, bloody mess. His chin and neck were scarlet with blood that drooled from his mouth and broken lips. His neck and chest were dotted with angry, blistering brands where his flesh was seared with a cigarette. Three fingers of each hand were twisted and broken, the digits swollen and jutting at disturbing angles. One of the men left and came back with a large set of rusty pruning shears from the back garden. Abu Ali, dazed, peered with his one good eye as we placed the thumb of his already horribly disfigured hand into the ugly mouth of the gardening tool.

That's when Abu Ali began sobbing and babbling in Arabic. Tarek leaned close to hear the broken man's guttural words and raised a finger to halt us.

"He says he'll talk," Tarek said, then returned his attention to the cadaverous Abu Ali.

"About fucking time," I cursed, wiping my forehead with a bloodied hand.

I sat and rested, my body weary from exertion. My reeling mind was playing a rapid-fire slideshow of images from the last few hours—things I will never forget. The smell of blood and burnt skin filled my senses. I looked down at myself to find my clothes disheveled and stained with blood. My knuckles were torn and bloodied, and it hurt to make a fist.

Tarek interrupted my introspection. He left Abu Ali to weep, broken and in unbearable pain. "He says he had given Bilal to a Turkish man who is an ISIS agent in Turkey, the same man who supplied him with drugs to sell in the camps. He would recruit people to go fight with ISIS as well. They wanted Bilal because they needed someone who was good with computers. He doesn't know what happened after he left Bilal in Turkey."

Visibly shaken, Tarek flinched at a choking sob that erupted from Abu Ali's throat, then went on. "He said that they tricked Bilal. They told him he was going to a job interview in a European country. What they actually did was take him across the border to Syria." Tarek's shoulders slumped in exhaustion, and he exhaled heavily. "I'm convinced he's telling us the truth."

I reached out and clasped Tarek's shoulder, leaving a bloody handprint on his shirt, "You did well. We could not have done this without you." I pretended not to notice his flinch when I laid such responsibility at his feet and stood.

Watching me approach, Abu Ali whimpered and his bare feet scrabbled at the blood-slickened floor tiles in front of his chair. "Calm down," I whispered gently. Tarek translated from behind me. "Give me the name of the Turkish man."

"He says he'll need his phone," Tarek translated from Abu Ali's blubbering.

I retrieved his phone from his belongings. It was powered off, of course. Someone might be trying to track him with its GPS. His phone password turned out to be the most easily extracted piece of information of the night. I turned it on and accessed his contacts myself. The Turkish man's name was Nazar, and I had his phone number. I powered down the phone again. Perhaps I was paranoid, perhaps not.

"Tell me all about Nazar," I commanded Abu Ali, "And if you leave anything out, I promise you won't leave this house in one piece." His one, bloodshot eye watched me pitifully—the other was a blue-purple mess—and Tarek translated. Broken as he was, he didn't hesitate to spill what he knew.

Tarek turned to me moments later, "Abu Ali was not really with ISIS. He just sold the drugs they supplied and occasionally fooled people like Bilal into going to Turkey where he delivers them to Nazar who takes them to Syria. He does not know what happens to them after they are brought from Turkey to Syria. He says he has never met anyone from ISIS, himself. He gets the drugs delivered to his house in Lebanon, and he insists he just gives the people to Nazar in Turkey and that is all."

I turned and stood before Abu Ali with my arms crossed over my chest. I was silent again as I stared at the ruined man. "He must be guarded," I said to Tarek while continuing to regard our captive, "Two of these men will do. Keep him cuffed in that chair. This place is so remote that if he recovers enough to scream, there will be no one to hear him." That thought led to another: "If the landlord comes back for any reason, and if Abu Ali even opens his mouth... put a bullet in their heads."

"Yes, sir," Tarek replied, and I could feel him taking careful mental notes of every instruction.

"When I go?" Abu Ali mumbled, his one-eyed stare utterly hopeless—perhaps for good reason.

Uncrossing my arms, I noted the splattering of blood on my sleeves and then saw my ruined shirt and pants. I sneered at the cloying mess, disgusted, and turned that sneer on Abu Ali. I said nothing to him. To Tarek, I said, "I'm going to wash up. You and I are leaving. Bring his phone and be sure it remains off."

I regarded myself in the bathroom mirror. The face that women looked at twice, that helped me get whatever I wanted with a smile, and that looked insightful and rugged on the jacket covers of my books stared back at me, drawn, haggard and spattered with blood. I barely recognized myself.

I very nearly allowed my thoughts to wander inward, but I refused any introspection. I scrubbed the blood from my face, my neck, my arms and my trembling, bruised-knuckled hands. They ached. The nagging questions and possible realizations remained in the periphery where I would keep them forever. The night's vile actions would haunt me enormously if I let them, so I forbade my mind to focus on anything but the mission and the book. The water was stained with blood as it swirled around the drain and disappeared.

Tarek and I left, and the two guards remained with Abu Ali as I instructed. The sun was well above the horizon as we drove toward Beirut and the scenery was exotic, even alien for a man from New York, but I was exhausted and had far too much to think about.

"What next, Mr. Henry?" Tarek asked as he adjusted the car's air conditioning.

I furrowed my brow and peered at him from under leaden eyelids. It surprised me that he spoke at all. He was as tired as I was though, so I chalked his indiscretion up to that. "I'm thinking," I said, "Let's have silence until we arrive at the hotel."

My subordinate pursed his lips but nodded tacitly.

It was impossible to devise any plan for our next steps with my mind in such a fog. I was weary of body, mind, and soul—though I didn't dwell much on the last. I knew that I had to get back to the hotel and write. I had to write even before I allowed myself to sleep. The peculiar way I was composing my book—living it as I wrote it—made me think that perhaps my next plan would occur naturally while I was typing the chapter in which we were currently living.

When we arrived at my hotel, Tarek leaned back and fetched his sports jacket from the back seat. "Here, sir," he said, looking down at my shirt that could be mistaken for a butcher's apron, "So people won't ask questions."

I nodded my approval, "I *am* the lucky one. Thank you."

He didn't say anything to that.

"Tomorrow," I went on, pragmatic as ever, "You'll pick me up in the morning and take me someplace... let's say... by the sea, far from the hotel, where we can search more thoroughly through Abu Ali's phone. Do not turn it on before then, but make sure it is fully charged."

The jacket was a little tight around the chest, and the sleeves were two inches too short, but it certainly kept the blossomed bloodstains from curious eyes as I hastily returned to my room. Thankfully, the early hour assured that I didn't encounter anyone but the counter staff, whom I ignored and walked by brusquely.

A shower settled my nerves, and some coffee from room service staved off my drowsiness long enough for me to write. And write I did. The words spilled onto my laptop screen as I recounted every detail of the prior night. Sweat beaded on my brow and I typed as fast as I could, loathe to keep any of the abhorrent images in my head.

I remembered how there was a tiny tendril of smoke when I pulled the cigarette away from Abu Ali's skin. A tiny, blackened crater of burnt flesh continued to cook for an instant after I branded him. His seared skin had smoked, not the cigarette; I was sure of it.

The phone rang.

Tala had gotten used to my calling every day. "Is everything okay?" she asked, concerned.

Abu Ali's roaring scream was still reverberating in my memory, but I lied, "Yes, Tala. Why?"

"Ever since you got to Beirut, you've called me every night to say goodnight. Last night you didn't."

She was right. During the time I usually called her, I was breaking a man's fingers.

"I'm so sorry," I said. "I didn't mean to worry you." I decided to give her half of the truth. "I've captured Abu Ali." I heard her gasp. "He hasn't told me anything yet," I explained, sounding entirely sincere to my ear. I hoped she was fooled.

"You are amazing," she said after a pause, "To have accomplished that. In a foreign country where you know no one. Incredible."

I thought a moment about how her tone sounded something like mine when I fed praise to Tarek, or Dimitrij before him.

"So, he hasn't told you anything about Bilal? Or where he might be?" The disappointment in her voice was like a weight on my chest. I wanted so badly to please her.

"Not yet," I lied, "But I'm sure he will give us what we want soon."

"Henry, listen to me," she said, her voice as captivating and familiar as it had been in the vast bathtub we shared and the warm, sumptuous bed in which we held one another. I found myself remembering how her skin glistened in the cooling bath water. "Abu Ali is a criminal. He is responsible for so many kidnappings, addictions, overdoses, and probably murders. Do not go lightly on him. He would not do the same for you. Be cruel. I know you are not like that. You are a gentle soul, a writer. I know. But you must be savage. Violence is the only way a man like that will give up Bilal's location."

I paused, briefly startled by Tala's suggestion that I torture Abu Ali. I drank in her words though, and I felt what I faintly recognized as guilt lift from my shoulders. A mordant smile found my lips. Tala had unwittingly justified my brutal treatment of my captive. I was going to enjoy writing this part of the chapter.

"Don't you trust me?" I asked.

"Of course I do," she replied, placated.

"Leave it to me. I will get it out of him. It's just a matter of time," I assured her. "I promise I'll call you tonight."

It would have done no good to tell her that Bilal was with ISIS now. She would lose hope. I thought about that and finished my second coffee. But I *did* want her to lose hope, didn't I? I certainly wanted her to give up on trying to find Bilal and move on. On the other hand, I was determined to fulfill my promise to her—to accomplish my mission—to win. Also, the book was literally writing itself. All I had to do was record it. I wanted urgently to see how it ended.

Despite my lack of sleep, I soldiered on and wrote and wrote. The sun was setting when I finally finished the chapter. My ingenuity was as exhausted as I was. I had no imagination left to think of a plan. What would I do with the information that I brutally took from Abu Ali? I needed to rest and clear the fog from my mind.

Finally, in bed, I stared at the ceiling, begging inwardly for sleep. I was restless and blamed all the caffeine I had drank. I teetered on the edge of sleep for a long while, smelling seared flesh, tasting the coppery tang of blood, hearing wails and begging in frantic Arabic. Until finally, I slept. It was a deep sleep, and I was grateful that I didn't remember dreaming.

The phone woke me.

Tarek was waiting downstairs.

"I will need a few minutes. Wait there for me. I won't be too long," I said, my voice still grainy from sleep. I quickly made coffee and found my mind to be clearer now. Crystal clear. I was able to think of my next step: The only way to get to Bilal was the Turkish man, Nazar. Abu Ali's phone might be key in tracking the man down. If it wasn't, I still have Abu Ali, and I would find out where to find Nazar the same way I got the rest of the information from him.

As planned, Tarek took me to the seaside. People, both tourists and locals enjoying the morning sun and the view of the pristine sea walked along the corniche. I watched them from Tarek's car as he translated some of the cryptic exchanges that were in Abu Ali's phone. He was diligent about deleting messages; that did not surprise me. But there were a few recent messages remaining in the history.

The last exchange between the two was written in code.

"I have a new flock of birds for you," Abu Ali wrote in Arabic.

"Instructions to be sent when hunters are ready," Nazar wrote back—in broken Arabic, according to Tarek.

I surmised that they were talking about a new batch of men to be sent to join ISIS, or rather, to be tricked into joining them.

There were other messages from just last night. They were from Abu Ali's wife, concerned when he didn't come home last night. In her texts, she also suggested that other people were asking about him.

I turned off the phone and said to Tarek, "Let's get going. Take us to the rental house. I have a few more questions for Abu Ali."

On the way, Tarek turned the radio on. I blinked at his hand when he reached for the tuner dial, but decided not to say anything. He knew I normally preferred total quiet on these trips to facilitate my thinking, but he was showing some wear. I still trusted his loyalty, but I thought it wouldn't hurt to let him get his mind off the mission for just a short while.

To me, the music was alien and bewildering tonally. At least a familiar-sounding drum machine gave the beat. I focused on that. After the tune had ended, the announcer came on the air. A moment later, Tarek turned up the volume. "They found the car! The police found Abu Ali's car!" he gasped.

"Don't wor—"

Tarek cut me off. "They found drugs and weapons in it. They are looking for Abu Ali." He was frantic.

Once again, it was left to me to calm him down. "Why are you worried? That is actually good for us. It's good news," I said, smiling unperturbedly.

"What? Why do you say that?"

"Wait, and you'll see," I replied. "Have I steered you wrong yet? No. I want you to trust me in this, just like you have with everything else so far."

"Okay, sir. Okay," he said, gripping the wheel tightly and trying to control his panic with deep, chest-heaving breaths.

"This will be all over soon, my friend," I soothed, "And you will be on your way to America."

That, as I had learned, was the right button to press when Tarek felt doubt. And just as I suspected, it worked. I watched him relax bit by bit, and by the time the next undulating song started to play, he was back to being stoically quiet.

Abu Ali was cuffed to the chair where I had left him the day before. He looked up and sneered. The effect wasn't what he had hoped though. He was missing a couple of teeth, and his lips were split and swollen. "Let me go," he wheezed, "I have family. Wife. Children." The cuffs rattled as he tugged at them. His broken fingers—six altogether—jutted grotesquely from his hands, twisted and hooked. Most of his wounds were scabbed over, but many festered. I saw that some of his cigarette burns were weeping and probably infected.

With the help of Tarek's translating, I communicated with my captive.

"Of course," I said, "You'll be going home shortly. That is, as long as you give me every piece of information I ask for. Understand? I'm still sore from yesterday, as I'm sure you are. I won't bother hurting my fists again. Instead, I'll go to the kitchen down the hall, find a nice, sharp knife and start removing parts of you. Got it?"

As Tarek interpreted, Abu Ali's disfigured visage looked as hopeful as a brutally beaten face could. Then, as Tarek described how this interrogation would be different, panic widened his one good eye, and he nodded desperately.

"Yes," Abu Ali said in tight-throated, broken English, "I tell. I say all. All you ask."

"That's better," I replied, and I dragged a chair in front of my captive into which I sat and casually crossed my legs. "That pleases me."

It took only minutes to glean everything Abu Ali could tell us. I felt a foul satisfaction having broken this man who had ruined so many lives including my Tala's. It gave me wicked pleasure to watch him grovel and betray his criminal associate.

Nazar lived in a town called Antakya, close to the Syrian border. He had been supplying Abu Ali with drugs that he gets from ISIS affiliates in Lebanon. Nazar's mission was to provide ISIS skilled men or fighters. Abu Ali preyed on young people who were desperate or simply drug addicts.

I was happy to let Abu Ali speak. I wanted to know everything, and it was preferable to having to torture him any further. He described, in detail, how he infiltrated the refugee camps with drugs because it was the easiest environments in which to recruit fighters and skilled people; they were desperate for jobs, tired and frustrated with their lives of displacement and oppression. Some, like Bilal, got into trouble and were especially susceptible to Abu Ali's trickery. He was easy to coerce and deliver to Nazar. Others got hooked on drugs, and, poor, soon could not afford their addiction. Abu Ali offered them jobs and they were then given to Nazar. It was a well-orchestrated system of recruitment.

I wanted to know more about the Turkish man's motives.

Abu Ali's simple response, in English, was, "Money."

"So, he is not a supporter of ISIS ideology?" I asked.

"Nazar's only interest is money," Tarek translated. "Men from ISIS pay him well to get his recruits through the Turkish border and to sell drugs. He makes an enormous profit."

"How much money are we talking about?" I asked Abu Ali through Tarek.

"I do not know," Abu Ali whined in English. "Please. I do not know."

I believed him. "How close are you two?"

"I consider him a good friend. We spend time when I am in Antakya."

"How would you describe him and his motives?" I asked, not hopeful that my captive would have a satisfactory response. I was wrong.

"He is a manipulative money lover."

That was all I needed to hear. When money is the motivation, and not an ideology, I was in the perfect position from which to win against a man such as Nazar. I had what he wanted: money.

Abu Ali winced at the sight of my broad smile, but I raised a hand and chuckled, "No, Abu Ali. You just earned yourself your freedom." The man's shoulders slackened in relief when Tarek translated. "We are going to clean you up, give you some food, and you are going to make a phone call for us. After that, we are going to bring you to the hospital closest to your house and leave you there to get those nasty fingers set and the rest of you looked after. How does that sound?"

The man wept.

"We are going to take a little drive and make the call from there. We can't chance anyone tracing the call to this house," I said, and Abu Ali happily agreed.

A couple of hours later, Abu Ali was tidied up, though he was still in a great amount of pain. We gave him a good meal, and he ate it as fast as his broken teeth would allow. We drove two cars down the highway and found a quiet spot on the shoulder of a side road, away from the sight of passing vehicles. The two men who were guarding him had their guns out and were pointing them at Abu Ali's head. Once I was sure he understood precisely what he was to say, I reached through the window and handed him the disposable cell phone that Tarek had purchased an hour prior.

"Dial," I said, leaning on the roof of the car, and my captive pressed the call button with one of his good fingers.

To his credit, Abu Ali was very convincing despite his painful injuries and the handguns trained on his head. He knew that if we sensed he was unconvincing, we would shoot him. Tarek translated Abu Ali's conversation for me after he hung up.

"Ah, my good friend! I have a special bird for you this time," Abu Ali said jovially once the Turkish man answered. "What? Oh, I had to get a new phone. Yes, again. I know. It's so inconvenient, but in our business, we can't be too careful. Am I right, friend?" His chuckle was surprisingly authentic as he held the phone to his ear with a mangled hand. "In a few days, I'm going to get in touch with you from another number—Yes, another one. I'll send to you this special bird I've found. I expect this new one will be very, very useful. I think we'll make a great deal of money once your associates see what help he can be. Good things will come of this one. Oh yes, I'm sure he's looking forward to meeting you as well. Oh! And he's a foreigner. Don't worry. Your English is still good? It will be fine. You'll see. Yes. You're welcome. Hm? Yes... what? Oh yes. Of course. I'll say hello to her for you."

The call went as planned—better even. Nazar showed no obvious signs of suspicion. In fact, he seemed excited by the prospect of a keen recruit that didn't require any coercion. Nazar trusted Abu Ali; they had been working together for years.

Tarek and I got into the car, and I tossed the phone out of the window. Abu Ali and his two guards left to return to the house and Tarek drove us back to the hotel. I suspected that Abu Ali's objections to not being driven to the hospital as I'd promised would be quickly silenced. I gave my men instructions to beat him only to the point of unconsciousness if he gave them too much trouble. Now, I understood that I might have to get rid of Abu Ali, but I had to wait until I met with Nazar. I would reconsider Abu Ali's usefulness only once I had Bilal in front of me.

Upon returning to my hotel, I told Tarek to meet me the next morning. Then, I went up to my suite energized and ready to formulate the next phase in my plan. I showered and sprawled on my bed and called Tala. I would get my laptop after that and record today's success and finish that chapter.

"Is something wrong?" Tala asked, "I have an uneasy feeling. You've been acting strangely. What's going on?"

It was lovely to hear her voice, as always, but I was distracted by the sight of my laptop on the table, and I wanted desperately to be typing the remainder of the chapter into it. "I thought you trusted me," I said, smiling into the phone, "Didn't I tell you everything was going well? In fact, today was a very productive one. I'm much closer to finding Bilal."

"Really? That's wonderful. What did you learn?"

"You leave that to me. But I can tell you this: I'm leaving for Turkey tomorrow. Didn't I tell you I'm getting close? You trust me, right?" I asked.

"Yes," she conceded, "I do."

"Good. I will be calling you from Turkey tomorrow night. Now, stop worrying. I have this under control."

I hurriedly booked my flight for the next morning and settled down to work on the end of the chapter. I typed enthusiastically, describing every detail while fresh in my mind. I was living these events, and my words dripped with authenticity because of it. I think I was addicted to this story—my book—as much as I was in love with Tala.

In the morning, Tarek came, and I invited him to my suite this time. I had several envelopes waiting on the coffee table. One, the biggest, had his name scrawled on it while the others were blank. "That one is for you," I said, gesturing toward his envelope, "Obviously. You'll find I paid you more than double our agreed price. It's the same with the others. I'll trust you to pay them."

"You're very generous, sir," he remarked and came to sit on the sofa.

"You more than earned it. There will be more for you when I get back."

"Get back? Where are you going?"

"We need to leave in the next fifteen minutes if I'm to make my flight to Turkey," I said, smirking.

"Turkey?" he said, only partially surprised, "You're going to see Nazar?"

"Yes, I am."

"Isn't that dangerous?" he asked, his brow furrowing in concern. Whether it was concern for me or the second envelope I had promised, I wasn't sure.

"On a mission," I said grandly, "Winners don't think about the danger. That is something left to the losers. Winners don't doubt their imminent victory."

Chapter Seven

I have said it before: I'm a winner. As such, I have learned what it takes to prevail over challenges and conquer obstacles. The mission is paramount. They say there is always the right tool for the job. When that job is a mission like the one I was on, the tools aren't the sort one keeps in a toolbelt. No, these tools are things like observation, leverage, motivation, insight, and resources. With tools like those handy, no mission is insurmountable.

I boarded my flight to Istanbul after which I would be making a connection to a second flight to Hatay. Planes were always a good place for me to think— if I didn't manage to fall asleep, that is. A vantage point from 39,000 feet gave me a good perspective on things. I was perfectly solitary and disconnected, and it gave me the time to, once again, plan and plot my next moves that were going to get me closer to the success of my mission.

Success could be defined in more than one way. Finding Bilal was the next step, and that would be a success, of course. But, if I brought him back to Tala—which would be how she and Bilal would identify their own success—I would have lost Tala, the woman who I loved. If I found Bilal dead, that would be a success for me; I could return to Tala and take his place in her heart. In either of these scenarios, I would be a winner though: I would have my book, *Tale of Tala*, no matter which of those endings I wrote in the last pages.

There may have been another circumstance where I could be the ultimate winner, a scenario I hadn't yet considered. Mulling over *that* is what I spent my time on the flight doing.

In Istanbul, before I boarded the plane to Hatay, it occurred to me that Tala and Bilal had made this same journey, perhaps the same flight. They were going on their honeymoon and then intended to emigrate to Europe to start a new life together. They would settle in Europe where Bilal's education would help him find a job in computers. Their goal was to leave behind their home of persistent suffering, relentless fear, and abysmal squalor.

I arrived at Hatay Airport in the late afternoon and took a taxi to a hotel in Antakya, close to the Syrian border. When I described Amsterdam and

Ljubljana as "old world," I hadn't set eyes on Antakya yet. Antakya was a truly ancient city; the centuries-old churches, modest spires, and antiquated homes fought for air from the encroaching—and equally drab-colored—modern buildings. The Asi River cut a channel through the center of the old city, only slightly greener than the concrete and stone through which it ambled. According to a tourist pamphlet left in the taxi, I was following in the footsteps of Alexander and Julius Caesar, Peter and Paul, and Anthony and Cleopatra. It was, admittedly, with a smug sense of pride that I considered myself among those. If ever I were in the company of historical, fellow winners, it was here in Antakya.

"They are taking our jobs and ruining our streets—sleeping on them!" the taxi driver was complaining.

I was roused from a daydream, a vivid picture of ancient rulers and myself sharing drinks at a party, and looked up from the colorful tourist pamphlet in my hands to squint at the driver. "What? Who?"

"Those damned Syrians," he grumped, "Refugees."

My nostrils flared, and I glared at him through his rear-view mirror, "If you have to flee your country because staying might kill you and your family, I hope you get a better reception." His eyes widened at the tooth-bared snarl on my face. There was venom in my voice; I was defending Tala, the refugee with whom I had fallen in love. "I hope you're looked upon as a human and treated fairly and with compassion. I hope, if you're displaced because of war, that you, the victim, aren't blamed for any conflict or become the target of thoughtless bigotry."

The driver seethed, grinding his teeth and sneered at me, wordless.

"Just take me to my hotel and don't say another word," I demanded and dismissed him by staring out the window at pedestrians and the occasional moped driver.

My hotel was close to the city's bustling center. I caught snippets of conversation as I checked in, none of which I comprehended, but I was able to recognize Turkish as well as Arabic being spoken by the locals. The hotel wasn't to my usual level of comfort, but I made my travel arrangements in a hurry. The lobby was connected to a small but not inelegant restaurant that looked out on the brick-paved street where locals and tourists alike traveled to and from the nearby market that was bustling a block away. The room was comfortable, though not the equal to the lavish suite I was used to.

I wasted no time before contacting Nazar.

"Am I speaking to Nazar?" I asked after the other end of the line picked up, and I was hailed in a brusque, monosyllabic greeting I did not understand. "Abu Ali told you I would be in touch, I believe."

There was only the slightest pause, and I could hear the smile in his voice when he said, "Yes! Our mutual friend has told me about you. I'm very excited to meet you." His English was quite good and was uncommonly understandable despite his strong Turkish accent. Nazar was exceedingly pleasant on the phone. I wasn't surprised; he stood to make a great deal of money from me, and he knew it.

"Let's not talk details on the phone, Nazar," I said, taking control of the conversation, "We should meet tomorrow morning. There is a nice restaurant here at my hotel. Meet me there."

Of course, he agreed. "I know the place," he said, "Ten tomorrow? Okay?" He tried unsuccessfully to hide his eagerness from my ears. He was as money hungry as Abu Ali was.

"I'll be there," I said.

I wrote for a bit, recording my arrival in Antakya. It was a shame I was only here on business. It was a fascinating spot. Then I called Tala.

"Turkey?" she asked. There was a catch in her voice, an edge that hinted at fear that someone who didn't know her might not notice. In those two syllables, I could hear the raw, painful memories of what she experienced in Turkey: she was raped, she lost a friend to organ harvesters and another friend to the Mediterranean, and she had her husband taken from her. The country represented some of her most brutal experiences in her life.

"Yes, Tala. I'm getting very close to finding Bilal. I will tell you more in the next few days," I said.

"I trust you," she said. "I owe you so much for this. I fear to hope, but you make hope possible." The words, so sincere and brave, justified the vicious methods I was using and steeled my resolve. I was ready to do anything to accomplish my mission.

I woke up early and took my time preparing for the show I was about to put on with Nazar. I would employ every possible tool to ensure my success. I sculpted my hair perfectly, shaved my face impeccably, and donned my clean, crisp suit that was clearly worth more than enough to indicate I was incredibly wealthy—which I was. My business card was ready in my breast pocket, and my iPad was in a designer, leather case.

Nazar was waiting for me in the lobby by the entrance to the restaurant. He was precisely as Abu Ali described him, shaggy hair, dirty nails, basically awful. His shirt was baggy, and his jeans were faded and worn. He stood and rushed to greet me, recognizing me at once because I was the only foreigner in the lobby, and I certainly stood out in a crowd. As I had rehearsed in my mind earlier, I casually approached him with a deliberate nonchalance. I looked down my nose at him with eyebrows raised, and when he offered his hand to shake, I considered it with a con-templative pause before deigning to touch the unclean extremity.

"Nice to meet you," he said in passable English.

I nodded my head and shook his hand with a firm, confident grip. His palm was clammy, and I reminded myself to use hand sanitizer as soon as we parted company. Then, with my contaminated hand, I led him with a cool patience toward the little bistro. We sat, and I ordered us tea.

The way the man shifted uncomfortably in his seat made it clear how imposing I was to him, how conscious he was of his unkempt appearance. It all worked to my benefit. Unconsciously, he crossed his arms over his grubby shirt. "How can I help you, sir?" he asked finally.

I smiled benevolently. "Call me Henry," I said. I didn't answer his question because I wanted to watch him twist in the wind for a bit before we got down to our business. I produced my card and handed it to the man.

"A best-seller author?" he said, impressed. I didn't bother correcting his grammar, though I had the urge.

"Well, among other things," I replied with a know-ing smirk. He idiotically mirrored my expression, per-ceiving a nonexistent private joke. I took my iPad from its case and quickly googled myself and passed the tablet to Nazar. "After my father's passing, I dedicated my time to writing. My father left me with the comfort of millions. I invested well in certain projects. I love business."

He scrolled with a fingertip, scanning the screen. I could see the greed in his eyes as he read headline after headline. I had him.

"How can I help you?" he said, his voice tremulous with excitement.

"I have a very simple request from you. And I will pay whatever you want for it."

"Tell me, sir—Henry. Tell me, Henry. Anything for you. We love America and Americans."

"Abu Ali told me about what you do for a living," I said, letting the statement hang between us.

The waiter brought our tea at that moment. I could not have timed it better. Nazar's hands were shaking when he raised his cup to his lips. He considered me nervously from over the rim of his cup, then said, "What did Abu Ali tell you?"

"That he brings men for you to take to ISIS for recruitment, to fight or in other capacities. You also coordinate drug pick-ups for him in Lebanon," I said, casually picking up my own tea and then blowing across its steaming surface before taking a preliminary sip.

"He told you this?" he said, eyebrows creeping up his greasy forehead.

"Listen," I said, leaning forward and leveling my narrowed gaze at him, "I'm not judging you. I, myself, do worse things than that. I assure you."

"You do?"

I chuckled and leaned back with my tea, crossing my legs and picking some nonexistent lint from my pant leg. "Yes, of course. How did you think I made my billions? Certainly not from selling books or inheriting from my father, a mere millionaire."

"Billions?" he said, his jaw dropping.

"Yes," I said, waving off the question, "So tell me, in the last years, how much have you been making?"

"You are not CIA or something, are you?"

I rolled my eyes and then calmly blinked at him. Patiently, like I was addressing a child, I said, "A CIA agent would not meet you at a hotel in Antakya. The CIA would simply arrest you without question through your Turkish government. No, Nazar, I am *not* CIA. I'm just a man with means who has a simple request of you."

"How can I help you then?"

"As confirmed by Abu Ali, a while back, you helped take a young man to ISIS. His name is Bilal; he is a computer engineer. I need to know where he is. Every useful piece of information you give me will be paid for in kind." I took an envelope, fat with bills, and put it on the table. "This is for the information, and there will be more."

"Are you writing about it? They will come after me. They will kill me if they find out I told you even the smallest detail."

I sighed, "Nazar, if you help me, no one will touch you. You will make enough money that you won't need them anymore. Anyway, how much do they pay you? Hm?"

"Not much, not much," he admitted. "First, they paid a lot, but now it's getting less because they are having financial problems." He straightened then, finally recognizing the gravity of the situation and how much he stood to gain from working with me. "I am just a messenger. I am not a terrorist."

"That's good to hear," I said, replacing my cup on the table and lacing my fingers over one knee unconcernedly, "I am not writing about this. I just need to know where this guy is because his wife has been looking for him. I promised to at least get her some information."

Nazar's eyes drifted down to the envelope which was too full of bills to be properly sealed. I had stuffed it with 10,000 US dollars. "Well, my friend," he said, smiling like a contented shark. He leaned forward and slipped the envelope into his rear, jeans pocket. "I take so many guys across the Bab El Hawa border. It is not that difficult. You take them across, then people on the other side load them into buses. Some buses leave to Raqqa, where ISIS is, some leave to Idlib, where other terrorist groups are, and some go to Aleppo to fight with the opposition of the Syrian army. I am in the business of importing people for whoever pays me. I do favors, and I can see you are a gentleman who is more generous than all my clients put together."

He paused and searched his memory, looking at the ceiling for a moment. "I took Bilal across, and he was loaded on a bus headed to Raqqa. ISIS was looking for someone who knew computers. I am not sure what happened to him after that. I gave him to the guys on the other side. It is all I know."

I was getting somewhere. At least Nazar knew people on the other side of the border. With all his trips, he must have access to Bilal. For clarity, so I could write about it convincingly—which was as important to me as getting to Bilal—I asked more questions. "Is it that easy to take guys over?" The book was never far from my thoughts.

He laughed. It was an unpleasant thing to hear, and it provoked an ugly smile on the man. "Money in this part of the world can get you an appointment to meet God Himself if you wish," he said, pleased with his joke, "Many Turkish border control officers are making a living out of these imports and exports of people, terrorists, women, you name it."

"Great. Then you are going to work for me. Let me make you an offer: I will pay you 50,000 dollars if you can find out exactly where Bilal is."

Nazar's mouth gaped. It took a moment for him to recover, but not too long. "That's not a problem," he said, "I will get that information. Most of the guys working on the other side of the border are working for the money anyway. ISIS financing is deteriorating, so it won't be hard. They will put their lives in danger and share information for just a few thousand dollars."

I nodded once, then struck him with the next question. "What will it cost me if I wanted Bilal delivered to me here?"

He looked at me, then down at his fidgeting hands. A fresh sheen of perspiration glistened on his brow and upper lip. "You know, if I get caught trying to smuggle someone out without their permission... They will behead me and shoot him. Then they will come find you here in Antakya. Are you crazy?"

Calmly, I tilted my head and gave him my gentlest smile. "I am crazy about getting Bilal here safely, yes. And you are crazy about being a rich man. Don't you want to be a rich man Nazar?" Money was the best tool, the best leverage for a man such as Nazar. "Imagine how your life will change when you have enough money to live without dallying in this unwholesome business any longer. You could have a nice house far away from all of this. You won't have to put your family or yourself in danger anymore. I could even try and find a way to bring you to America." I could feel my words sinking in. I had him, I knew it. And I was happy about that. It was making me sick having to deal with this piece of human trash.

Eager to be done with this business, I dropped a bomb on him, "One million."

He flinched and nearly toppled the table as he stood up, "Dollars?!?" he gasped, incredulous.

"To get him here, to me. Yes. One million dollars. American dollars."

"I have only dreamed of money like that," he said.

"Well, let me make your dreams come true."

"If I bring him and you don't pay me, you won't even have time to leave Turkey. You know that, right? The sort of trouble you will be in, you won't survive." Despite his warning, he settled back into his seat. A thought occurred to him. "What if he is dead?" he asked.

"Then I will give you 50,000 dollars. If you bring indisputable evidence, I'll pay more."

"And what if we get caught?"

I shrugged and crossed my arms over my chest. "I'm confident you won't. How much confidence does a million dollars give *you*?"

He tapped his lower lip, thinking. "Well... everyone there feeds on money. I will find a way."

"I will be waiting," I said, "And if you play games with me, you will not like the outcome." The threat was delivered as amicably as the rest of our conversation, simply matter of fact.

"No, no games. I don't play games when that kind of money is involved. I will bring him."

"Good. I knew Abu Ali wouldn't disappoint me. You're as clever and resourceful as he described," I lied. "You will call me with *any* news. Understood? I'm trusting you with this. You are the expert. I don't know how things work on the other side of the border. I'm leaving this to you." I did not trust him so much as I trusted his greed. With that much money, I felt my trust was warranted.

I dismissed him with a benign flit of my fingers, "You have my number. Don't make me wait too long."

After the sniveling human trafficker had left, I returned to my room to pack. I would change hotels immediately. I was rather sure he would not try anything foolish, but I had to take precautions in case he somehow got a counter offer or had information pried from him. It was too dangerous to stay here.

I had to think of everything. Getting vast amounts of money was a challenge when it was in cash. Luckily, I was able to contact an old family friend, a friend of my father's, and he made all the arrangements for me and knew better than to inquire after any details. He put me in touch with someone at my European bank, and I was able to pick up my cash in just a couple of days. I would wait.

In the meantime, I spent most of my time in my hotel room, rarely leaving it. I wrote, spoke to Tala and to my bankers. I should admit that I was anxious the whole time. I wasn't so overconfident that I didn't realize the possible danger I was in. There was always the chance Nazar would be caught, but, at the same time, I *did* change locations and kept a low profile. The prize was worth the gamble.

Wasn't it?

Selfishly, I wanted Nazar's attempt to free Bilal to fail. They would be caught and probably killed. Then I could finish my book with the ending I had always wanted from the beginning: Tala and I would be together. I would bring the horrible, brutal news back to her, she would collapse into my strong, soothing arms, I would comfort her, and, quickly or gradually—I didn't care which—Tala would see all I had done for her and would realize she had been in love with me all along. What a perfect ending for my book!

Then there was Tarek and the issue of Abu Ali. I still required Tarek to keep our prisoner safe in case I lost contact with Nazar. Without Abu Ali, I would have no way of finding other people who might have information on Bilal. I had left a great deal of money with Tarek, but his reassurance wasn't easily bought.

"Authorities are looking for him, Mr. Henry. I am scared we will get caught with him," Tarek said during one of our many phone conversations.

There was a slight chance that he would get so nervous that he might tell the authorities. I had to get through to him and help him calm down. I wired him still more money, and it seemed to appease his doubts for the time being.

After days, I felt the cold hands of dread reaching for me. Nazar hadn't called. How would I know if they got caught? Then I reminded myself that I could not let myself be shaken. I had to remain vigilant. Winners did not give in to fear and doubt.

I was forgetting about my worries with the help of a glass of whiskey, along with five or six before that, when my phone rang. I expected it to be Tala, calling to ask me for the hundredth time how my search for Bilal was going. I took the phone from the table and stared in shock at the caller identification. It was Nazar! I answered immediately.

"Hello?"

"I have him. He is with me," he said, his voice shaky and rushed. "We are in Turkey. I need my money. I need to get out of here before they find me."

My world collapsed. Bilal was alive, and he had made it to the relative safety of Turkey. The fact that he allowed Nazar to rescue him at all meant he wanted out of ISIS and certainly be reunited with his wife, the love of his life. The love of *my* life.

"Are you there? Sir?" Nazar's voice was brittle with panic.

During the long hours I spent in my hotel room, I prepared plans for every eventuality I could imagine.

While this was not the one I hoped for, I was ready for it.

"Yes, I'm here," I said, my voice calm and assertive despite my racing pulse. "Ok. Don't worry. You will have your money. I need you to meet me, with him. Antakya is too close to the border for this to be a secure transaction. We need to change locations. You will meet me at my hotel in Ankara, Latanya Hotel." I had chosen the Turkish capital because it was further from the border, yes, but it was also much larger and a city where it was easier to remain anonymous and hidden.

"Ankara?" he sputtered. "That's so far..."

"Get a car," I said through my teeth, losing patience, "Get yourself and our mutual friend into it and then drive there. Got it?"

"Yes, sir," he said. "I've already moved my family to a more secure place."

I didn't care, but I replied, "Good. Maybe have them meet you there then. Call me when you have Bilal in Ankara." I hung up.

I rented a car and started the drive to Ankara. During the drive—more than seven and a half hours—I was in a state of shock. At least I had plenty of time to think and plan my next moves. I reached for my phone several times with the intent to call Tala and to let her know that I had found him. I couldn't. I had to wait. I had to see if I could still manage to have our story, my book, end precisely the way I wanted. At the same time, I wanted to hear her voice. I *needed* to hear her voice. I had been under such stress for so long; I just needed to call.

For selfish reasons, I didn't want to call her, and for selfish reasons, I just had to.

I called Tala.

"Henry?" She sounded drowsy. I must have woken her.

"I'm sorry, Tala. Did I wake you? I won't keep you. I just wanted to check in on you," I lied.

"That's sweet, Henry," she said, then yawned. "Is there any news?"

Again, I lied, "I'm sorry, Tala, no. But I think things are about to happen. I can feel it."

"Alright, Henry. Call me the minute you hear something," she said, obviously hoping to get back to sleep.

"Of course. Sleep well."

The sweetness in her voice made me feel even worse for having lied to her. But I quickly shrugged off such feelings; my guilt didn't last longer than a few seconds. I simply reminded myself that I was a winner. I had won so far at everything. I won when I met Tala, I won when I found Abu Ali, I won in my search for Bilal, and I won in my writing career. *Tale of Tala* was going to bring me back into the public eye when it was published. It was going to put me back on the top of the best-seller lists.

My state of mind, relishing my success and supremacy, got the better of me. That was when I picked up my phone again to call Tarek.

"Yes, sir? It's late. Is everything alright?" he asked, as nervous as I had ever heard him.

"Oh yes," I assured him, "Better than alright. Our mission is almost finished. We can start cleaning up and getting ready to celebrate our success."

"That's very good news," Tarek said, relief obvious in his sleepy voice. "What next then?"

"Get one of the guards to kill Abu Ali and throw his body somewhere on the highway before morning."

There was silence on the line. It gave me almost enough time to consider the gravity of what I had just said, but Tarek spoke before I could manage any real introspection.

"I will take care of it," he replied. He had to focus entirely on his own mission of finding a new life in America. All he had to do was order the death of a lowlife. He was decided.

It was only a matter of a few, short hours before Abu Ali's body was found by the police. They would assume that it was a drug trafficking deal that had gone wrong, and Tarek would be on a flight to Istanbul. The two men who guarded then killed our captive-turned-victim were paid an enormous amount of money. Everyone was pleased, except for me. For, at around the same time, I would meet my competitor in the race for Tala's heart, her husband, my rival.

I was going to win. I just didn't know how I would do it.

Not yet.

I got to my hotel in Ankara, checked in, and called Nazar on the number he had texted me a couple of hours prior. I had instructed him to change phones once he was on his way.

"We will be there in a couple of hours, maybe two and a half," he said, sounding weary from the travel and, of course, from the strain and pressure he was feeling.

"Good. I'll be waiting."

While I waited, I wrote. I had to update the story up to the point where I arrived at the hotel and was waiting for Bilal's arrival. It was my hope that the suspense I was feeling would be felt similarly by my readers at this point. Bilal was coming. What was I going to do? How was Bilal going to react to the mastermind of his rescue when he heard what I was going to tell him?

My mind chewed on those questions like a dog worrying at a bone. Then, I knew. I knew exactly what I was going to tell him.

I was going to win at this too, just like everything else up until that point. Nothing would keep me from my goal, to have Tala and to live and write a book that was going to be as much a winner as I would be. Every lie I told Tala would be worth it. In fact, I didn't think of it as lying any longer; I thought of it as storytelling to secure a better life for her, for her and for me.

That thought made my mind work all the harder. How could I win? What leverage did I have? What tools could I use to win over Bilal? I just didn't have enough information, criteria on how to beat my rival. I had to meet him. I had to know him, who he was, and how to bring him down. My future with Tala was in the balance, and, just as important, so was the ending of my book.

Chapter Eight

The road you travel can lead to victory, or it can lead to defeat; the destination depends on the decisions you make. The outcome of each decision leads to the next fork in the road and that one to the next. Each choice has its consequences. For a man born a winner like me, every winding path is presumed to lead to victory. For a loser, roads are often blocked by their despair; decisions are frightening things. For those who live somewhere between those two routes, doubt and uncertainty are roadblocks to overcome.

I sat on the edge of the cream-white leather sofa in the lounge area of my suite. My elbows rested on my knees, and I massaged my temples, eyes closed as I stoked the fires of my brain, searching for the insight I knew would come. I recognized, first and foremost, that I had to get the story from Bilal for my book. Only then could I tell him anything about Tala.

Tala. What would I tell him about Tala?

That was the decision that would break my heart. The way I saw it, there were two options: I could tell the truth and reunite Bilal with his wife, or I could lie and tell him whatever it would take to keep him from her, and I could have her for myself. I couldn't stand the notion of losing. At the same time, could I take from the woman I love her future with this man? How contemptible would my lying to them and stealing Tala from her husband have been? Had I not already done worse? Was I not beyond moral dilemmas like this by now?

My unwelcome moment of introspection was interrupted by my phone. It was Nazar.

"We are here," he said, his voice unmistakably tired.

Goosebumps prickled on my arms and perspiration beaded on my forehead. I hesitated at the notion of leaving the safety of the room. "I will be right down," I said, and bloody images of my beheading at the hands of hooded men flashed suddenly into my mind. "Meet me in the lobby," I added with a confidence I did not feel.

I stood and squared my shoulders, steeling myself against my anxiety. It only took a moment. I exhaled a long, steadying breath and strode to the door. As I opened it, I assured myself that Nazar could not have led them to me. He certainly would not have made it this far before they found him and killed him, right? What I had to trust most of all was his greed. As well, he must have been cunning enough to extract Bilal in the first place. Nazar was clever and greedy; he would be sure to survive long enough to get his money. My plan to use him was a good one.

The hallway was empty. I pressed the button and waited in front of the elevator doors, staring at my indistinct reflection in the burnished elevator doors. My heart was in my throat, and the hair stood up on the back of my neck at the sound of the elevator drawing nearer to my floor. I was ready to run if there were men waiting inside. Why did I not keep a gun? The light above the door flickered on, and the gentle bell chimed deafeningly. The doors slid open.

It was empty.

I didn't realize I was holding my breath until I stepped into the elevator and my lungs sucked in a relieved gasp. My fists relaxed at my sides, and I drew a slow, calming breath before forcing myself to calm. I chastened myself for this fear. You are a winner, I repeated in my head, a winner. I had come this far and lived. I had survived so far in the face of danger; I would survive this. One more deep breath and my nerves were finally under control.

I was seconds from meeting Bilal. There was a mirror on either side of me in the elevator. I was impeccably dressed as always, tall, and Hollywood handsome, and I took a moment to admire one reflection of myself and then the other. There was no way Bilal was better looking than I was. He didn't have a fortune like me. He had nothing to offer Tala. By the time the elevator descended to the lobby, my back was straight, my jaw set, and my eyes narrowed with determination and self-assurance.

The door hissed open, and I stepped into the lobby as Henry, the mastermind, the man of means, the one in charge. The heels of my Italian loafers articulated my confident strides across the stone tiles toward the small lounge to my right. Nazar spotted me from around a man who had his back to me and stood, eyes bright with anxiety. The man had to be Bilal.

Bilal stood and turned to face me as I approached. With no preamble, in surprisingly elegant accented English, he said, "Where is Fatima?" He was pale, had a beard, no mustache, and he wore black pants and shirt. I was taller than he, and, without question, better looking. I was not proud to find myself relieved by that fact.

"This man, Nazar, said you knew where she is. Where is she?" he repeated, his gaze unwavering.

I tilted my head, staring at Bilal for a heartbeat before I turned to Nazar. "Give us some privacy, Nazar. I'll call you after our mutual friend here and I have had some words."

The Turkish man half turned to go, then paused. I wasn't surprised. "What about... our business?" Nazar asked. Of course. He was worried about his money. I didn't blame him; it *was* a vast amount of money.

"Don't worry," I soothed, as one might soothe a hyperactive lapdog. "And don't go far from the lobby here. Go get a drink from the bar," I suggested.

Without waiting for Nazar's reply, I turned back to Bilal and gestured politely back toward the elevator from which I had made my entrance. "Please," I said, "Let's talk up in my suite, shall we?"

"Fine," he said, his thick, unkempt brows furrowed over dark, wary eyes.

The silence was leaden during our trip in the elevator until Bilal spoke, "So, where is Fatima?"

Perhaps my having remained silent for the few moments we had been aboard the elevator suggested weakness on my part. I made sure to correct that assumption with an even stare and a calm, cold reply. "We will talk when we get to my room." He opened his mouth to speak, but closed it again and stared up at the numbers climbing in sequence, floor to floor.

I was buying time as much as flexing my supremacy muscles. Maintaining my dominant status in every exchange was of utmost importance if I was going to achieve every goal on my way to winning this. Part of me wanted to tell him right there, in the elevator, that Tala—Fatima—was dead. I spent the remainder of our ride considering and comparing our reflections in the wall mirrors. My chest puffed up reflexively as I sized him up.

When we entered my suite, I gestured him in and followed after. I closed the door, and Bilal spun on his heel. "Fatima," he said, "Where is she? Tell me."

I walked passed him, unconcerned, and settled onto the sofa, reclining and leaning an elbow casually on the armrest. "Bilal," I said, waving a hand to the set plush chair opposite me, "Before I tell you anything about Fatima, I need you to tell me what happened when you were taken."

Bilal looked to the chair and then back to me. The air between us sizzled with tension. "And who are you to ask me?" he said, his lip curled in a derisive snarl.

Unmoved, I said, "I, my friend, am the man who rescued you from the most dreaded terrorist organization in existence." Somewhere in the back of my head, I marveled at that fact myself. I truly was a winner of extraordinary scale. "Or," I went on, my gaze darkening, "would you prefer I send you back?"

There. I saw him wince almost imperceptibly— the crack in his veneer. I had found the leverage I was looking for.

"No, no," he said, the iron no longer in his voice, "I am glad to be out of there." He cleared his throat and then sat in the chair I had offered him a moment before. "I might owe you an apology," he conceded reluctantly. "Thank you for freeing me. But, why did you do it? Who are you? And where," he implored, "is Fatima?"

"Do you drink alcohol?" I asked.

"No," he said, frowning. "Where is Fatima?"

"Would you like a glass of water or something?"

"No. Why are you not answering the question?"

I stood then, and I crossed the room to the wet bar. I opened the magnum of whiskey and poured myself two fingers, neat. "Bilal," I said, rolling the amber liquid in the tumbler and then raising the glass to my nose, contemplating the whiskey's quality, "Before I give you even one piece of information, I'm going to need to hear your story. Understand?" My tone changed, and my gaze grew cold. "Now, start from where you and Fatima were separated."

Bilal recognized my iron resolve and nodded. "Abu Ali took me from Fatima, thinking I am going to do a job for a European country. We went in a car, for hours and hours. Then, this Turkish man, Nazar—I just learned his name hours ago—came to the car and said I need to go to another minivan. I got nervous and asked why Abu Ali wasn't coming with me. Abu Ali said that it is a sensitive job and he would wait for me. I got into the van; then we were stopped. Nazar drove the van. He handed some men in uniform some papers, and they let us pass."

I nodded, listening closely and didn't look away as I settled back down on the sofa, drink in hand.

He continued.

"On the way, I asked him where we were going. He did not answer. I was in the van alone with Nazar. Then we drove another few kilometers, and two men got into the van. They were armed, and from their looks, I could tell they belonged to a terrorist organization. I had seen men like them on television.

"They pointed their guns at me and told me not to say a word. Nazar drove a bit longer and then, when we stopped, the two men dragged me out of the van. That is when Nazar left. It was the last time I saw him until yesterday.

"The two men put me into another car. We drove until we met a checkpoint where I saw the ISIS flag. It all became clear to me, finally. I had been tricked into joining ISIS."

As Bilal was speaking, I took mental notes and planned how best to portray him and describe his story in my book. Perhaps I ought to have been sympathetic, hearing this man's tragic story, but he remained my rival. All I thought about was how his story would impact *Tale of Tala*. That is, until I thought about how Tala may not accept him back after knowing he was affiliated with terrorists. I was in love, and in love we are selfish.

"I arrived at a camp," Bilal said, "for what may have been two days—it might have been four or eight—I was left in a small cell, alone. No light, water or food. The heat and the darkness were like a hell. I did not know what would come of me. All I thought about was Fatima. I thought of what might have happened to her, and whether I would see her again. I never stopped thinking about her during my whole time there. I didn't even know if she was alive or not."

I should have felt something other than contempt for Bilal as he talked about his painful experience, but here was the only man who could thwart my plan to have Tala for my own. We were both competing for her heart, even though he didn't know that, yet. It rankled that he had the advantage over me: he was Tala's husband. But, I risked my life for her; I was the one who rescued her from prostitution. I could find leverage. I could gain the advantage.

"Then, after two days," Bilal explained, "a man came and gave me lessons on ISIS—attempting to indoctrinate me. Omar was his name. Omar told me how the organization is misrepresented in the media and that most of what I had heard about ISIS is fabricated. He told me how Sunni Muslims have been persecuted and how Bashar al-Assad and other Arab leaders had been committing crimes against Muslims.

"During the following days, I attended these sessions where we were told about Islam and the importance of establishing a strong state for Muslims amid the discrimination against us in the west as well as within the Middle East itself. We were shown atrocities committed by American troops in Iraq, Afghanistan, and elsewhere.

"Then, Omar came to explain to me what they needed from me. He was ruthless. He threatened that if I did anything wrong or even tried, that I would be more sorry than I could ever have believed. They wanted me to join a group of people working for them with computers. Our job was to try and hack government websites and email accounts, also social media accounts, collecting data and giving it to our supervisor. My group consisted of just a few people who were skilled at that sort of thing. They were from all over the world, even foreigners like yourself.

"Sometimes," he said, troubled, his eyes drifting to his lap where he clasped his hands, wringing them, "they would bring us to witness beheadings. It was a way to intimidate us. That would be our fate if we tried to escape or did any wrong against the plan. And that is how my life went for the last year: working all day, witnessing beheadings, and living in war because of all the bombardment of the area by the Russians or the Americans, or whoever."

Then Bilal said the vilest thing. It should not have pleased me, but it did. He looked up at me then and winced slightly before confessing, "They forced me to do the most horrible things." I inclined my head and silently waited for him to proceed. I tried to make my interest seem sympathetic, but inside, I was hoping for the worst. He sighed and said, "They forced me to rape women. It had nothing to do with Islam, nor did anything they did. I could say nothing. I did what I was told, because to do otherwise would have meant my death. All I could do was maintain hope that somehow, I would be out of there and be reunited with my wife, Fatima."

"Then, in the middle of the night, a guard came to me and asked me to go with him. I obeyed as I did in everything. He was paid well by Nazar. You see, people there are of two kinds: those who believe in the ideology of ISIS, who have been brainwashed, and those who don't want to be there. On both sides, there are those who are driven by money above all. Nazar knew who was who. That is how he found a way to get me out.

"I did not know where I was going, but anywhere was better than there. At that point, even death might have been better. In the car, he told me that a man who knows my wife had paid for my release. And here I am, with you," he said, leveling his stare at me at last and folding his arms over his chest.

"Where is my wife? What happened to her?"

At last, the point where I had to decide what to say—which route to take at this fork in my road—had occurred. Bilal had held up his end of the bargain in telling me his brutal story. Suddenly, fear hit me. It reared its dreadful head. I feared losing Tala if I reunited them—feared it terribly.

I would never try to defend my choice, but it is for victory a winner strives; it is for love a lover desires. If we yearn for these things keenly enough, it can bring out the worst in us.

I hid my fear behind a kind face and leaned close in such a way that Bilal grew wide-eyed, worried about what I was about to tell him. Quietly, sympathetically, I said, "After you had left, Fatima waited for you. But, she soon ran out of money..."

I let that hang in the air for several heartbeats and watched Bilal's eyes reflect the doubt and anxiousness that I was purposefully inciting behind them. He was experiencing fear now. I saw him draw in a breath to speak, but I went on before he could utter a word, and toyed with him like a cat with a mouse.

"She could not return to Lebanon," I explained with convincing tenderness. I continued as though I were delivering sorrowful news to a fond friend rather than striking my adversary with words for weapons—the preferred weapon of writers. "She was cleaning houses, saving up for her passage to Europe. Smugglers don't offer their services cheaply." I paused as though there were a lump in my throat and considered Bilal, my enemy, with a facsimile of a tortured expression before continuing, "One of her clients raped her, savagely."

Bilal's face melted into ghastly misery at my vicious statement. I held up my hand, gently halting any objection or discussion. "I'm so sorry to have to tell you," I lied, "There's more." Helplessly, the distressed man balled his fists and grimaced, preparing himself for still more distressing news.

"She was reduced to selling her body for the money she needed to pay for her passage to Europe," I said, my brow knitting with the pain of having to say such a thing aloud. In front of me, Bilal was stricken, in shock and trembling with outrage.

I described Tala's voyage from Turkey to Greece. "She watched her friend die, and she nearly died herself, alone and afraid," I said, hitting my foe this time with guilt. I could see it in him: in his slumped shoulders, in his unblinking stare. "Without you, she had no one to protect her," I went on, shaking my head woefully, stoking the fire of his misery.

"I need to speak to her! I need to see her!" Bilal groaned, dark anguish making his features look haggard.

"Please," I said regretfully, "I'm so very sorry, Bilal. I'm not finished."

Bilal bared his teeth and snarled tacitly, a man awaiting the bullets of a firing squad. "Tell me," he said, glaring.

"When she finally arrived in Europe, after enduring violence, death, rape..." I paused to sigh, building the suspense. I imagined showing Bilal a gaping, bottomless pit, black and sinister and cold. I imagined standing next to him and placing a kind hand on his shoulder as we both peered into the implacable void, just before I shoved him in. "...She was taken by human traffickers and forced into working all this time in a prostitution ring in Slovenia. It is where I eventually met her."

A primal scream erupted from Bilal's throat, and he leaped over the table, swinging at me with both fists.

I was ready though. In fact, I was surprised it took this long for him to attack me. I was taller, bigger, and stronger. I pinned him down and screamed in his face, "Bilal! Wait! You don't understand!" He and I were both panting, and he snarled ferociously up at me. "I fell in love with her, Bilal," I admitted with a passion that may have been the truest thing I had said to him so far. He deflated under me, arms falling to his sides and he turned away.

I stood and offered my hand to help him up. He batted it away, and I said, "I care for her." Even a truth like that had a knife's edge after all I had said to Bilal.

Bilal took to his feet and scowled at me, his face still flushed from his outburst. "Did Fatima ask you to come find me?"

I lied. "Fatima—Tala now—asked me to write her story. To do so, I had to find you. I had to finish my book."

He squinted at me for a moment, then asked, "Does she love you?"

I lied again. "We are deeply in love. She wants a fresh start. I want to finish my book, take her to America, and start a life together."

Bilal was silent. He looked away and sat on the chair again. "But I need to talk to Fatima."

His persistence was a challenge, and for every challenge there is a solution.

I did not know much about Bilal but for everything that Tala had told me about him and the information I garnered from his own storytelling. I knew enough though.

I returned to my seat and was thankful to find my drink undisturbed on a side table. "You have just fled ISIS. They will be looking for you. It is just a matter of time before they find you. You have no documents and, I'm assuming, no money. I have a proposition for you."

He looked at me, then away, then back at me. I was pleased to see this. He was with me so far.

"I will get you a passport from the Dominican Republic, and I will give you enough money to go somewhere, like... say... South America. You can start your own business or something, find a woman to fall in love with, and you can live happily ever after. In return, you forget about Tala—Fatima." It took me a heartbeat to correct myself and use Tala's given name.

There is an equation for manipulation: remind your subject of the problem, offer a solution, and draw a hopeful future.

"How much money?"

I knew he would go for it.

"I will give you one million American dollars. That's enough for you to do whatever you want." I added then, my tone severe, "But you can never..." I paused, ensuring his eyes were focused on mine, "... never try to contact Fatima again."

He was silent for a long moment but gave little hint as to what he was thinking. Then, "Okay. I was to ask for one favor though," he said.

"Anything you want. Just say it," I said, trying my best not to let my relief show itself in my voice.

"I want you to tell Fatima that not for one day did I not think of her. I want you to tell her that I have forgiven her for what she had to do to survive."

"I will tell her. I promise," I lied.

I secured rooms for Bilal and Nazar. They were, justifiably, exhausted after all they had been through in the last twelve hours. I returned to my suite and called Tala.

When a lie is uttered, it naturally brings with it more lies. It is an art, a form of fiction writing. Perhaps that's why I took to it with such proficiency. But, I became a liar out of necessity and for the sake of love.

"How is the search for Bilal going, Henry?" she asked, "Are you getting close?"

"Yes, Tala," I said, feigning excitement. "I'm almost there. I'm sure of it."

"Oh, good. I'm so lucky to have met you," she said, "You have given me so much. And now, you are tracking down my husband. I placed my trust in the right man."

It stung to hear her talk about trust.

I spent the night writing. It was a means of escaping the guilt that was beginning to nag me. Whenever I felt a pang of guilt though, I reminded myself of the doctrine of winning. I thought of the happiness my success in this mission was going to bring Tala and me and I felt justified. It helped to have my book to work on, and I had a lot to type after the day I had.

That night, I lied in my book for the first time. I wrote that when Nazar came back after searching for Bilal, he reported that Bilal had been killed. When *Tale of Tala* was to be released, it must never include the truth about Tala's husband. I wrote that section of the book how I wanted Tala one day to read it: the fateful news of Bilal's death being a poignant a dramatic turn of the plot.

The following days went by quickly and in a guilty haze.

First, I paid Nazar, but not before I had him rehearse and perform a script I prepared. It was the story of how Bilal had died, heroically defying his ISIS captors. I needed collaboration for my story. For money, that man did whatever I asked. He took his money, enough to change his life and the life of his family forever. I was glad never to have to see him again.

Dimitrij, the concierge who was taking care of Tala for me, arranged another passport, this one for Bilal. It was complicated and a big challenge, but, for money, anything can be obtained in this world. Bilal would take his passport, a plane ticket to Columbia, and his freshly filled million-dollar account I opened for him, and I would never see him again.

I went to Istanbul where Tarek was waiting for me. I paid him more than I agreed because he certainly earned it. Every one of my plans came off perfectly while he was helping me. I owed him for his hard work. He was a very helpful and loyal assistant. It would be months before he would arrive in New York, but I fulfilled my promise to him and got the process started. He would most likely work for me once he joined me in New York.

Then, I was ready to return to Slovenia. I didn't tell Tala I was coming back; I didn't want her to know because I was going to have very bad news to deliver. I would use the time on the airplane to formulate yet another plan: how to gently break the news to Tala that her husband was dead. I would console her and protect her. That is how I would win her heart, no matter how long it took. All that I had done, the lies, the violence, they were for Tala. The last chapter of my book would detail my success, my victory, and my claiming of my prize, Tala.

It was a long, dangerous, and twisting road to travel. I did not regret one decision I had made regarding which path to take when I was faced with a fork in my road. I planned and schemed with one thing on my mind: to win. I was a winner, and I deserved the fruit of my labor.

Chapter Nine
Part One

I have been obsessed with the notion of winning since I was a boy. After having met Tala, to win, to have her, to have her love, and to succeed with the book became my goal, my journey, my mission. That success would bring her story, and my name, into the world's collective awareness where they belonged. To succeed in those aspirations would be my great triumph.

To secure my victory, I would perform violence, order a man's murder, and defy death. I lied, betrayed, schemed, and sabotaged.

To win, I would overcome challenges that others would consider insurmountable, travel to dangerous places, love with a passion that lesser men could only imagine, and save my lover from a cursed past to grant her a blessed future.

There are two sides of the winning coin, and two edges to the sword of victory. For my prize, I would embrace this dichotomy: light and dark, good and evil, losers and winners—without one there cannot be the other. To win, I would endure whatever was necessary and do anything that was required, because my purpose was paramount. Tala would love me.

On the plane to Slovenia, like I always seemed to do, I thought. I pondered what lay ahead. I was eager to see Tala. I hadn't laid eyes on her in far too long. I missed her terribly. I could imagine her smile: dark eyes sparkling and lush lips parting in shocked, elated surprise.

I remembered the first time I ever saw her. She was, even dressed in her distressed jeans and leather jacket, the most beautiful and provocative woman I had ever seen in my life. She trusted me with the gift of her story. Since then, it grew into *our* story, and I would make it evolve into my book, *Tale of Tala*.

It was going to take preparation to ensure she would believe me when I lied right to her face. I fulfilled my promise and found her husband. But I would have to hurt her. She would despair, I knew, but it would be worth it for her—for us. For me.

I *had* to lie to her. The pain she would undoubtedly experience was going to be temporary though. She was a survivor, I knew. After all she had been through, learning her husband was dead—something she partially suspected already—was just to be one last modicum of grief in comparison. In fact, the truth would hurt her even more. She would be crushed if she ever discovered Bilal had been convinced to forget about his wife for mere money.

By the time my plane had begun its descent into Ljubljana, I had added to my list of justifications for my lying to Tala. The life Bilal would have given Tala would be just a continuation of her misery to date. He had no money, no future, and no home. Now both of them had a nationality and hope for the future. They had money—enough for each to live comfortably for the rest of their lives, she with me and he with and wherever he likes. This deception may have been the best thing to ever happen to them, really.

In the taxi from the airport, I rehearsed what I was going to say. I had to keep my composure and break the news to her gently. I would comfort her, give her space if she needed it, and, above all, I would win her over, no matter how long it took.

Dimitrij positively beamed, flashing his garish teeth at me, when I arrived in the hotel lobby. "You're back! I'm so very happy to see you!" he gushed. "I took very good care of Ms. Tala for you, Sir Henry," he said, crossing the lobby to take my hand and shake it heartily, "But with all the traveling, shopping... oh the shopping! Ms. Tala has expensive tastes." I found his insolent grin vulgar, but I smiled blithely and shook his hand. I knew he was digging for more money, so

I slipped a few folded bills into his breast pocket and patted his chest amicably.

"I'm going up to our suite," I said laconically.

"Of course!" he exclaimed before he took up my bag and followed me to the elevator.

He stepped toward the opening door, and I stopped him. "No, Dimitrij," I said, "I would like to be alone when I see Tala for the first time in so long." I took my bag from him, and he chuckled.

"Oh, yes. I understand," he replied with a sly cant to his head. I had a powerful urge to punch him in those unsightly teeth when he winked at me just as the elevator doors closed between us.

I knocked on the door to our suite out of respect for Tala's privacy. She wasn't expecting me after all. My heart crept into my throat at the sound of Tala's footsteps approaching the door. I watched the tiny bead of light flicker in the door's peephole and heard a gasp of surprise from the other side of the door. During the eternity it took for Tala to unlock the door, my palms grew clammy, and I wiped them on my pant legs. There was no reason to be uneasy, I told myself, the worst was over, and I had come back to Tala after accomplishing my mission. There was just one thing left to do before the unsavory experiences would be over; one last lie and it would be done.

"Henry!" Tala exclaimed. She flung the door open and hugged me fiercely enough to crush the wind out of me. The feel of her touch, the smell of her hair, the warmth of her hug, it was all worth it. I would do anything for these sensations, for this affection. I did unspeakable things for it already, and if I had to, I would do it all again. Lying was the least of it all, and it was the last vile thing I had to do. I would do it—I would do whatever it took.

Tala broke the embrace and walked into the suite. After such a welcome, her absence made the room just a little bit colder. "Did you find him?" she asked without a pause.

This was the performance for which I was pre-paring and rehearsing. The lies I was about to tell her were for the greater good, I thought to myself, they were necessary and are just barriers I needed to hur-dle on my road to victory. She would only suffer for a short while, and, in the long run, it would be far less hurtful than the truth.

"Tala," I said, "please sit down."

Her smile departed her face in response to my tone. She sat on the sofa, and I settled next to her, avoiding her gaze.

In those few seconds, I questioned my actions one last time. I had to do it. I had to lie to her. I convinced myself that my motivation and my justification were both sound. There was no turning back now.

I met her eyes, and the words spilled free from my lips as though they were under great pressure. "I tracked him down, Tala," I said. She did not allow herself any hope; I could see it in her eyes that she knew what was coming next even before I said it. "Bilal was killed by ISIS, Tala," I told her, reaching out to touch her arm, but she flinched away.

"No!" she blurted, her lower lip trembling with both rage and sorrow. "I don't believe it."

"I'm so sorry, Tala. I wish it weren't true," I said. "I was worried you might not be convinced, so I filmed Nazar, Abu Ali's associate, an eye witness. I didn't want to show you this. You don't have to watch it if you don't want to." I took out my phone and showed her the screen on which the first frame of the cued-up video showed Nazar's face looking into the camera. "I don't have to press play," I said. My concern for her feelings was real. I hoped she didn't need the proof, the evidence I manufactured.

"Press play," she whispered, her tear-filled eyes fixed on my phone's screen. I tapped the play icon.

I watched as her every hope evaporated. Tala's shoulders shook, and, wracked with grief, she emitted a guttural, shuddering, groan. When she looked at me, her misery took my breath away. It was in my power to tell her the truth then; there was a chance yet to set things right and relieve her of this wretched sorrow. I would not though. I did not come this far only to give up on my victory now.

Tala did not refuse my touch this time. I pulled her to me, embracing her, and she threw her arms around me and held me like I was a life ring and she was shipwrecked on the Mediterranean once more. Her tears wet my shirt, and she clawed at my back, trembling as she wept. I comforted her and gave her what refuge I could in my embrace. She was grieving, and I would be there for her.

For the next few days, Tala went through the usual stages of grief. I was there for it all and did what I could to ease her suffering. She cried abruptly and often, threw petulant tantrums where she would deny my claim that Bilal was dead, and spent hours in bed, despondent and numb, before finally arriving at the final phase, acceptance. I never left her side the entire time.

I knew what she was going through. I had lost loved ones too: my father and my mother. The presence and affection of those you care about can be like a drug. Losing them can be akin to going, as they say, cold turkey. Only after enduring the extensive suffering of withdrawal symptoms can someone come out the other side of the ordeal, healed.

It was after a week had passed that the moment for which I was waiting finally arrived. On that night, while I was holding her, comforting her in bed while the forgotten television illuminated us with flickering, blue light, we both looked up at each other at the same moment, and Tala looked away. I reached out and, with the soft touch of a fingertip under her chin, I guided her to face me. First, I pressed my brow to hers, then gently, lovingly, I pressed my lips to hers.

At once, Tala kissed me in return. Our tentative kiss suddenly intensified into something more frantic and urgent. Our breathing came in hisses and gasps, and Tala reached for my shirt, raking at it with her fingers. "You," Tala breathed against my neck, "have been so good to me, Henry. Like an angel." She kissed, bit, and then soothingly kissed my bare shoulder. "You saved me," she said, kissing a path up along my throat and over my stubbled chin, "protected me." Her lips found mine again, and she sucked my bottom lip between her teeth before tugging it passionately only to release it with a flushed, feral smile. "You risked your life to fulfill your promise to me," she said, unfastening my belt and pants.

Tala straddled my hips, and she lifted herself upward, reached behind herself to position me. She looked down at me from under her tousled hair. "You've waited a long time for this," she said, breathless, then she pressed downward, and we were one. The world disappeared but for the feel of flesh on flesh, the sounds of sighs and gasps, and the pleasures for which I had waited what seemed an eternity. We made love, at last.

Since that night, things were even better than I could have imagined. Tala's heartbreak seemed to be mending quickly, perhaps because she had suspected Bilal might be dead this whole time. She may have come to terms with the loss a long while ago, and it was just the shock of its verification that opened the wound again. Tala cried only occasionally and, in the meantime, allowed me to distract her with affection and tourist-style adventure in Slovenia.

Every night, I would spend some time writing, finishing my book. I still needed the perfect ending, and I had yet to tell Tala that it was her story I had been writing all this time. Well, it was almost her story. I had made necessary modifications when it came to Bilal. It was imperative that Tala didn't read the truth; to her, Bilal's death had to remain a fact instead of a fabrication I had devised.

It was time to come clean about the book, at least in part. We were enjoying an exceptional dinner by the river in Ljubljana, and the sky was russet and violet through the whispering trees lining the restaurant's patio. "I have a secret," I said, putting my fork down and folding my napkin.

Tala looked at me, a cautious smile on her lips. "A secret?" she asked, intrigued.

I laid my napkin on my empty plate and nodded. "Yes, Tala," I said, "Since having met you, I have been writing your story—our story now."

That's when I experienced the first of many shocks to follow.

"I love you, Henry," she said.

The world halted. It was as though the river stopped flowing; the breeze quieted in the leaves, and the world ceased to rotate. Had I heard that correctly? I blinked at her. In that instant, the sins I had committed, the deceptions and manipulations, the violence and killing, they were all worth it. I felt the weight of those acts lifting from my laden shoulders. "I..." I stammered, staggered for a moment, "I love you too, Tala."

We shared a smile, and her eyes glittered with brimming tears of happiness. I reached across the table and cradled her face in my hands. I stood and kissed her tenderly. There was no need for regret any longer. My plans had all come to fruition and Tala was mine, mine at last.

Even as I kissed Tala, held her hand, and uttered soft, affirming words, I was writing the scene in my mind and planning how I would describe this pivotal moment in my book. My readers were going to share the elation I felt at this moment; I knew it. So many plots and lies had to be devised and executed perfectly for this flawless victory to have occurred. There was just one last thing I needed to do, and it would truly secure my win.

"I want you to come with me to America, Tala," I said, holding one of her hands in both of mine. "And the fastest way to do that is to be married."

"Are you proposing?" she said, raising her free hand to her mouth in surprise.

"Well," I said, a little embarrassed, "I would need to get on my knees for that."

"No," she assured me. "You don't have to. You have done so much for me. You have put your life in danger and have been nothing but a loyal and loving man to me. I am such a lucky woman, and even luckier now. Yes!" she exclaimed, "Yes, yes, yes!"

I leaped from my chair and rounded the table to gather her up in my arms, lifting her from her seat. "She said yes!" I cried. Other patrons and passers-by smiled broadly and some pattered congratulatory applause. I didn't worry about what sort of spectacle we were making; I dismissed such reservations just as I had the vile things I had to do to get to this perfect, pristine, magical moment.

I took her back to the hotel and made love to her. Our lovemaking was a celebration. We were relentless and generous, intimate and adventurous. We fell asleep, exhausted and deeply satisfied, until morning when we made love again, lazily and tenderly.

We were enjoying breakfast on our balcony when Tala looked up from her plate, eyes twinkling with excitement. "So, when are we going to get married? We have to do it soon, right? So, let's start planning."

I chuckled, spreading jam on my toast, "Of course. Do you want anything special for our wedding?"

She thought a moment and beamed, "Yes! I didn't get to wear a proper wedding dress for my last wedding. All women are supposed to wear a lovely, white dress at their wedding."

"Done. We are getting you a white dress, the most beautiful of them all," I announced.

"But you can't see it," she warned with a smirk, "It is bad luck."

"I won't see it then, not until our wedding ceremony. You go pick it up. You're the boss."

"I also want to walk down the aisle with you waiting for me at the end of it, just like in the movies."

"Deal. No problem. I wouldn't have it any other way. Just name it—anything you want for our wedding. It's yours," I said, grinning a big, and admittedly dorky smile.

"And I changed my mind. I *do* want you to go down on one knee. You never did," she teased.

"We can save that until I get the ring."

Right after breakfast, Tala went shopping for her dress. I went to jewelry stores and looked at rings. The ring I chose for Tala was, in my opinion, perfect. When I saw it in the display case, the emerald, elegantly surrounded by a ring of sparkling diamonds, I knew I had found her ring.

I waited for her at the café near our hotel, prepared this time. When she rounded the corner, she didn't spot me until I had stood up from my table and had settled onto one knee before her. This time, I had a ring. She stopped mid-stride when I knelt on the sidewalk in front of her, and she laughed. When I opened the black, velvet box, her beautiful, dark eyes widened in amazement.

"Tala," I intoned. The patrons of the café stopped their chatter, and they all looked at us, wistful and approving smiles all silently directed our way. "Be my wife. Marry me."

"Yes!" she proclaimed, "Yes, Henry!"

I slipped the ring onto her finger, and there were hoots and raucous cheers from the other tables. Tala drew me up by my hands and threw her arms around me, squeezing me tightly. I was beaming ecstatically, and I declared, "I love you, Tala. I love you, I love you, I love you!"

Moments like that one justified the methods I employed to get us both to this point: in love, at last. Nothing could have made me regret anything I had done. Not after that moment, in particular. I would have done it all again. I hoped that Tala's joy would help her to forget Bilal and focus on her love for me. I was sure it would.

Tala had picked a stunning dress. I, as well as the witnesses and officiant at the city office, were taken aback by her incredible beauty. She had gathered her voluminous, shimmering, dark hair into a loose bun with tendrils brushing her creamy shoulders. The dress, strapless, displayed those shoulders to breathtaking effect. The exquisite garment's deep, lace-trimmed bust line elegantly accentuated Tala's enthralling figure. Smooth, shimmering satin was gathered around her midriff and hips by a graceful crisscrossing of ribbons that marched down her lower back to the top of the dress's mid-length train.

It was a sight that would be impossible to forget in a groom's lifetime.

When our eyes met, I was disconcerted by the forced smile on her otherwise stunning face. Valiantly, she was trying to look as happy as she could, but I knew her too well not so see through it. It was disappointing to see that she wasn't as thrilled and overjoyed as I felt. I knew it had to be Bilal. The ceremony must have brought back memories of her first wedding, and subsequently, thoughts of her husband's death.

For a split second, I thought she would stop and turn around to leave. She did not. My brave, lovely bride walked down the aisle, just like she told me she would, though her smile was more tentative than I would have liked. When she arrived beside me, I placed my hand fondly on the soft skin of her back, and we shared a timid smile. I inquired with a glance if she was okay, and she nodded almost imperceptibly.

We exchanged our vows. The ceremony was very basic and thankfully short, and after we had promised to be there for one another in times of sickness and in health, we were united for the rest of our lives. I was her husband, she was my wife, but I was disappointed that she couldn't enjoy this momentous and joyful day as much as I would have hoped. I could hardly blame her. We were married; that's what truly mattered.

We spent a few more weeks in Slovenia where I put my energy into helping Tala make happy memories of our first days of marriage. Newlyweds, we treated the time like a honeymoon, taking tours and sightseeing. There were times when Tala was content and even cheerful, but it would be some time before she could allow herself real happiness with the fresh loss of her first husband. I had to accept that and be patient.

One day soon, she would recognize how she had overcome so much and deserved the happiness I helped to bring her. I wanted her to look back on the life she came from, if you could call it that, and then look at herself now. Tala, Fatima then, grew up and eked out a miserable life in a genuinely dreadful place, the refugee camp. She defied the odds and survived unspeakable experiences in Turkey and a near-death incident on the Mediterranean. I rescued her from a detestable existence as a mere commodity of human traffickers in a prostitution ring. The next step was to bring her to her new home in America.

The time marched by quickly, and during that time, I wrote the final chapter of my book, ending it with our wedding day. Soon, Tala's American visa came through, and we were on a plane that day, flying to America. I was optimistic, expecting that once home, there would not be anything to remind Tala of Bilal. She could finally let herself experience the bliss and peace she deserved.

I had been gone for months. I was finally back and was ready to pick up my life where I had left off before loss and failure stole me away for a time. I was home, my new wife was with me, and I was happy and ready to release my next novel, *Tale of Tala*. I hadn't announced it yet, but I soon would, along with my marriage to Tala. I had no doubt that America, and the world, would love the book. It was sensational, timely, and controversial. It touched on hot topics like the refugee crisis, terrorism, and human trafficking—all things that were constantly in every headline in the newsstands. I told the story precisely as I wanted to tell it, without any mention of the untruths I told my wife-to-be. I would take that secret to the grave.

Chapter Nine
Part Two

When a winner is driven to anger, the same part of him that leads him to success and victory is the part of him that makes him ruthless and unwavering. If one is born to be a winner, he insists on getting what he wants, when he wants it, the way he wants it. It is dangerous to cross such a man. He will do everything in his power to win, and if that winner is a writer, he will use words as his weapon.

It was a long flight from London, where we boarded our connecting flight to New York. Like I always did, I spent the time on the flight making mental observations and planning. Somewhere over the Atlantic Ocean, I acquired an objectivity that I could only get at the highest cruising altitudes. I had a clear mind, free of the subjectivity of emotions, even love.

Tala was sleeping next to me in her aisle seat, huddled under my jacket that I had given her to keep warm in the cool, recycled air in the cabin. Staring at her, I tried to imagine exactly why her behavior had changed so markedly and suddenly. She still took care of me, shared laughter with me, and we had some of the best sex I had ever experienced. When I took a mental step back and altered my perspective just a little, I found I was suspicious. Was it all an act? It was normal for her to mourn, and perhaps our wedding was a harsh reminder of her loss. I had to do something to help. I couldn't rely on time alone to mend her heart.

I would succeed in this too, to bring Tala the happiness and better life she had been seeking since the day she left her home in the refugee camp. I thought I had won her heart, but that was only partially true. There was a part of her heart that Tala still devoted to Bilal. Her whole heart would be mine. It would take more acts of love and kindness, and that was something I was more than willing to provide for my new wife. In this too, I would be the winner.

My thoughts, as always, drifted back to my book. I recognized that it was thanks to Tala that I was back to writing. I was grateful for her story and for the good luck of having met her. Luck? Is there any such thing as luck? I was confident that *Tale of Tala* would be a hit. There was no doubt in my mind. I just wished I could have written the events as they actually occurred. It would have been a relief, in a way, to tell

Tala the truth. She may have been upset at me, furious even. But wouldn't she be even angrier at Bilal, who sold their love for a million dollars? For the sake of my book, did I want to tell her the truth? I thought to myself that I was a writer before anything else. I tried to convince myself, but it was too much to risk. It was difficult to say how she might react. At the same time though, people would appreciate the real story, and couldn't I include Tala's reaction in the final chapter?

I made up my mind.

Moments later, I had my laptop in front of me, and I was typing. I kept glancing over at Tala, wary that she might wake and read what was on my screen. Writing was truly a drug for me. Only an addict would be unable to stop himself from writing those passages within sight of Tala, regardless of the consequences. I typed the aspects of the story I failed to include in the first draft: how Nazar brought Bilal to me, the deal I made, the story I fabricated, and how I manipulated events in order to win Tala from Bilal.

I decided that when we got home to New York, I would let Tala rest. She was in a new city and starting a new life. I would wait a few days until the manuscript was done, and then, before sending it to my publisher, I would tell Tala the unpleasant truth.

"Are you still writing?" Tala asked, rubbing her sleepy eyes with her knuckles.

I closed my laptop at once and flashed a too-brilliant smile at my wife. "Yes, Darling, I am."

"So, tell me more about America, about New York. Is it true that it is where dreams come true?" she asked sleepily.

"Yes," I replied, chuckling, "It is where dreams come true. It is where my dream of living my life with you will come true. And yours can come true there as well."

She paused, looked at me with a fierce expression and grasped my hand tightly. "My dream has already come true," she said.

I smiled at her and leaned close to kiss her. "Mine too."

Later, we were going through customs, and Tala was pulled aside for a secondary inspection. I got frustrated and, placing my arm around Tala's shoulders, I addressed the officer. "Is there something wrong?" I asked.

The man paused and gave me a double-take. He stared at me a wide-eyed look of recognition. "Oh, it's a routine procedure; it's her first time in America," he told me apologetically. "I've read all your books. I loved them all, even that last one that the critics didn't like."

I could not have cared less. I spent all of this time and energy on winning Tala; I could not stand the notion of losing her if they figured out that I had bought her passport. We had already prepared a story to share with customs agents: she was Dominican but had lived all over the world because her parents worked as diplomats. That would also explain why she didn't speak Spanish.

Tala was very nervous. I squeezed her shoulder and whispered gently, "It is going to be fine. Just cooperate and answer their questions when they ask. Don't say anything beyond that. You'll be okay."

"This way, Maam," the officer said, holding the door to an adjoining room open for Tala.

I put on a smile, the sort that I reserve for my most ingratiating fans, and I asked him, "It's alright if I come along, right?" I was already casually following Tala through the door. He replied in the affirmative, but I didn't pay him enough attention to hear what he said.

We found two seats in a room already filled with shoulder-to-shoulder immigrants. It was before the 2016 presidential election. The rhetoric of fear and the scapegoating of refugees had become deeply entrenched in the American psyche. Nowhere was that more apparent than at borders and customs checks like this one. The influence of the media was obvious when I watched the underpaid and overworked customs agents inspect and question other people entering America from abroad. They were unnecessarily discourteous, impatient, and tough.

Tala's name was called, and I walked to the counter with her, holding her hand. The agent had her passport in a blue file. He entered some data into his computer and asked her dispassionately, "When did you get married?"

I answered, smiling proudly, "We are newlyweds, married just two months ago."

The man's expression darkened with annoyance, and he leveled his gaze on me. "I was asking *her*. Have a seat. I will call you if I need you."

"Do you know who I am?" I couldn't keep the petulance from my voice.

The man rolled his eyes as only someone hiding behind a badge can do to another human being, safe in the knowledge that they are in the position of power. "No," he replied flatly. "Take a seat and wait."

For some people, that feeling of superiority they get from a uniform and badge is the only sense of control they have in their lives, and they derive deep satisfaction from lording over other people. If this man weren't directly responsible for Tala's safe and trouble-free entry into America, I would have eagerly explained to him why I thought he was an asshole.

"Go ahead," Tala said, "I will be alright."

I nodded and took a seat.

I watched Tala from a nearby bank of seats. I was sandwiched between a morbidly obese man whose hips were encroaching onto my chair and a large family with four children who were all fighting over the seat on my other side. Things seemed to be going better than I thought they might, until the officer asked, "Do you have a cell phone?"

Tala stiffened. I could tell she was anxious, but I couldn't imagine why. She had the phone I gave her; why would it be a problem for the agent to see it? "I have a Slovenian number, but I will get an American one when I get home," she answered. I could see her fist tighten around her phone. Though Tala could conceal her fright from the agent, I knew her so well that I could read it from her rigid posture and tight jaw.

"Can I please see your phone?" the agent asked, his eyes still on his screen as he reached out a hand, palm up. She was hesitant, and the agent looked up at her, curious. Tala quickly complied before she was asked a second time. The agent barely glanced at the phone before he handed it back. Bored, he stamped her passport. "Welcome to America," he said and was already looking beyond Tala for the next person.

Tala smiled broadly, relieved. The smile I returned to her was anything but sincere. I was still wondering why Tala would be so nervous about her phone. I had bought it for her so we could keep in touch while I was traveling. I didn't know of any friends with whom she might have been in touch. She hadn't used her phone for anything but communication with me via calls and texts. As a writer, I was observant and inquisitive by nature, and her reaction to the mention of her phone had me vexed.

We hired an airport limousine to drive us to my house, Tala's new home. I would have enjoyed the scenery in my hometown, Manhattan, if I weren't distracted by my suspicion; I had to get my hands on Tala's phone. It was the first time my new wife had ever seen a city like New York beyond what she had seen on television, and, despite being tired from all the traveling, she was glued to her window, admiring the iconic metropolis's bustling crowds whose diversity of culture, fashion, and demographics varied more in one city block than she had ever experienced in her life.

She fixated on a couple openly engaged in a passionate argument; the man wore a high-collared wool coat, and glared at his girlfriend who, red-faced and teary-eyed, was screaming at him, her hands, in their home-knit mittens, gesticulating savagely. Bike couriers weaved in and out of traffic that was predominantly one particular shade of yellow.

"The energy," Tala remarked. "So many people."

She watched as we passed countless storefronts, many of which were sandwich shops with names that were familiar to me and everyone else in my neighborhood. Tala turned to me and asked, "Is this the deli district?"

I barked an unexpected laugh. "No," I said, knowing exactly what she meant, "This is just Manhattan.

You will never have to look far for a good sandwich around here."

My house hadn't been lived in for months. My maid kept it in order while I was gone though, so Tala was greeted with fresh flowers in the foyer. "What a lovely house," Tala said, turning in a circle just inside the front door.

"It is *your* house now," I said, pulling her close. "You must be tired. Let me show you to our room."

"Yes," she admitted. "I would like a shower and then a warm bed."

Moments later, she was showering in the en-suite bathroom. I sat on the edge of the bed, staring at the bathroom door from which came the sound of running water. She had brought her phone into the bathroom with her. There could be no reason to do that other than to keep it out of my hands. What was on that phone? I needed to know.

I didn't have long to wait before she was curled up under the fresh sheets that my maid had put on the bed that morning. Fortunately, Tala slept deeply, suffering from jet lag. I took the phone from the table next to her side of the bed and silently left, going downstairs to the living room.

The passcode on the home screen didn't slow me down. I was the one who set up the phone for Tala. I hadn't intended ever to need to, but I saved my thumbprint in case I had the need to bypass the phone's security. The way Tala reacted to the phone at the airport had me convinced that something was very wrong. I didn't know what to expect, but I had to investigate.

I was shocked and incensed by what I found on her phone.

Tala had been communicating with Bilal. I scrolled through the entirety of their correspondence on WhatsApp. It didn't take much work to translate the Arabic using a web-based translator right there on her phone.

Bilal had reached out to her through a friend she had apparently kept in touch with in Lebanon. Tala and Bilal had been talking and plotting. It was part of their plan for Tala to marry me and come to America where Bilal would eventually come, and they would be reunited. One translated text described how outraged Tala was that I had lied to her and how difficult it was for her to be with me. She admitted that it was an act. She didn't love me; she was just using me to gain American citizenship and to turn her dreams into reality. Those dreams included a reunion with her love, her husband, Bilal.

The two had even discussed, in detail, the steps leading to their reuniting. Bilal suggested that eventually, Tala and I would get a divorce, and she would rightfully claim half of my wealth. What Tala said in reply made my pulse race with fury. She joked, and a joke is always rooted in truth, that she would be more pleased if the two of them killed me. Tala said, in her text, "He deserves death because he lied to me, we deserve to live in peace and with money."

There was a call history as well. She and Bilal must have both known the truth after so many phone calls.

According to the dates of the messages, Tala had begun these communications just before our wedding. It was excruciatingly painful to relive what was one of my fondest memories in my life and realize that the woman I loved had cheated me and manipulated me on that of all days. Her apparent sadness was not grief for her late husband, but for the time she would be forced to be married to me.

Fighting the urge to throw the phone against the wall, I seethed and stared at the screen, at line after line of texts between the two of them. I almost missed one very important text in my rage but stopped and scrolled back to read it. Bilal was flying into JFK in two weeks and had given Tala his flight information. A wicked smile played across my face, my eyes narrowed, and my nostrils flared. They weren't the only ones who could plot and scheme.

I was angry, yes, incredibly angry. There was a part of me though, that recognized that these were the consequences of my lies. It didn't blunt the hurt or the fury I felt. They thought that they were going to win this. They didn't know who they were dealing with.

I went upstairs and quietly replaced the phone on the bedside table, and I watched her sleep for a long moment. She was beautiful. It made my heart ache to regard her. Her features were beatific in the tranquility of sleep. At that moment, I wished I could have killed her. I felt justified, and I was certainly angry enough. But no, I couldn't. That is not how my book would end. No. I would not be that merciful, and my book deserved a more creative ending than that.

My wrath had to be bottled for the moment. To win, I had to calm myself and plan for my victory. Nothing but writing could help. I recorded the events of the day: the journey from Slovenia to America, Tala's first experience in New York, and, of course, my discovery of Tala's vile deception. By the time I had finished up to the present in my book, I had devised a plan. I knew precisely how I would deal with Tala and Bilal.

I opened a fresh bottle of whiskey and finished it as well as *Tale of Tala* by morning after having stayed up the entire night writing and drinking. Until then, my process was to write the story day by day as I experienced it, as it happened. This time, I wrote the story before it occurred, as I knew it would unfold in the weeks to come. That was how confident I was in my plan. I was a winner, and nothing would deter me from succeeding in my victory. I was fiercely determined.

Tala awoke at four in the morning thanks to her jet lag. I was well past the point of drunk. Despite that, I had to play the part and act as though nothing were wrong. It was imperative that Tala not realize I was aware of her communications with Bilal in order for my plan—my revenge—to succeed. I took one last look at my screen, pleased with myself.

I turned that smile on Tala when she walked in and asked me, "Are you writing?"

"Yes, I am," I said, my vehemence hiding safely behind my imitation of a smile. "I'm just typing up the final chapter. It's nearly done."

Tala yawned and then grinned sleepily at me. "Congratulations. Are you happy with it?" she asked.

"You bet I am. It's going to be a hit." I stared at her with my forced smile, observing the dishonesty in her pleased expression. It hurt to think about how she had been maneuvering behind my back, lying and manipulating.

"I'm sure you're right," she said before turning back for the bedroom to go back to sleep. "Try and get some rest," she said over her shoulder.

I needed to be finished that same night, because, for the next two weeks, I would be busy putting into place all the components of my plan. A happy consequence of my heavy workload was that I would not have any time to spend with my new wife. It was for the best. While I was sure I could keep up the charade of affection and trust, it enraged me to look at her, much less speak to her.

In two weeks, Bilal would land in New York. My book launch would be that same day. The party would be held in one of New York's most exclusive venues. I would invite the most notable personalities, celebrities, and media. There would be complimentary copies of *Tale of Tala* for everyone at the event and, perhaps a few weeks or months later, copies would be on bookstore shelves. But it was of paramount importance that the launch of the book was on that exact day because that was how I had described it in my book.

The anticipation was building. I put in appearances on local and national television programs, and I answered questions about the book and about my personal life—the sorts of questions that make for scintillating television. In this way, *Tale of Tala* was an especially easy book to market, considering all the questions about the story were, in fact, about my life. My new bride was the book's namesake, after all.

Everywhere I looked, newspapers, magazines, tabloids, morning news shows, all had some mention of my upcoming book as well as gossip about my new marriage and my wife. Tala was a true beauty; her photo made it onto screens and pages wherever the book was mentioned. Her image may have been the biggest marketing tool for *Tale of Tala*.

My manager and publisher both thought I was crazy for rushing the release of the book like this. My manager booked as many appearances as possible for those two weeks, and my publisher complained that getting the book on paper would be a serious challenge under those time constraints. Both were easily placated though. They knew what sort of money my new book was going to be worth to them and they complied in the end.

Tala could see a change in me. I was distant and distracted, but she attributed it to my book and its imminent release. She played the role of supportive wife very convincingly. I wasn't fooled, but, luckily the tabloids and journalists were. I knew she was still in contact with Bilal because I continued to check her phone whenever I had the chance. He had attained his American visa according to the messages.

In those secret texts, I read one of Tala's where she apologized that she could not meet Bilal at the airport because of my book launch. He wrote back that he would check into a hotel and wait to see her the next day. Further texts described how much they missed one another and how they looked forward to their reunion.

As the day of the book launch approached, Tala grew more and more cheerful. She maintained that she was simply excited by the book launch and all of the public attention she was enjoying. It may have been partially true; she certainly liked the way the media couldn't get enough of her. Tala manipulated the journalists with words and photographers with her wide, dark eyes. She fooled them all, but not me. I was finally beyond her scheming.

It was very satisfying to turn the tables on her and to be the one manipulating. Regarding the book and the launch, Tala was becoming just a little anxious, perhaps because I had forbidden her from reading it. I told her she would read it the same day everyone else would at the release. I did not want *anyone* to read the book. In fact, I paid guards at the printers. My publisher thought my excessive security was brilliant marketing. Pictures of the guards made it into all the papers. The mystery I spun invoked intrigue and that lead to a great deal of attention in the media.

Publicity was exactly what I wanted. My revenge required a massive audience for my victory to be truly satisfying, and I would have that. My winning was only a matter of days away.

Chapter Nine
Part Three

Only the typesetter and I had laid eyes on *Tale of Tala*. There were 250 copies sealed in boxes awaiting the 250 guests attending the launch that night. I hired the same guards I had hired during the publishing process to watch over the boxes of books. The day had finally arrived.

It was also the day that Bilal would arrive.

Tala and I were both eager for this day to come. Of course, Tala was excited to have her story shared with the world; we both were looking forward to that. She would be a household name by tomorrow, loved by many—something she had yearned for since her attention-starved childhood. Her story would also garner awareness and sympathy for those with similar stories to hers.

Refugees all over the world would likely benefit from the book's release and popularity, people like her

family back home in Lebanon. Tala never spared them
a thought though. They would likely hear about her
success in America as well as what they will identify
as shameful, dishonorable acts, but it didn't matter in
the least to Tala. She was no longer Fatima; she was
Tala now.

I knew Tala's growing cheerfulness as the day
of the release approached was mainly due to Bilal's
impending arrival. She would see him again for the
first time since they were separated in Turkey when
he was taken by ISIS, and she was left on her own.
Bilal was her childhood love, the love that was taken
from her—the love she dreamed of every night.

My excitement rushed through me the moment
I woke up that morning. I sat up, eager to start this
long-awaited day. Tala was sleeping next to me,
sheets bunched up around her bare legs. With the
early-morning sun warming her body through our
bedroom window, her slumbering form reminded me
of our first morning together. That sunrise was mere
months ago and yet an eternity. That was the morning
Tala finished telling me her tragic and heroic story.

It was no wonder she was sleeping so soundly; we
had made love savagely until we were utterly spent
and exhausted. The feral way we took our pleasure
from each other was a provocative power play. The two
of us were planning deceit and betrayal, and I believe
that for both of us, the wild lovemaking was deeply

spiteful, even vindictive. I thought of it as my victory lap to celebrate my triumph of having both won and conquered her. The quote came to me then: "Confuse not love with the raptures of possession..." It was something another novelist had observed during the beginning of the last century. It was an apt quotation.

The memory of the energetic, cathartic, and, at moments, adversarial sex we had, caused fresh arousal to stir in my loins. I considered waking my treacherous wife to satisfy my urges, but there was no time. I had preparations to make for the launch. I set to it immediately, getting showered and dressed before going to my office to make calls and confirm details.

Tala and I had a taciturn lunch together. Perhaps neither of us wanted to give the other any hints that might reveal our mutual duplicity. Instead, we stared at our phones, chewed our food, and betrayed each other with pecks and taps of our thumbs, texting and emailing plans of treachery against the person on the other side of the table.

I knew she was communicating with Bilal, right there, right in front of me. I knew from having seen his flight details that he was scheduled to arrive at four that afternoon. A smile blossomed on her face after she read something on her phone. I tilted my head and, feigning ignorance, I asked, "Oh, are you as excited as I am about tonight?"

She was startled but recovered quickly. Placing her phone face-down on the table, she nodded too quickly and smiled too broadly, "Yes, Henry. I can't wait." She glanced at her phone and then once again at me from across our lunch table and added, with a cryptic quirk to her lips, "This is a very important day."

I wanted to laugh in her face, seeing through her weak disguise. She was so sure that I thought her anticipation was for the gala book launch, but I knew she was only thinking of Bilal who was on his way at that very moment. "Yes," I agreed, "Very important." I wiped the corners of my mouth with a napkin and said, "I can't wait for the world to see you the way I do, Tala. You deserve it."

Our limo pulled up to the red carpet at six o'clock sharp. I sat across from Tala, admiring her body in the custom-tailored, designer gown I had commissioned. Tala had no shortage of designers who wanted to dress her. With a figure like hers and the promise of so much publicity, fashion houses were lined up. The dress managed to be provocative while remaining relatively modest. Despite looking so exquisite, Tala was nervous. Who could blame her? She had never been the center of attention on a red carpet before, and also, I doubted very much that she had heard much from Bilal after his plane touched down at JFK.

I was smirking when I opened the limo door and was assaulted by rapid-fire flashes and shouts of,

"Henry! Over here! Look this way!" It had been a long time since I was acknowledged as a winner like this. I didn't always enjoy many aspects of my celebrity, but tonight, I relished it. I turned and offered my hand to Tala who I helped step onto the carpet from the limo. At the first sight of her long, lissome legs exiting the limousine, the cameras began to flash relentlessly. Tala squinted and winced at the blinding strobe effect.

"Everything is alright," I soothed, holding her hand and guiding her toward the heart of the crowd. Linked ropes of velvet held back the throng of press and photographers. "They all want to see you. Let them. Smile for them, Tala. They are here to celebrate you. It's all about you, Tala."

She put on a false smile and hugged the crook of my arm. Tala was distraught, and I knew why. The people around us would most likely assume that she was simply overwhelmed by the flood of attention she was getting. "Tala!" they cried, trying to get her to turn their way and smile. "Over here! Tala! Who designed your gown?!? Tala!" The cacophony assailed us all the way to the door, and we were obligated to stop and pose several times and put on broad smiles. Mine were exultant and mischievous, while Tala's were aloof and even vacant. We were the couple of the year.

Of all the hundreds of people present, only I knew what was going to happen that night. I planned meticulously, and things would go exactly as I predicted in the book. Everyone at the launch, when they read their complimentary copy of *Tale of Tala*, would only then learn the details of a love story that had gone tragically wrong. They would read an account of displacement, violence, love, and deceit and then they would have an understanding of the things that they would witness tonight at the gala book launch.

Persistent, journalists shouted over one another, asking questions about everything from her dress to her citizenship. I held up a hand and pulled Tala possessively close to my side and said, grinning, "There will be a time for questions later, at the press conference. Let us enjoy the party until then." I lead Tala into the venue, leaving the flashing lights and the noisy crowd behind us.

I planned every phase of the evening, and, of course, everything went precisely as I desired. All of the guests arrived and were given similar treatment by the photographers and journalists hedging the red carpet; they drank from the open bar and socialized; then, after everyone had taken their seats, I would step to the podium as their host, and I would make a speech.

Tala stood at my side, smiling dazzlingly but insincerely at me from a pace to my left. I pretended her expression was genuine and smiled back before placing my hands on the podium and enthusiastically addressed my many guests. When the applause died down, I took a deep breath. The moment for which I had been single-mindedly planning and anxiously awaiting was finally here. It was time for my speech.

"A year ago," I began, "I quit writing." The room sobered noticeably, quieting completely. "I, of course, gave up because of a book that none of you liked," I said and broke the tension with a hearty chuckle. "I don't blame you. The book was... How was it put? Derivative drivel?" I laughed and shrugged, "I can't disagree with that. But it was not a failure; in fact, it was one of my most notable achievements. I feel like I won with that book because it led me on a journey on which I met my wife." I gestured grandly toward Tala and said, "This is Tala, the subject of my new book and my beautiful bride." The crowd cheered in adoring tribute, and I clapped along with them. Tala demurely turned to the audience and bowed her head, modestly acknowledging their applause.

"Tala's story begins in a refugee camp in Lebanon from which she escapes her bleak life with her childhood love. She loses him in Turkey and then embarks on a dangerous and tragic journey across the Mediterranean to Europe. In Slovenia, she is forced into prostitution by human traffickers, and that is where I meet her." The audience hissed with whispered remarks about the last point, and I looked at Tala who didn't react to the mention of prostitution in any discernible way. Her smile was unnaturally painted on her perfect, lovely features.

"Tala is hearing all of this for the first time like all of you in this room," I explained, glancing once at Tala before returning my attention to the room full of faces focused on me. "I committed myself to the task of finding Tala's husband, Bilal." At the mention of her husband's name, Tala blinked and focused on me once more. I looked at her with a level stare as I spoke into the microphone, "And I did. I found him. I lied to her, this beautiful, resilient woman standing before you. I lied and told her that Bilal was dead."

Finally, Tala showed some recognition and some semblance of emotion: shock. It was the first genuine expression she had shown all evening.

I went on.

"I lied to her and told her that he was killed by ISIS. He wasn't. He was recruited by ISIS in Syria and used for his computer expertise. I rescued him." I watched as Tala slowly began to back away from me toward the stairs at the side of the stage. I let her and directed all of my attention toward the audience. I saw shocked faces; the guests were scandalized and riveted. I was being recorded on countless video cameras and smartphones. In moments, the world, through social media, would be buzzing with the story. The fact of her sudden and sordid rise to celebrity dawned on

Tala's face. Fear blanched her features, and she turned and walked quickly from the stage.

"In fact, today her husband arrived here in America—just over two hours ago. While I was enjoying lunch with my wife, Tala, this afternoon, I sent an anonymous message to Homeland Security with Bilal's flight information and a thorough description of the man who I knew was a recruit of ISIS. That is a serious charge," I went on, shaking my head in mock disappointment. "Another is conspiracy to murder," I said. "I found evidence on Tala's phone that he and she were plotting to kill me. Aiding and abetting terrorists and conspiracy to murder: two serious charges."

There were two uniformed officers waiting for Tala at the bottom of the stairs. Recording devices were all aimed at her and documented, with embarrassingly clear images and video, the officers handcuffing her and exiting through the nearby exit.

I shook my head, watching Tala as she was taken away. Inside though, I was laughing and celebrating my undisputed victory over Tala and Bilal, and, when I looked back at the audience who were stricken and delighted by the scandal unfolding before their eyes, I knew my book would be an incredible success: yet another win I had predicted.

When those audience members returned home that night and started reading their copies of *Tale of Tala*, they would all realize just how gifted its author truly was. I had predicted the events that followed my speech with flawless accuracy. I knew Bilal would have called Tala from the airport. I could have guessed by her disposition while we were in the limo, but, days ago, I had foreseen it and knew it would occur exactly that way.

My next prediction was thanks to how well I had grown to understand my wife in the short time we knew each other. She was a manipulator, she was selfish, and, above all else, she was a survivor. When Bilal called from the airport to ask Tala to help him obtain a lawyer, she asked him, "Who are you? Why did you call this number?"

"My love, Fatima, what are you talking about?" he asked, frightened and miserable.

"I don't know of any Fatima. My name is Tala. Who is this? Don't ever call this number again." Tala feared the authorities. She was afraid that her life was crumbling again like it had so many times already. Resilient and self-serving, she betrayed Bilal in the face of losing her freedom and being incarcerated for being associated with a suspected terrorist. Just as essential, she would not be denied her new life of luxury and wealth.

I observed the tumult among the guests and media in the room. Looking down at them from under the spotlight and behind the podium, I raised my hand for calm. When Tala and the officers left, relative quiet returned. "Ladies and gentlemen," I said with gravity weighing on every syllable, "You will all get a copy of *Tale of Tala*. Enjoy reading it. The final chapter was written just days ago and includes the events of today as I—*accurately*—projected they would occur."

"My friends," I went on, "Always remember to look inside and define yourself. Are you a winner? Or are you a loser, or maybe neither—someone who is uncertain as to which side of the same coin you exist on. If you are a loser, you will finish last and with everything you deserve. Success is beyond the realm of a loser. If you are unsure if you are a loser or a winner, don't bother. Leave the journey to the winners. But if you are a winner..." I said, pausing for effect. I had them. I could feel the palpable energy of their unwavering attention, and I hoped that energy was apparent on video as well. "If you are a winner," I said, a crescendo building in my voice, "You *must*," I sneered dramatically, "at *any* price," I said, brandishing a fist and pointing meaningfully toward the door through which my vanquished foe of a wife had made her shameful exit, "...finish as the winner."

Chapter Nine
Part Four

It was thirty years ago that I released *Tale of Tala* at a notorious and controversial event where the principal character of the book was arrested after having tried to betray me. That day, she, and my readers, learned how unwise and dangerous it can be to fool with a man like me—a man born a winner.

Today, I sit on my patio. The view from my home's vantage is extraordinary: low mountains, green with grass and ferns, framing a post-card picture of the peaceful city of Jericho. Palestine has been my home for many years now. There are two palm trees reaching for the clouds that drift gracefully across the pale, blue sky, one for me and one for my wife. One day, I will be buried under one and my wife under the other to share eternity next to each other on this sacred land.

The novel was a best-seller. My manager and publisher were over the moon with my brilliant marketing ploy. The book launch was a thing of legend in the industry. Footage of Tala's arrest and my speech went viral, and, without one cent spent on promotion, I made *Tale of Tala* a topic of conversation, scandal, and gossip all over the world. Bookstores worldwide were sold out constantly. I released modified editions every other year or so. For three decades, the book has been consistently a top seller. You would be hard-pressed to find someone who hasn't read it.

I sit here, scribbling my signature into the inside cover of book after book, leisurely preparing for the release of this final edition in just a few weeks. Like the former editions, I had read it carefully and amended the last chapters, adding new events as they occurred in our lives. I, of course, modified things here and there for the sake of readability and to bolster the story. Tala was my proofreader, and she was never shy with her red pen and astute suggestions for edits. Then, my assistant, Tarek, a man who was invaluable to me in some of the most dreadful and dangerous legs of my journey, would dutifully take the manuscript to the publisher.

Tala is inside now, preparing supper for me and our son and daughter, Bilal and Fatima, who are visiting for two weeks, and who will join us at the launch party of this final edition of *Tale of Tala*.

Like I had always lived, I will die: a winner who invariably got what he wanted in life. Over the years,

I learned from further journeys; each had important lessons for me. Winning offers the sort of satisfaction that is spectacularly intense but fleeting. The triumph of which I'm proudest, and that I celebrate every day, is love. In love, there is no resentment, no hate; there is no shame or regret; there is forgiveness, and with it, merited and hard-fought victory. I am almost seventy, and I am still a winner, more so now than ever.

Printed in Great Britain
by Amazon